UNSEASONABLY COLD

She had just paused to look through one of the cabin's windows at the period furnishings inside when she heard a man say, loudly and distinctly, "If you try anything like that, I'll kill you."

Phyllis stiffened in surprise at hearing such a threat expressed like that. The man's voice came from in front of the cabin. Phyllis was torn between the urge to see what was going on and the natural caution that told her to stay right where she was, out of the would-be murderer's sight.

As she stepped around the corner of the cabin, she saw a man standing there with his back to her. He laughed and said, "No, really, I'll kill you." He seemed to be talking to himself, because there was no one anywhere around except Phyllis. Then she noticed the earphone tucked into his ear and realized he was talking on one of those Bluetooth cell phones, or whatever they were called. As Phyllis watched, the man put some sort of pill in his mouth, then took a drink from the water bottle in his hand. He laughed again, then froze as he noticed her standing there. . . .

continued . . .

The Pumpkin Muffin Murder

A Fresh-Baked Mystery

LIVIA J. WASHBURN

AN OBSIDIAN MYSTERY

OBSIDIAN

Published by New American Library, a division of
Penguin Group (USA) Inc., 375 Hudson Street,
New York, New York 10014, USA
Penguin Group (Canada), 90 Eglinton Avenue East, Suite 700, Toronto,
Ontario M4P 2Y3, Canada (a division of Pearson Penguin Canada Inc.)
Penguin Books Ltd., 80 Strand, London WC2R 0RL, England
Penguin Ireland, 25 St. Stephen's Green, Dublin 2,
Ireland (a division of Penguin Books Ltd.)
Penguin Group (Australia), 250 Camberwell Road, Camberwell, Victoria 3124,
Australia (a division of Pearson Australia Group Pty. Ltd.)
Penguin Books India Pvt. Ltd., 11 Community Centre, Panchsheel Park,
New Delhi - 110 017, India
Penguin Group (NZ), 67 Apollo Drive, Rosedale, Auckland 0632,
New Zealand (a division of Pearson New Zealand Ltd.)
Penguin Books (South Africa) (Pty.) Ltd., 24 Sturdee Avenue,
Rosebank, Johannesburg 2196, South Africa

Penguin Books Ltd., Registered Offices:
80 Strand, London WC2R 0RL, England

Published by Obsidian, an imprint of New American Library, a division of Penguin
Group (USA) Inc. Previously published in an Obsidian trade paperback edition.

First Obsidian Mass Market Printing, November 2011
10 9 8 7 6 5 4 3 2 1

Copyright © Livia Reasoner, 2010
Excerpt from *The Gingerbread Bump-Off* copyright © Livia Reasoner, 2011
All rights reserved

OBSIDIAN and logo are trademarks of Penguin Group (USA) Inc.

Printed in the United States of America

*This book is dedicated to
my husband, James Reasoner,*

and

*my two daughters, Shayna and Joanna,
who are very tolerant of my craziness
when deadlines loom.*

Chapter 1

One thing you never forgot about being a parent, Phyllis Newsom thought, was the feeling of helplessness that comes over you when your child is sick. Of course, Bobby was her grandson, not her son, but that didn't matter. He felt miserable, and she had done everything she could to make him feel better, but he still sobbed in pain as she held him and carried him back and forth across the dimly lit living room of her house, trying to calm him down.

"It'll be all right, Bobby," she told the four-year-old. "Don't worry; everything will be just fine. You'll be all well soon."

Not soon enough to suit her, though. The pediatrician had said that it might be a week or more before Bobby's ear infection cleared up. And it would have to heal on its own, because this wasn't like the old days when doctors prescribed antibiotics for such ailments. Phyllis remembered giving her son, Mike, the wonderful pink liquid when he was little and came down with something like this. That stuff seemed to cure anything.

Now the doctors claimed that it really didn't, and Phyllis supposed that they ought to know what they were talking about. They were doctors, after all. But she missed being able to feel like she was accomplishing something, like she was helping her child get well sooner.

Ah, well. She sighed and held Bobby closer, letting him rest his head on her shoulder. She was wearing a nice thick robe over her pajamas, so she supposed it almost felt like a pillow to him.

The sound of footsteps made her glance toward the stairs. Sam Fletcher's long legs came into view, followed by the rest of his lanky form. He was dressed in pajamas, a robe, and slippers, too, although his were a nice manly brown rather than the purple of Phyllis's nightclothes.

"Thought I heard the little one carryin' on," Sam said as he came from the foyer into the living room.

"I'm sorry, Sam. He just can't rest comfortably with his ear hurting that way. I gave him some pain reliever like the doctor said, but . . ."

Sam nodded. "Yeah, I reckon it must hurt, all right." He held out his arms. "Here, let me hold him for a while."

Phyllis hesitated. Not because she didn't trust Sam, of course. In the nearly two and a half years that he had rented a room in her house here in Weatherford, Texas, she had grown to know him very well. He was both strong and gentle, just the sort of man who wouldn't think twice about offering to comfort a sick child. But Bobby was her responsibility, not his.

"It's the middle of the night," she told Sam. "You should be sleeping. I'll be all right."

A smile spread across Sam's rugged face. "Shoot, I wasn't asleep anyway. Seems like the older I get, the less easy it is for me to sleep. I was on the computer lookin' at YouTube. You know they got clips on there from all the TV shows I used to watch back in the fifties? I hadn't seen George Burns and Gracie Allen in a long time."

Phyllis couldn't help but smile back at him. They were roughly the same age, in their late sixties, and it wasn't unusual for either of them to discover something new and wonderful on the Internet that most younger people had probably known about for years.

"I'll have to check that out sometime," she said. "Are you sure you don't mind . . . ?"

Sam motioned with his fingers to indicate that she should give Bobby to him.

"Well, all right." She handed the whimpering youngster over.

Bobby immediately threw his arms around Sam's neck and buried his face against the man's shoulder. His sobs began to subside.

"I think I'm jealous," Phyllis said with a laugh. "He appears to like you more than he does me."

"Oh, I wouldn't say that. He just senses that we're kindred spirits."

Phyllis raised an eyebrow. "How so?"

"Normally, I sleep like a baby, too. I kick and fret all night."

"I wouldn't know," Phyllis said as she arched an eyebrow.

Sam chuckled as he started walking slowly back and forth across the living room. Bobby quieted even more. Within a few minutes, he appeared to be sound asleep.

Sam looked at the boy, then grinned at Phyllis. "Say good night, Gracie," he whispered.

"Good night, Gracie," she responded. She held her arms out. "I'll put him in bed."

"No, I got him. We start passin' him around like a football, he's liable to wake up again."

Sam left the living room and started carefully up the stairs. A couple of days earlier, when Bobby had come to stay with Phyllis, Sam and Mike had climbed up into the attic of the old house and brought down the crib Mike had slept in twenty-some-odd years earlier. Bobby had complained that he wasn't a baby and shouldn't have to sleep in a crib, but that was really the only place Phyllis had for him to sleep. They had compromised by leaving the sides down when they put the crib in Phyllis's bedroom.

She was in the kitchen brewing some herbal tea when Sam came back downstairs. "Figured I'd find you in here," he said.

"Did he keep on sleeping?"

"Like a rock. I reckon that medicine finally caught up with him and made him conk out."

"You want some tea?"

"Is it made from flowers and stuff?"

"Well, I'm not going to drink regular tea at this time of night. I never would get to sleep."

"All right, sure. I guess I don't need anything else keepin' me awake, either."

Phyllis poured the tea when it was ready, and they sat down on opposite sides of the kitchen table. She sipped from her cup, then said, "I wish Bobby had been able to go to California with Mike and Sarah. This may well be Bud's last Thanksgiving."

"That's Sarah's dad?"

"Yes."

"At least she's gettin' to spend this time with him."

"Yes, and that's a blessing."

Phyllis thought about her daughter-in-law. She knew from experience how terrible it was to have to face the impending end of a loved one's life. She had lost her husband, Kenny, a number of years earlier. And Sam had gone through the same thing when cancer claimed his wife. But Phyllis also knew that the last days spent together could be some of the most precious of all, easing the passing of the one who had to leave and creating memories that those left behind would carry with them for the rest of *their* days.

So when Bobby had come down with the ear infection the day before Mike and Sarah were supposed to leave to spend a couple of weeks in California with Sarah's parents, and the doctor told them they couldn't take him on the airplane, Phyllis hadn't hesitated. She had urged them to make the trip and leave Bobby with her. "I'd love the chance to spend that much time with him," she had told her son and daughter-in-law. "That way you can make your trip without having to worry about him."

"Oh, I'll worry about him," Sarah had said, and Phyllis knew exactly what she meant. Worrying was a parent's permanent job. Mike was a grown man, and not a day went by that Phyllis didn't spend some of the time wondering where he was and what he was doing and worrying about whether he was all right.

The fact that Mike was a deputy in the Parker County Sheriff's Department didn't make things any easier. But Phyllis knew she would have worried about him no matter what he did for a living.

Phyllis realized that she'd been sitting there quietly, musing over the events of the past few days, without saying a word. Sam had been silent, too. Yet she didn't feel the least bit awkward or uncomfortable because of the silence, and from the looks of him, neither did Sam. It had been a good thing when she'd had a vacancy open up in the house a couple of years earlier, she thought. Her old superintendent, Dolly Williamson, had suggested that she rent the room to Sam, and even though there had been some rough patches at first, caused by having a man in a house full of retired female teachers, it hadn't taken long for Sam to become a member of the family.

And that was the way she thought of him and Carolyn Wilbarger and Eve Turner, the other retired teachers who lived with her. They were all family now.

"This tea's not bad," Sam said. "Bein' a good Texan, though, I'm not sure I'll ever get used to drinkin' any kind of tea without a bunch of ice cubes in it."

Before Phyllis could respond, a key rattled in the lock of the back door.

She and Sam looked at each other in puzzlement. Who in the world could be coming in at that hour? It was after midnight and, anyway, no one had a key to her house except the people who lived there and Mike. Carolyn and Eve were upstairs asleep, and Mike was in California....

Phyllis felt a little twinge of apprehension. Maybe someone was actually trying to break in. They could be attempting to pick the lock. But would a burglar do that when the lights in the kitchen were on and someone was obviously in here?

Sam was on his feet, facing the door. He had braved danger to protect her in the past, and she wasn't surprised that he would do it again. She wouldn't let him do it alone, though. She stood up as well and started looking around for some sort of weapon.

The door swung open, and Carolyn said, "I'm sorry. I didn't mean to disturb anybody."

Sam, bless his heart, didn't miss a beat. He crossed his arms, frowned at Carolyn, and said, "Young lady, do you have any idea what time it is?"

Carolyn looked flabbergasted for a second, but then she glared as she closed the door and said, "I don't need any sass from you, Sam Fletcher. I'm tired."

"Well, I'd imagine so, what with you out gallivantin' around until the wee hours of the morning."

Carolyn looked at Phyllis, who came around the table and got between them. "I thought you were upstairs asleep," Phyllis said to her old friend.

"I would have been if I hadn't gotten a call from Dana Powell," Carolyn said as she took off her coat. "Logan was supposed to help her with some decorations for the Harvest Festival, but you know how undependable *he* is. I've been over at Dana's house all evening, giving her a hand."

Phyllis shook her head. "I didn't hear the phone ring."

"She called me on my cell. Anyway, you were busy with Bobby."

Like seemingly everyone else in the world these days, Phyllis carried a cell phone, but having lived for decades before the things were even invented, she sometimes forgot how ever present they were. Occasionally she had to remind herself when she was out that she didn't have to look for a public phone if she wanted to make a call.

"Like I said, I didn't want to disturb anyone," Carolyn went on. "So I just slipped out and went on over there."

Dana Powell was about twenty years younger than Carolyn—and Phyllis and Sam, for that matter—but she and Carolyn had taught together at the same school before Carolyn retired, and they were still friends. Phyllis liked her as well, although she thought sometimes that Dana was a little too skinny and a little too blond for an elementary school teacher. But there was no denying that

Dana was good with the kids and was also heavily involved in the community, including being in charge of some of the plans for the upcoming "Harvest Festival."

In recent, more politically correct years, that term had been adopted in a lot of places for Halloween celebrations, but this year, in Weatherford, Texas, the festival was taking place the Saturday before Thanksgiving, which as far as Phyllis was concerned was a more traditional and appropriate time for it, anyway. The festival was being held in a city park on the south side of town that surrounded a small lake known for the flock of ducks that lived there most of the year. The ducks would be gone now, having migrated south for the winter, but the park was still a pleasant, picturesque place with playground equipment for the children, hiking trails, picnic areas, and a couple of old settlers' cabins that had been moved in from farther west in the county. Phyllis remembered taking some of her history classes to the park on field trips so the students could see the bullet holes left behind in the walls by Indian battles, and check out the interiors, which were furnished in pioneer fashion.

A couple of days from now, on Saturday evening, the park would be full of games and rides and craft displays, along with an assortment of food and drink vendors, much like the Peach Festival that was held in Weatherford every summer. There would also be a cooking contest centered on traditional Thanksgiving foods such as pumpkin pies, creative uses of cranberry, unusual stuffings to go with turkey, and things like that.

The cooking contest was especially interesting to Phyllis, who entered nearly every such contest that came along, and she was usually in competition with Carolyn. There wouldn't be any rivalry this time, however. Carolyn had already agreed to serve as a judge in the contest instead of entering it. That was fine with Phyllis, although in a way she would miss their friendly competition.

She might miss the contest entirely, she thought, depending on how Bobby was doing. She might not have the time to prepare her entry.

"What were you working on with Dana?" she asked Carolyn as she got another cup from the cabinet and poured some tea for her friend. Phyllis hadn't asked whether Carolyn wanted one, but knew she loved herbal tea.

"Scarecrow costumes, of all things," Carolyn said as she took the cup. "Thank you."

Sam said, "I thought they were tryin' to get folks to *come* to this festival, not scare them off."

"Oh, there are going to be scarecrows and bales of hay scattered around the park as decorations," Carolyn explained. "Logan was going to pick up the supplies to make the costumes, but then he had some sort of business emergency, so Dana called me and we went to Wal-Mart and Dollar Tree together to get what she'd need. When I saw how much work she had in front of her, I said I'd stay and help." Carolyn stifled a yawn. "I didn't expect to be quite so late getting back, though. But we got to talking while we worked, and, well, you know how that goes."

Phyllis nodded. "Yes, of course. I hope Logan was at least properly apologetic when he got home."

Carolyn took another sip of tea. "He didn't get home. At least, he hadn't when I left."

"Wasn't Dana worried? I would have been."

"I suppose she's used to it," Carolyn said with a shake of her head. "She should know by now that her husband is as much married to that real estate business as he is to her." She looked back and forth between Phyllis and Sam. "Enough about the Powells. What are the two of you doing up at this time of night?"

"Bobby's ear was hurting and he had trouble sleeping," Phyllis said. "Sam was able to get him to doze off, though."

"Well, I'm not going to have any trouble falling asleep. I'm exhausted." Carolyn stood up, quickly downed the rest of her tea, rinsed the cup out in the sink, and put the empty cup in the dishwasher. "Good night, both of you. Don't stay up too late."

"We won't," Sam said, then added, "I'm gonna go look at YouTube some more."

He started to follow Carolyn out of the kitchen, but Phyllis stopped him with a hand on his arm. "Thank you for helping with Bobby."

"Anytime," he said with a smile. "He's a good little fella. Hate to see him hurtin'. You think he'll feel good enough to go to the festival on Saturday?"

"I hope so. We could all use some good times."

"Yeah." Sam nodded. "Hope it goes well."

"Why wouldn't it?"

"Well, you never know. . . ."

"Yes, you do," Phyllis said firmly. "*I* know. There's not going to be any trouble at this festival. Nothing unusual is going to happen."

"That's right." Sam leaned over and planted a quick kiss on her forehead. "Good night."

She told him good night and watched him go up the stairs, wishing he hadn't brought up all the things that had happened in the past. He hadn't meant anything by it, of course.

It was hard to forget, though, that for a while there, murder had seemed to make a habit of following her around.

But more than a year had passed without any sort of trouble, she reminded herself. There was no reason to think it would crop up again now.

With that thought in her head, she turned off the light in the kitchen and went upstairs.

Chapter 2

Bobby seemed to feel better the next morning. He acted more like his usual self, anyway, and didn't complain too much about his ear.

Phyllis wasn't surprised when the phone rang and she answered it to find her daughter-in-law, Sarah, on the other end. Sarah had been calling every day to check on Bobby, and Phyllis couldn't blame her for that. She would have been just as worried if she'd been in Sarah's position.

"He had a little trouble last night," she said in answer to Sarah's question about how Bobby was doing. "His ear hurt enough that he had trouble sleeping, but he settled down after a while."

"Oh, the poor little guy. Is he still running a fever?"

"No, not anymore. How's Bud doing?"

"Hanging in there," Sarah said, but Phyllis heard the sorrow in her voice. They all knew the end was coming for Sarah's father, but knowing didn't make it any easier to take.

"I'm sorry it won't be much of a Thanksgiving for you, dear."

"Well, I'm thankful we were able to have this time with him," Sarah said, "and I'm grateful to you for making that possible. And for helping to keep my dad cheered up."

Phyllis frowned a little in puzzlement. "What do you mean by that?"

"Mike's been telling him all about those murder cases you've been mixed up in."

"Oh, good grief. Mike shouldn't be bothering him with all that nonsense."

Sarah laughed. "No, no, Dad loves it. He says it sounds just like a TV show."

It hadn't *felt* the least bit like a TV show when she was living through those tumultuous times, Phyllis thought. Having friends accused of murder, trying to sort out all the trials and tragedies of human lives, even finding herself and those she loved in danger at times . . . She was glad Bud found Mike's yarns to be entertaining diversions, but going through those events certainly hadn't been.

"It'll be just fine with me if there aren't any more murders for me to solve," she told Sarah.

"Amen to that. How are *you* holding up, Phyllis? It's been a long time since you had to keep up with a little ball of fire like Bobby."

"Oh, I'm fine," Phyllis answered without hesitation. It was true that she was a little tired this morning from the sleep she'd missed the night before, but she wasn't going to tell Sarah that. Sarah didn't need anything else to worry about. Phyllis went on, "Mike was always on the go when he was little, too, and it doesn't take long to fall back into the old routines. Having Sam and Carolyn and Eve around has been a big help, too. Sam was actually the one who got Bobby to sleep last night."

"That was nice of him. Sam's a good guy."

"Yes," Phyllis agreed, "he most certainly is." She didn't particularly want to discuss how she felt about Sam with her daughter-in-law, so she went on, "It's nice and warm today, so I thought I might take Bobby to the park this morning. If that's all right with you, that is."

"Oh, sure. Whatever you think is all right is fine with me. I trust you, Phyllis; you know that."

"Yes, but you're Bobby's mother. I thought since we were talking anyway, it wouldn't hurt to check with you."

"You go right ahead. Have a good time. Is he around so I can talk to him for a minute?"

"I believe he's in the living room, watching TV." Phyllis leaned out the door of the kitchen, where she had answered the phone, and looked along the hallway toward the living room. She heard the sound of the television coming from there, playing cartoons. Cupping her hand over the phone, she called, "Bobby? Your mother wants to talk to you."

He appeared in the hall and came running toward her, holding up his hands for the phone. "Mama! Mama!" he said.

"Here he is," Phyllis told Sarah, then handed the cordless phone to her grandson.

"Hi, Mama!" Bobby said breathlessly.

Phyllis went back to the counter, where she had set down her coffee cup when the phone rang. Bobby stood in the door between the kitchen and the hall, talking rapidly as he told Sarah about the TV shows he'd been watching and the games he'd been playing and how Sam was teaching him how to shoot a basketball. Phyllis sipped the still-warm coffee and smiled. Bobby's enthusiasm for life was contagious.

After a few minutes, the little boy said, "Bye, Mama," and turned to hold the phone up to Phyllis. "Mama wants to talk to you again, Gran'mama."

"Thank you, Bobby," Phyllis said as she took it. "You can go back and watch TV again if you want to."

"Okay!" He hurried off toward the living room.

Phyllis was laughing a little as she held the phone to her ear again. Sarah chuckled, too, and said, "He does go on, doesn't he?"

"It's wonderful having him here. I wish he'd been able to go with you to see his grandfather, but since he couldn't, I'm glad I was able to help out. And this way he'll get to go to the Harvest Festival, too, if he feels like it."

"Oh, that's right. That's this weekend, isn't it?"

"Yes, it's all day Saturday and Saturday night."

"What are you going to bake for the contest?"

"I've come up with a recipe for pumpkin cheesecake muffins that I think will be good." Phyllis explained how she would make the muffins, along with the pecan crumble topping she thought would go well on them.

"Oh, that sounds good," Sarah said. "I'll have to try them when we get back. Of course, by then, you'll have won the Harvest Festival cooking contest."

"Not necessarily," Phyllis said. "I'm sure there'll be a lot of delicious entries." But not one from Carolyn, she thought, which would improve her chances of winning.

She chatted with Sarah for a few more minutes, then hung up after promising to call immediately if Bobby's ear infection got worse. After finishing her coffee, she called him into the kitchen again and said, "Would you like to go to the park this morning?"

His eyes widened with excitement for a second before he grew serious again and asked, "You think it's all right? Mama said I had to stay in while I was sick."

"I talked to her about it, and she thought it was okay since it's warm here today. You probably shouldn't play too hard and wear yourself out while we're there, though."

"Okay!"

"Go get your jacket. It's still cool enough that you'll need it."

Bobby hurried upstairs, dashing past Sam, who was coming down, on the way. "We're goin' to the park!" he told Sam.

Sam walked into the kitchen as Phyllis was rinsing her coffee cup. "Bobby says you're goin' to the park."

"That's right." Phyllis put the cup in the dishwasher. "Would you like to come along?"

"That's a mighty appealin' invitation, but I was fixin' to head for the lumberyard. Need some stain for those bookshelves I'm buildin'."

Phyllis thought about telling him that could wait, but then she restrained herself. The way Sam spent his days was his decision to make, not hers. She enjoyed his company, but she enjoyed Bobby's company, too.

"I suppose we'll see you later, then."

He lifted a hand in farewell. "So long," he said as he

headed for the front of the house. His pickup was parked at the curb. Phyllis's car took up half of the two-car garage attached to the house, and Carolyn, as the boarder who had lived there the longest, had seniority and claimed the other half of the garage for her car. The broad, tree-shaded street was in a quiet neighborhood a handful of blocks from downtown Weatherford, and there wasn't much traffic along it. So parking on the street had never been a problem.

Phyllis got her purse and a sweater from the closet just inside the front door and was ready to go when Bobby came downstairs wearing a lightweight jacket. They went into the garage through the kitchen, and as they were getting into the car, Bobby asked, "Are we goin' to the park where the fest'val's gonna be?"

"That's right," Phyllis told him. There were several city parks scattered around town, but the one that surrounded the little "lake," which was more like a pond, was the one she liked the best.

"Will the ducks be there?" Mike and Sarah had taken Bobby to the park to feed the ducks on numerous occasions, according to Bobby. He liked to describe how the birds squabbled and quacked over the bits of stale bread he tossed to them.

"Probably not," Phyllis told him. "But you never know. The ones who live there during the summer have all gone south for the winter, I imagine, but there could be some others stopping by on their way down from Canada or someplace."

"I hope so. I like the ducks."

With the red lights and the heavy traffic on South Main Street and around the junior college, it took them about ten minutes to reach the park. Since school was in session, the place wasn't very busy during the day. Most of the people who came there were either retirees who found it a good place to walk for exercise or young mothers with preschool-age children. Today when Phyllis pulled into the parking lot, she saw only three vehicles there, and one of them was a white pickup belonging to the city parks department.

A large sign was draped over and tied onto the wooden fence that separated the parking lot from the park itself. The sign announced that the first annual Harvest Festival would be held there that Saturday. Calling something the "first annual" anything was a sign of confidence, Phyllis thought. Even though it was likely that the festival would be a success, no one could know that for certain at this point.

Bobby had the seat belt off and the door open by the time Phyllis could get around to the passenger side of the car. Since he was a little small for his age, Bobby had graduated from a car seat to a booster seat only a year earlier and was still proud of being able to ride in the seat like a big boy. He also liked being able to unfasten his own seat belt but was good about not doing so while the car was moving, unlike some kids. Phyllis was old enough to remember when hardly anyone had worn seat belts, especially children. Even though she thought that in some cases society had overreacted to perceived dangers, this was definitely not one of those cases.

"Remember, don't run around and play too hard," she called after Bobby as he trotted around the cabins toward the swing set not far from the lake. Phyllis searched the water but didn't see any ducks. She hoped Bobby wouldn't be too disappointed by the lack of fowl.

While Bobby climbed onto one of the swings and began pushing himself back and forth with his feet, Phyllis strolled toward one of the old, historical cabins. They were built in the dogtrot style, two cabins with a common roof that also covered the open area between them, the so-called dogtrot.

She had just paused to look through one of the cabin's windows at the period furnishings inside when she heard a man say, loudly and distinctly, "If you try anything like that, I'll kill you."

Chapter 3

🧁

$\mathcal{P}$hyllis stiffened in surprise at hearing such a threat expressed like that. The man's voice came from in front of the cabin. Phyllis was torn between the urge to see what was going on and the natural caution that told her to stay right where she was, out of the would-be murderer's sight.

Caution lost that battle, for one simple, very good reason. Bobby was down there at the swing set, and the man was between him and Phyllis. She had to find out what was going on if some sort of danger might be threatening her grandson.

Anyway, a woman and two small children were walking on the far side of the lake, which was only about fifty yards wide. Phyllis didn't think anybody would commit murder in plain sight, on a warm, sunny autumn morning like this.

As she stepped around the corner of the cabin, she saw a man standing there. He laughed and said, "No, really, I'll kill you." He seemed to be talking to himself, because there was no one else anywhere around except Phyllis. Then she noticed the earphone tucked into his ear and realized he was talking on one of those Bluetooth cell phones, or whatever they were called. As Phyllis watched, the man put some sort of pill in his mouth, then took a drink from the water bottle in his hand. He laughed again, then froze as he noticed her standing there.

Phyllis felt a wave of embarrassment go through her. Even though it was unintentional, she had been eavesdropping on a private conversation and had wound up spying on the man for a few seconds before he realized she was there. He seemed more surprised than upset, though. He gave her a little smile and a friendly nod, then went on talking to someone on the phone.

"You try to steal NorCenTex Development out from under me, Ben, and you'll regret it; I promise you. I'll cut your throat, bucko. Hey, we still on for golf next week? . . . Fine, I'll see you then. . . . Yeah, take it easy, buddy."

Phyllis told herself not to feel embarrassed. If people were going to wander around apparently talking to themselves like they'd lost their minds, they couldn't complain if people heard what they were saying.

The man took another drink from the water bottle and then said, "Hi, there. Beautiful day, isn't it?"

"It certainly is," Phyllis agreed. "A little bit of a late Indian summer, I suppose."

"Yeah. Where I grew up, it's winter by now, and it will be for a long time."

"Where's that?" Phyllis asked, wanting to be polite.

"Chicago. Haven't been back there in a long time, though. I'm a Texan now." The man looked curiously at her. "Say, we've met, haven't we?"

Phyllis had already recognized him. He was a wiry man of medium height with dark hair. He wore jeans and a gray shirt with the sleeves rolled up a couple of turns.

"You're Logan Powell, aren't you?" Phyllis asked.

"That's right."

"I know your wife. I used to be a teacher, too. I'm Phyllis Newsom."

"Oh, sure," Logan Powell said as a grin spread across his face. "We've run into each other at school board meetings, football games, things like that."

Phyllis nodded. She felt relieved and a little bit silly

for being worried now. Still, you could never tell for sure what might happen, and it was better to be careful.

Powell went on, "You probably thought I was a crazy man, telling somebody I was going to kill him."

"Well . . . I did wonder what was going on," Phyllis admitted.

"That was my buddy Ben Loomis I was talking to. He's another real estate guy. He's been making noises about trying to cut himself in on a deal I've been working on, and I was just lettin' him know what he can expect if he does." Powell laughed again as he fished a red-and-white-striped peppermint candy out of his pocket and unwrapped it. "But we're old friends. He knows I didn't mean it. I'm still not gonna let him get his grubby paws on my deal, though."

"But you wouldn't resort to murder."

"Of course not." Powell popped the peppermint into his mouth, then made a gun out of the thumb and index finger of his right hand and let the hammer drop. "Doesn't hurt to let a guy worry a little, though." He nodded toward the swing set. "That your little guy?"

"My grandson," Phyllis said. She knew good and well that Powell hadn't mistaken Bobby for her son. She looked all right for her age, and there wasn't *too* much gray in her brown hair, but no way did she look as if she could have a four-year-old.

"Cute kid. Are you bringing him to the festival?"

"I plan to if he feels up to it. He's been battling an ear infection."

"Sorry to hear that. I hope both of you can make it. It's gonna be quite an event. I'm on the chamber of commerce planning committee, and we've been working really hard to make sure it's something the town can be proud of."

That wasn't exactly the way Phyllis had heard it the night before, when Carolyn arrived home in the wee hours of the morning after helping Powell's wife, Dana, with preparations for the festival because Powell himself was missing in action. She didn't bring that up, though.

"And of course it's all for a good cause," Powell went on.

"Feeding the homeless and disadvantaged, right?"

"Yep. That's why the only admission we're charging each family is a bag of canned goods or other nonperishable food."

The way he said that made Phyllis think that it was a statement he'd uttered a lot.

"Of course, if anybody wants to donate more than one bag, we'll be happy to take it," he continued. "We'll be delivering all that food on Thanksgiving morning, along with free turkey dinners for some of the families. We're in need of volunteers to help with those deliveries, if you're interested."

"Well, I don't know. I'm taking care of my grandson while my son and his wife are out of town. . . ."

"Sure, I understand. But if it works out where you can lend a hand, we'd be happy for the help."

"I'll keep it in mind," Phyllis promised. She wondered whether Carolyn planned to help distribute the food collected at the festival. That seemed like something she would do. Carolyn could be as tough as nails when she wanted to, but she had a kind heart.

"Well, I guess I'd better be going," Powell said. "I just swung by here to have a look around and figure out where some of the decorations are gonna go. We'll be working all day tomorrow to get everything ready, and probably half the night. I hope this good weather holds."

"It's supposed to, although we may get a cool front during the day Saturday. At least that's what I've heard."

"It'll be all right with me if we do. Some nice crisp autumn air will make it seem more like Thanksgiving, you know?"

Phyllis nodded. "You're right."

"So long," Powell said. He started walking toward the parking lot. He hadn't gotten out of earshot when his phone must have vibrated, because he lifted a hand to his ear to touch a button or something and said, "Logan Powell . . . Hey, babe, how you doin'?"

Phyllis headed toward the swings. She had already

inadvertently listened in on Powell's side of a business conversation this morning. She didn't need to eavesdrop while he talked to his wife.

Bobby dragged his feet in the sand to stop the swing as Phyllis came up. "I wanna do somethin' else, Gran'-mama," he said.

"Well, go ahead," she told him, waving a hand to take in all the park around them. "First, though, are you feeling all right?"

"Yeah, just a little tired. But I wanna play some more, anyway."

He ran over to an old covered wagon, of which nothing was left except the wheels, the iron framework, and some thick sideboards. Children climbed on it as they would on monkey bars. Bobby swarmed up one of the wheels and began walking along the top of the sideboard, holding on to the curved frame over the top that had once been covered with canvas. Phyllis stood close to him, ready to catch him if he started to fall, but he made his way nimbly all around the wagon.

From there Bobby went to the play horses, each with its thick spring base that bounced back and forth, and the teeter-totter, where he sat on one end while Phyllis pushed the other end up and down. She was getting tired, and he seemed to be, too. Besides, it was almost lunchtime.

"Why don't we walk around the lake once and then go back home?" she suggested.

"Okay. Can we get Happy Meals?"

"No, I'll fix you something for lunch when we get back."

"Okay." He trotted ahead of her until he reached the wooden bridge spanning the deep drainage ditch that fed into the lake. Then he stopped and waited, and Phyllis knew he didn't want to walk over the bridge until she caught up with him to hold his hand.

How many times had she walked over this same bridge holding Mike's hand, twenty years earlier? Phyllis had no idea, but she knew that each and every one of them had been a special moment. She hoped that Mike remembered them with as much fondness as she did, and that someday Bobby would have good memories, too, of the days when his grandmother had brought him to this park.

She swallowed hard as she walked along the far bank of the lake with him. She wasn't going to be a foolish old woman and cry over some memories, she told herself. She wasn't.

Well . . . maybe a little. She brushed away a tear without Bobby noticing.

Sam was back, staining boards at the workbench in the garage when they got home a little later. Carolyn's car was gone, though, Phyllis noted.

"Do you know where Carolyn went?" she asked Sam as she and Bobby got out of the car.

"Yeah, she was just leavin' when I came back in," he replied. "Said to tell you she was goin' to see Dana Powell and would probably eat lunch with her at school, so you shouldn't worry about her."

"More planning for the festival?"

"I suppose so," Sam said with a shrug as he worked some of the stain into a board with a cloth. "She didn't really say."

"Bobby and I ran into Dana's husband at the park this morning. He was checking things out and seeing where decorations need to go."

"Do I know him?"

"You've met him."

"I'll take your word for it. My memory for names isn't what it used to be." He smiled. "But then, what is, when you get to be our age?"

"Speak for yourself. After following a four-year-old around a park all morning, I feel positively young."

Sam frowned at her. "Really?"

"Lord, no. I'm worn out," Phyllis admitted. She watched Bobby as he opened the kitchen door and went into the house. "But I feel young inside."

"Only place it really counts," Sam said.

Chapter 4

$\mathscr{B}$obby went to sleep on the sofa while he was watching TV after a lunch of grilled cheese sandwiches with apple slices in them, one of his favorites. He didn't take regular naps anymore—he was a big boy now, as he liked to point out—but sometimes all the playing caught up with him and caused him to doze off, Phyllis had discovered.

When she came out of the kitchen after cleaning up the lunch dishes, she found Eve Turner sitting in the living room watching Bobby sleep. The much-married and as-often-divorced Eve had an affectionate smile on her face. She got up from the armchair where she was sitting and motioned for Phyllis to follow her back into the kitchen.

"He's just adorable," Eve said when they were in the other room and their voices wouldn't disturb Bobby. "I'm not surprised that he's so cute, though. Mike's a very handsome young man, and Sarah is lovely, of course."

"All sleeping little boys are cute," Phyllis pointed out. "Like puppies."

"Well . . . yes, I suppose."

Phyllis knew that Eve, despite all her marriages, had never had any children of her own. She hadn't inquired as to why that was. Some people probably thought she was just a nosy old busybody, but she truly didn't like to pry into her friends' personal lives ... although sometimes circumstances had thrust the necessity to do just that onto her.

"This is the longest I've kept him since he was born," she said. "It's been wonderful."

"There's some good to be found in almost everything, I suppose. Even something as sad as Sarah's father being sick."

"I suppose," Phyllis agreed.

Before she could say anything else, the back door opened and Carolyn came in. She seemed rather distracted, but she nodded pleasantly enough to Phyllis and Eve and said, "Ladies."

"How did your meeting with Dana Powell go?" Phyllis asked.

"All right. It wasn't just Dana, though. There were several other teachers there ... Jenna Grantham, Barbara Loomis, Kendra Neville, and Taryn Marshall. They've all been working on decorations for the festival, and Taryn had her art classes make posters advertising it. I have a lot of them in my car right now. I thought I'd take them around town and put them up this afternoon."

"It's a little late for something like that, isn't it?" Eve asked. "It seems to me like posters should have gone up at least a week ago."

Carolyn inclined her head in agreement, then said, "That's the way I would have done it, but I think Taryn just didn't get around to it until now. These young teachers are always so busy these days."

Phyllis knew that was true. The state demanded so much more paperwork now than it had when she was teaching, and there were more extracurricular activities that had to have coaches and sponsors, too. And she knew the teachers Carolyn was talking about had to be young, with names like Taryn, Kendra, and Jenna. Barbara Loomis was the only one Carolyn had mentioned who had what Phyllis considered a more common name, and she suddenly thought about the conversation she'd had that morning with Logan Powell.

"Is Barbara Loomis married to a real estate man?" she asked. She had probably met all the teachers Carolyn had mentioned but didn't really remember any of them.

"That's right," Carolyn said. "Why do you ask?"

"Oh, I took Bobby to the park this morning, and while I was there I ran into Logan Powell. He was talking on the phone to some other real estate agent named Ben Loomis."

Carolyn nodded. "That's Barbara's husband, all right. What in the world was Logan Powell doing at the park?"

"He said he was getting ready for the festival and seeing where the decorations needed to be placed," Phyllis explained.

Carolyn made a scoffing sound. "Of course he was," she said. "I'm sure he'll be there tomorrow and Saturday, too, taking credit for everything when it was his wife and the other ladies who did most of the real work. Logan's just interested in putting on a show and having everyone tell him how wonderful he is."

Carolyn didn't believe in pulling her punches when it came to her opinions of people, so her comments didn't really surprise Phyllis.

She went on. "I suppose it's worth putting up with grandstanders like him, though, if it helps put food in the bellies of people who really need it. There's not much in the world that's worse than being hungry, let me tell you."

Phyllis noticed that her friend's voice held an unusual vehemence, and so did Eve, who said, "Goodness, dear, you sound like you're speaking from experience."

"I am," Carolyn said. "My family was poor when I was a child. I mean, really poor." She gave a curt shake of her head. "But you don't want to hear about that."

"Actually, I would like to hear about it," Phyllis said. "You've never talked much about your childhood, Carolyn. Why, I probably know more about what Sam's life was like when he was growing up than I do about yours, and I've known you a lot longer than him!"

She realized that maybe she was being insensitive.

Perhaps Carolyn's childhood had been so bad that she just wanted to put it behind her and never even think about it again.

But there was a candor that came with age, and Phyllis wanted to believe that there was nothing old friends couldn't say to each other.

After a moment, Carolyn sighed. "If you really want to hear about it, I need some tea."

"I just happen to have some brewing in the pot," Phyllis replied with a smile.

A couple of minutes later, the three women were sitting around the kitchen table, each with a cup of orange spice herbal tea in front of her. Phyllis quickly checked in on Bobby and saw that he was still sound asleep on the sofa in the living room, so she wasn't worried about him waking up anytime soon.

"Go ahead," Eve said to Carolyn.

"But you don't have to tell us anything you don't want to," Phyllis added.

Carolyn sipped her tea. "I'm just worried that you're going to be terribly bored." She took a deep breath. "I come from a little farming town down close to Waco."

Phyllis nodded. "You've mentioned that before."

"I never told you, though, that we never really had a home of our own. My father was a mechanic, and when things were going well, my parents were able to rent a house in town, but when they weren't, he had to take jobs on the big farms around there, and we'd wind up living in one of the little houses that the owners provided for workers. There were seven children, plus my grandfather, my mother's father, lived with us, so there would be ten people crowded into a house that wasn't much more than a two-room shack."

"That's terrible," Eve said. "It sounds like . . . like slave quarters."

Phyllis, who had taught eighth-grade American history for many years, said, "I'm sure it was hardly that bad, but it must have been terrible anyway."

"Yes, it could have been worse," Carolyn agreed. "That's what my mother and father told me all the time, and my grandfather, too. They had all lived through the Great Depression, after all. They knew what real hardship was like."

Like Carolyn, Phyllis had been born a little too late to have been through the Depression. She'd been alive when Pearl Harbor was attacked but had no memory of it. She could vaguely recall, though, the celebrations sparked off by the surrender of Japan at the end of the war.

"It's a funny thing," Carolyn mused as she stared at her cup and saucer on the table in front of her, "but when your belly is empty it hurts just as bad whether it's 1932 or 1948. And the shame a little girl feels when she has to go to school in a flour-sack dress that's more patches than dress because three older sisters have already worn it doesn't really change, either."

"You poor dear," Eve murmured.

"Don't feel sorry for me," Carolyn said firmly. "Growing up like that taught me a great deal. I learned the value of hard work, for one thing, and I learned that if you want to get out of a bad situation, you have to actually *do* something about it. Sitting around and complaining won't accomplish a thing."

"That's the truth," Phyllis said.

"Even with its drawbacks, I liked school better than anything else. That's why I decided I wanted to be a teacher. I started saving my money for college when I was a sophomore in high school. I got a job at a department store in Waco and hitchhiked into town every day after school to work, then hitchhiked home at night."

"Dear Lord!" Eve said. "You're lucky you weren't killed . . . or worse!"

"I was willing to take that chance," Carolyn said. "Anyway, the world was a different place then, at least for the most part. It wasn't as mean."

Phyllis wasn't sure about that. Judging by what she knew about some of the things that had gone on in the past, there had always been a lot of meanness in the world. People just hadn't been as aware of it back then as they were now.

"I was able to save enough money to pay for my first semester at Mary Hardin-Baylor College, as well as a little room in a boardinghouse," Carolyn went on. "I kept working all through college and was able to get my degree and my teaching certificate. My older brothers and sisters helped a little, too, when they could, just like I helped the younger ones after I graduated and got a teaching position. I tried not to look back . . . but I never really forgot what it was like to be hungry on Thanksgiving. I don't want any other child to have to experience that, if there's anything I can do to help it." She smiled. "There you are. The sad story of Carolyn Mahoney Wilbarger."

"It *is* a sad story," Eve insisted. "I'm sorry you had to go through that."

"I'm sure that neither of you grew up in a bed of roses, either. A lot of people had it tough back then, and even tougher the generation before."

"Yes, and now people worry about being in an area where their cell phone reception isn't quite as strong," Phyllis said. "I guess it's all just a matter of perspective."

Before any of them could say anything else, Bobby came wandering down the hall to the kitchen, rubbing his eyes with his knuckles. "I went to sleep," he said. "I missed my cartoons."

"I'm sorry, dear," Phyllis said as he climbed up into her lap and laid his head on her shoulder. She patted him on the back and added, "Life is hard sometimes."

Chapter 5

Carolyn's story had touched Phyllis, so later that afternoon when Carolyn was back from putting up the posters and they were both in the kitchen again, she said to her friend, "I'd like to help more with the festival."

"You should have come with me to help with the posters."

"I know. I'm sorry, I didn't think about it in time, what with dealing with Bobby."

"Well, you're entering the cooking contest, aren't you?"

"That's right."

"Then you'll be helping to get people to come and donate canned goods," Carolyn said. "What are you going to make?"

Phyllis felt a moment of instinctive hesitation. She and Carolyn had gone head-to-head in so many of these competitions, often finishing first and second, or at least in the top five, that she was in the habit of being secretive about the recipes she planned to enter. The rivalry between them was so keen that she didn't want to give Carolyn any unnecessary advantage.

But of course in this case that wasn't a consideration, since Carolyn wasn't entering the contest. So Phyllis smiled and said, "Pumpkin cheesecake muffins with a pecan crumble on top."

"My, that sounds good. People know what wonderful

bakers we have here in Weatherford, so I'm sure a lot of them will show up just to sample the contest entries. So you see, you're doing your part."

"I'd like to do more," Phyllis insisted. "I'll bet that you're going to be delivering canned goods and turkey dinners to disadvantaged families on Thanksgiving, aren't you?"

"Yes, I volunteered to do that," Carolyn said.

"Well, then, I'll help you."

Carolyn frowned. "Aren't you planning to have a big Thanksgiving dinner here?"

"Yes, of course. It's tradition." Phyllis had been preparing a veritable feast for Thanksgiving almost every year for so many years that she couldn't even remember how long it had been anymore.

"So you'll be busy with that."

"Oh, goodness, not so busy that I can't afford to take a few hours to help people who've been less fortunate than I have. Thanksgiving isn't just about counting your own blessings. It's about sharing them with others."

"That's true," Carolyn admitted. "And we can certainly use all the help we can get."

"Then it's settled," Phyllis declared. "Anyway, I'll be doing a lot of the cooking the day before, so things will just have to be heated up on Thanksgiving Day. The turkey will take a long time to roast, and Eve can check on it now and then if she needs to."

Carolyn frowned. "I don't know if I'd give Eve any responsibility for such an important part of the meal. She's a fine woman, but I'm reasonably sure that none of her husbands ever married her for her cooking, if you know what I mean."

"I know what you mean," Phyllis said with a smile, "but I think Eve can handle it."

"Let's just hope you don't wind up with a burned bird." Carolyn added, "If you want to help more with the festival itself, you can always come with me tomorrow and help get the park ready."

"I think that would be fun," Phyllis said. "But what about Bobby? I'd have to bring him along, and he might get underfoot while we were trying to work."

Carolyn thought about that for a moment, then suggested, "Let Sam watch him for the afternoon."

"Sam?" Phyllis repeated, surprised that Carolyn would come up with that idea. Even though Carolyn had been opposed to the idea of Sam moving into the house to start with, the two of them had become friendly, even though they weren't good friends and probably never would be. Phyllis would have thought that Carolyn believed Sam couldn't possibly take care of a four-year-old by himself, though.

"Why not?" Carolyn asked with a shrug. "Bobby's not really very sick now, is he?"

"No, I think he's almost over the ear infection."

"And Sam has children, doesn't he?"

"Yes, but they're grown."

"They were little once." Carolyn's tone took on a slightly caustic edge as she went on. "I'm sure he didn't take care of them nearly as much as his wife did, but he's bound to have watched them some. And he has grandchildren of his own."

"That's true."

"So I think he could take care of Bobby for a few hours without fouling up too much. Anyway, you'd only be a cell phone call and a ten-minute drive away."

"Also true," Phyllis said. "You've convinced me. There's just one thing you're forgetting."

"What's that?"

"I'll still have to ask Sam if it's all right with him."

Carolyn waved a hand and said, "Land's sake, Phyllis, you know that man will do anything that *you* ask him to. He's your boyfriend, after all."

Phyllis felt her face growing warm. "He's not my—"

She had started to say that Sam wasn't her boyfriend, but she stopped as she realized that, actually, he probably was. They had certainly enjoyed some romantic moments over the past couple of years, and they liked spending time in each other's company in general. And neither one of them was seeing anyone else. Eve had even given up her habitual flirting with Sam since it was so obvious that it wasn't going to get her anywhere. So, yes, maybe they were boyfriend and girlfriend. But after spending so many years around eighth-graders, Phyllis just couldn't bring herself to think of it that way.

"Why don't we just say that he's my gentleman friend?"

"Call it anything you want," Carolyn said. "You've got that man wrapped around your little finger, and you know it. If you ask him to watch Bobby tomorrow, he'll do it."

"We'll see," Phyllis said.

"Shoot, yeah, I'd be glad to watch the little fella."

"You're not just saying that because . . ."

Phyllis's voice trailed off. She and Sam were on the sofa in the living room and had been watching the ten o'clock news on TV. Bobby was settled in his makeshift bed for the night, and Carolyn and Eve were both upstairs, as far as Phyllis knew. During a commercial, Phyllis had taken advantage of the opportunity to mute the sound on the television and ask Sam about the possibility of him taking care of Bobby the next day.

He was looking at her now with one somewhat bushy eyebrow cocked quizzically. "Because of what?" he asked.

"Because it's me who's asking you."

A grin stretched across his rugged face. "You know I'd do dang near anything for you, Phyllis. But to tell you the truth, I'd been thinkin' that I'd like to spend more time with Bobby. No offense, but I don't get to do much male bondin' around here. Probably be good for both of us."

She had to laugh. "You mean you're getting tired of being the only rooster in the henhouse?"

"Well, it's not exactly like *that*. . . ."

"My goodness, Sam Fletcher, you're blushing."

"Yeah, I expect so," he said. "Anyway, Bobby's been after me to show him how some of those woodworkin' tools in the garage operate, so this would be a good chance to do that."

Phyllis leaned back. "Woodworking tools? Good

grief, Sam, he's four years old! He doesn't need to be working with tools."

"Didn't say that I'd let him use 'em. Won't hurt to let him start gettin' familiar with 'em, though. I can see to it that he knows how to handle each tool safely before he ever touches any of 'em."

"You'll be careful?" she asked.

"You know I will," he promised.

Phyllis hesitated a moment longer as she wrestled with an unexpected feeling. It should have been Kenny showing Bobby how to use those tools, she told herself, thinking of her late husband. He had passed away before Bobby was even born, though. That made one grandfather Bobby had never known, and with Sarah's father doing so badly, Bobby probably wouldn't remember his other grandfather, either.

But he would have a good friend in Sam, Phyllis realized, so she nodded and said, "All right, as long as you make sure he doesn't get hurt. He'll need to stay well back, and he should wear safety goggles, too."

"He'll love that," Sam said, grinning again. He gestured toward the TV. "Weather forecast is comin' on."

Phyllis turned the sound back on, and they sat there watching as the meteorologist, who looked like she had just graduated from college and was gorgeous enough to be a model, explained that Friday would be partly cloudy and Saturday would be mostly cloudy and cooler as a front came through. No rain, though, which was good. Rain would ruin the festival.

They sat there through the sports report and the latest explanation of why the Dallas Cowboys weren't playing as well as they should have been. Then Phyllis turned the TV off because neither of them cared to watch any of the late-night talk shows or any more news.

Before she could stand up, though, Sam said, "A while ago when you were askin' me how come I agreed to watch Bobby, you were afraid I said yes just because I'm your boyfriend, right?"

"No, of course not," she said. "I mean ... well ... I wanted you to be honest with me, Sam. I don't want you to feel like you always have to do what I want. Or what you *think* I want."

"I'm honest with you. Always have been. At least I try to be. I've always felt like you're honest with me, too."

"Oh, yes, of course."

"Like I told you, I want to spend as much time with Bobby as I can. He's full of questions, and he's a smart kid. There's nothin' like a smart kid for keepin' you on your toes."

Phyllis laughed. "That's the truth. You never know what he's going to say."

"Yeah. Like the other day"—Sam leaned closer to her—"when he said, 'My gran'mama's your girlfriend, ain't she, Sam?'"

"Oh!" Phyllis said. She punched him on the arm. "He didn't say that! Did he?"

"Swear to God. He's a perceptive little cuss."

"I'm just ... not sure I'm ready to be back in junior high again."

"Well, now, there's the difference between you and me. . . . Part of me never left junior high." His arm tightened around her shoulders.

Phyllis leaned against him and sighed. "Oh, well. I suppose there are worse things than feeling like you're in eighth grade again."

Chapter 6

The next day was breezy, and warm for November. After lunch, Carolyn told Phyllis, "We need to go by the school and pick up the scarecrows Dana and her friends made. She has them in the back of her SUV. She said just to come by her room and get the key."

That was fine with Phyllis, although she hadn't been to the elementary school where Dana Powell taught since the carnival just before Halloween a couple of years earlier, when a murder had taken place there. Those weren't good memories, but at least the killer had been caught.

"Will we need to take both cars to carry them?" she asked.

Carolyn nodded. "Probably. There are a dozen scarecrows. We can put two or three in each trunk, and the others can ride in the backseats."

Phyllis had to chuckle at the image that conjured up of her and Carolyn playing chauffeur for a bunch of scarecrows.

They left the house and drove to Oliver Loving Elementary School on the outskirts of town. Carolyn was a frequent visitor, but everyone in the office seemed to be glad to see Phyllis again when they checked in there and got their visitor passes.

Dana Powell had her fourth-grade students working

long-division problems on the whiteboard when Phyllis and Carolyn got to her room. She waved them in, told the kids to keep working, and went to her desk to get the key to her SUV from her purse.

"Phyllis, it's good to see you again," she said with a smile as she handed Carolyn a ring of keys with an attached remote control fob.

"Phyllis wants to help set up the decorations," Carolyn explained.

"That's great. We can use all the volunteers we can get."

"It's nice to see you, too, Dana," Phyllis said. "I ran into your husband at the park yesterday."

"Logan? What was he doing there?"

"He said he was looking the place over and deciding where to put the decorations," Phyllis explained, a little surprised that Dana seemed surprised. She would have thought that Dana would know what her own husband had been doing. Although there were some couples who just didn't talk much, she reminded herself. Whatever it took to make a marriage work ...

"All of that's been pretty much decided already," Dana said.

Phyllis shrugged. "That's what he told me."

"Oh, it doesn't really matter," Dana said with a wave of her hand. She wore rings on several of her slender fingers. "I guess he just wants to feel like he's being helpful."

Phyllis wasn't convinced that was what Dana really thought, but as Dana had said, it didn't really matter, at least where the Harvest Festival was concerned.

"Phyllis is going to help me deliver canned goods and turkey dinners on Thanksgiving, too," Carolyn said.

"Well, you're really getting into the spirit." Dana smiled.

"I have a lot to be thankful for," Phyllis said. "I'd like to pass some of that along."

"That's a good attitude." Dana motioned at the keys. "You can just drop those off at the front desk if you'd like. I can pick them up later."

Carolyn nodded. "All right. I'll see you after school."

They said their good-byes and left the classroom. As

they walked out of the building, Phyllis said, "You'll be helping with the preparations after school?"

"Yes. I'm sure it'll take until sometime tonight to get everything ready," Carolyn replied. "We may be working late."

"I'd offer to help you, but . . ."

"I know. You have Bobby to take care of. What you're doing this afternoon is plenty, Phyllis, really. Having the two cars means I won't have to make two trips."

Carolyn knew what Dana's SUV looked like. It was bright red and easy to spot in the parking lot, so she had parked nearby and Phyllis had followed suit. Carolyn pushed the button on the remote to unlock the vehicle as she and Phyllis came up to it, then pushed another button that opened the rear gate. With a loud beep, it started to rise.

At the sight of the scarecrows that filled the back end of the vehicle, Phyllis said, "They look almost like a bunch of bodies piled in there."

Carolyn frowned. "That's a rather gruesome thought, isn't it? Of course, given your predilection for finding bodies . . ."

"Don't even start," Phyllis said in a tone of mock warning.

The scarecrows had been made by stuffing overalls and flannel shirts with crumpled newspaper with wire running through them, so they were lightweight and flexible. The heads were stuffed burlap bags on which button eyes had been sewn. Noses and mouths had been drawn on with markers, and straw hats were pinned to the heads. The feet and hands were made of dried johnsongrass leaves that Carolyn had collected from a friend's family farm. They had been happy to get rid of the troublesome weed that reduced crop yields.

As Carolyn had predicted, they were able to put two scarecrows in each of the car trunks. Phyllis put one in the front seat of her car, on the passenger side, then lined up three more in the backseat.

"We could use the HOV lanes, if there were any in Weatherford," she told Carolyn with a smile.

Carolyn had loaded her car the same way. She stepped back, studied the grinning scarecrows for a moment, and then said, "That's just creepy. I suppose they'll look good sitting on bales of hay around the park, though. The hay was supposed to be delivered this morning, and the booths and decorations will go up this afternoon and this evening."

"I can take Dana's keys back to the office, if you'd like," Phyllis offered. "You can go on to the park, and I'll catch up to you."

"All right." Carolyn tossed the keys to her. "I'll see you there."

Phyllis walked back into the school while Carolyn got in her car and started the engine. A couple of teachers were standing at the counter in the office, talking to Katherine Felton, the school secretary, when Phyllis walked in. They looked over at her and smiled, and the one who was short, a little plump, and pretty, with curly dark hair, said, "It's Mrs. Newsom, isn't it?"

"That's right," Phyllis said.

"You may not remember me. I'm Barbara Loomis."

"Of course I remember you," Phyllis said truthfully. The woman's name had come back to her almost right away, possibly because Carolyn had mentioned her just the day before. She nodded to the other teacher, a tall blonde, and added, "And you're Ms. Grantham."

"That's right," the woman said. "Jenna Grantham. It's good to see you again, Mrs. Newsom. Carolyn talks about you all the time."

Jenna was around thirty, Barbara about ten years older than that. Phyllis didn't know either of them well but had seen them on numerous occasions, usually when Carolyn asked her to come along to some school function.

Barbara said, "Carolyn certainly has stayed involved with the school, even though she's retired."

"Well, she likes it here," Phyllis said. Carolyn had taught at this particular elementary for the final few years of her career, after having spent most of her time at one of the older schools. "She's always enjoyed being around the children and doing things to help."

"And we're glad to have her volunteering," Jenna said. "She's worked with some of the resource kids on their reading and made a big difference."

"You taught junior high, didn't you?" Barbara asked.

"That's right. Eighth grade. American history."

Barbara shook her head. "You couldn't pay me enough to teach junior high. All those hormones in the air."

"Yeah, and the kids can be a pain, too," Jenna said with a smile.

Phyllis handed Dana's keys to the secretary. "Mrs. Powell said we could leave these here and she'd pick them up later."

"I'll make sure she gets them," Katherine promised.

"What were you doing with Dana's keys?" Jenna asked. There wasn't any suspicion in her voice, just curiosity.

"Carolyn and I picked up the scarecrows," Phyllis explained. "We're going to take them over to the park and set them up on the hay bales."

"That's going to be cute," Barbara said. "I'm glad Dana thought of it."

"I didn't know it was her idea."

Barbara nodded. "Oh, yes. She's very creative."

"And she has her husband to help her."

"Logan?" Barbara asked with a puzzled frown. "I wouldn't say he helps all that much with things like this. He's like my husband. Too busy with his business all the time. They're in the same line of work, you know. Real estate."

"I know," Phyllis said. "I ran into him at the park yesterday morning, and as a matter of fact, he was talking to your husband on the phone."

"You were at the park?" Jenna asked.

"That's right. I took my grandson there to play. He really loves the place."

"It's a nice little park," Jenna agreed. She glanced at her watch. "Well, I'd better get busy. I still have a lot to do, and my conference period will be over before you know it. Talk to you later, Barbara. Nice seeing you again, Mrs. Newsom."

"You, too," Phyllis said. She hadn't meant to linger this long at the school. Carolyn was probably already at the park by now. But there was a bond between teachers, even between active ones and retired ones, and she always enjoyed visiting with people who knew what it was like to stand up there in front of a classroom full of students and try to plant some knowledge in their heads. It was one of the most frustrating but at the same time one of the most rewarding jobs in the world.

By the time Phyllis reached the park, Carolyn had already unloaded three of the scarecrows from her car and propped them up on bales of hay. Thin wooden stakes went down through the gap between the shirt collar and the back of the overalls and were driven into the hay to hold the stuffed figures upright. Phyllis thought they looked very distinctive and picturesque.

There were a lot more people here today than there had been the day before. City employees were unloading and setting up portable toilets and sawhorses for crowd control. The sound of hammering filled the air as other employees erected the booths that were being rented by local businesses to promote their goods or services. All the local civic clubs were sponsoring booths, too, that would be used for various arts and crafts displays, games and face painting for the kids, and concession stands. It was definitely a busy place.

And Logan Powell was right in the middle of it, Phyllis saw as she carried one of the scarecrows from her car across the park. Despite the things Carolyn and the other women had said about him, Logan seemed to be heavily involved, striding around the park and issuing orders, talking on the cell phone tucked into his ear, and popping peppermints. He saw Phyllis and gave her a grin and a wave, then pointed out to one of the workmen where a sign needed to go.

Phyllis came to a bale of hay with a stake lying on it. She set the scarecrow on the hay, positioned it, and picked up the stake.

"Careful," a voice said behind her. "You could kill a guy with that thing."

Chapter 7

Phyllis turned her head, looked over her shoulder, and saw Logan grinning at her. She positioned the stake, worked it through a precut slit in the overalls, slid it down the scarecrow's back, and pushed it into the hay until it was good and solid.

"There," she said as she straightened and stepped back. "How does that look?"

"It looks great," Logan said. "Very autumnal. I didn't know you were gonna help with the decorations, Phyllis. You don't mind if I call you Phyllis, do you?"

"No, not at all. I guess you could say I'm a late-blooming volunteer, at least in this case."

"We appreciate all the help we can get." That seemed to be a common sentiment. Logan looked around. "Hey, where's that grandson of yours?"

"Oh, I left him at home with . . . a friend of mine." Phyllis wasn't going to start referring to Sam as her boyfriend when she was talking to other people. It was one thing to come to an understanding between themselves, but quite another not to act her age in public.

"Well, be sure to bring him to the festival tomorrow. He'll get a big kick out of it. There'll be a lot of good food, too. You know there's gonna be a cooking contest." Logan smiled again and made a production of licking his lips. "I've got a real sweet tooth, I'm afraid."

"Yes, I've noticed you eating those peppermints."

"Yeah, I guess I, ah, picked up the habit when I quit smoking."

"It's a much healthier habit, I would think," Phyllis said. "I'm entering the contest, you know."

Logan's eyebrows went up. "Really?" He lowered his voice to a conspiratorial tone. "What are you making?"

Phyllis glanced around, falling into the same conspiratorial attitude. Then she said quietly, "Pumpkin cheesecake muffins. With pecan crumble topping."

"Ohhhh," Logan said. "That sounds delicious. I'll be sure to try one."

"I hope you like it."

"Well, got to get back to work," he said. "No rest for the wicked, as they say. I'll see you tomorrow."

Phyllis nodded. "Of course."

Logan walked across the park to talk to some of the city employees. Phyllis started back toward the parking lot to get another scarecrow out of her car.

Carolyn fell in step beside her. "That was Logan Powell talking to you, wasn't it?" she asked.

"That's right."

"He was *flirting* with you, Phyllis."

Phyllis stopped in her tracks and turned to look at her friend in surprise. "Flirting with me?" she repeated. "No, he wasn't!"

Carolyn nodded. "He most certainly was," she insisted. "I was watching. I saw the way he smiled and laughed the whole time he was talking to you. I kept waiting for him to touch you on the arm or the shoulder, but he never did. He thought about it, though."

"Well, that's just crazy," Phyllis said with a shake of her head. "I'm at least twenty years older than he is."

"Some men like older women, or so I've been told." Carolyn added grudgingly, "Anyway, you don't look as old as you really are. You could pass for—I don't know—sixty."

"Thanks . . . I think. But you're wrong about Logan. He was just being friendly. He's a salesman, Carolyn. I'll bet he's in the habit of talking like that to everyone he meets. It's a lot easier to sell something to someone when you've established some sort of connection with them first."

"Maybe," Carolyn said, but she didn't sound convinced.

"Anyway, there's no reason in the world for Logan to flirt with me when he's got a beautiful wife like Dana."

"Some men don't need a reason. Like you said, it's a habit."

Phyllis didn't want to continue with this conversation. As far as she was concerned, the very idea was just silly. So she said, "We'd better get the rest of those scarecrows out."

"I've only got a couple left. When I finish with them, I'll help you with the others."

It didn't take long for them to unload and position the rest of the scarecrows. When that was done, Phyllis asked, "Is there anything else I can do to help?"

Carolyn shook her head. "That's all I was supposed to do, and it went a lot faster than I expected it to, since you gave me a hand."

"I think I'll go back to the house, then, and mix up a batch of those muffins."

"One more test run, is that it?"

"I suppose you could call it that. Really, though, I'm just hungry for them."

"I'm looking forward to trying them," Carolyn said. "I can't let that influence any decision I might make as a judge in the contest, though."

"I wouldn't expect it to," Phyllis told her honestly. Carolyn was her oldest friend, but she knew that Carolyn would also be scrupulously fair when it came to judging the entries in the contest. Neither of them would have had it any other way.

They drove back to the house, Phyllis arriving ahead of Carolyn because of the traffic. When she pulled into the garage, she saw Sam and Bobby standing by the workbench. Bobby was wearing a pair of safety goggles that were much too big for him, but at least his eyes were completely covered and protected, Phyllis thought. The elastic strap attached to the goggles had been tied in a knot behind Bobby's head so it would hold them on.

"Look at me, Gran'mama," he called to her as she got out of the car.

"I see you," Phyllis told him. "With those big eyes, you look like a Martian."

"A what?"

"A Martian. A man from Mars."

"But there aren't any men on Mars," Bobby said, obviously puzzled. "My dad read to me about it in a book."

Sam said, "We didn't always know that, Bobby. Used to be, some folks thought there were people on Mars and Venus and most of the other planets."

"In other dimensions or alt'nate universes, maybe."

Phyllis and Sam exchanged a glance, and she could tell that he was thinking the same thing she was, about how much smarter in some ways children were these days. Four-year-olds knew about alternate universes, took iPhones for granted, and could even set the clock on a VCR ... although VCRs had already long gone the way of the buggy whip, Phyllis reminded herself. It was all DVRs and TiVos and Hulu now.

"Has Sam been teaching you all about these tools?"

Bobby nodded. "Yeah, but he won't let me use any of them yet. He says I have to be older first."

"That's right," Phyllis said. "I'll have to talk to your mother and father, and they'll decide when they think you're old enough to do things like that."

"Okay. The saws are really cool, though. And Sam really knows how to use 'em."

"I expect your grandpa Kenny was even better at it," Sam said. "These were his tools, you know—most of them, anyway. They wouldn't be here if it wasn't for him." Sam paused and chuckled. "Neither would you."

Bobby looked up and frowned. "How come?"

Phyllis put a hand on his shoulder and steered him toward the kitchen door. "You come along with me now, Bobby. I've got something you can help me with. I'm going to make a batch of muffins."

He switched his gaze to her. "What kind?"

"Pumpkin."

"Do I *like* punkin muffins?"

"You'll like these," she assured him. She pulled the goggles off his head and tossed them to Sam, who caught them deftly. She mouthed *Thank you* to him. He just grinned and nodded.

Carolyn drove in as Phyllis ushered Bobby on into the house. She had him wash up while she did the same and then got the mixing bowls out in the kitchen. Carolyn didn't come in the house right away, which was a little unusual, but Phyllis didn't really think anything of it. A few minutes later, when Carolyn walked through the kitchen, she didn't say anything.

Bobby stood on a chair to help him reach the counter as he and Phyllis worked together mixing up all the ingredients for the muffins. The bowl of cream cheese filling went into the freezer while they worked on the other two bowls. Phyllis poured the pumpkin batter into the baking cups Bobby had put in the muffin tins. She took the cream cheese mixture out of the freezer, where it had firmed. Carefully not touching the edges, she placed a spoonful in the middle of each muffin. She then handed the bowl of crumble to Bobby so he could add it on top. She had the oven preheating, and when the muffins were ready to go in, she said, "All right, we'll check them in twenty minutes."

"Then can we eat 'em?" he said eagerly.

"They might need to cook a little longer, and then they'll need to cool. Well, now that I think about it, that might be too close to suppertime. It might spoil your appetite."

Bobby's face fell. "Oh."

Phyllis couldn't help but feel sorry for him, and anyway, he had helped her get the muffins ready to bake. "Tell you what," she said. "Maybe we can split one of them, just you and me. I won't tell anyone if you won't."

That brought the grin back to his face. "Deal!"

"You can go watch TV or play a game now."

"Okay." He hurried off toward the living room.

Sam came in from the garage a few minutes later

while Phyllis was cleaning up the dishes she and Bobby had gotten dirty in preparing the muffins. He took a deep breath and said, "That smells mighty good. Nothin' smells much better than baked goods."

"You can have one of them at supper." She kept her word and didn't mention that she and Bobby intended to get a head start on the others.

Sam leaned a hip against the counter. He didn't sound quite as casual as he looked when he said, "Carolyn tells me that fella Logan Powell was flirtin' with you at the park."

Phyllis turned to face him, not quite sure whether to be angry or amused. "She said what?" Without giving Sam a chance to answer, she went on, "That's crazy. No such thing happened."

"Well, I wouldn't be surprised if it did. You're a mighty fine-lookin' woman."

"Oh, sure. Men who are young enough to be my son hit on me all the time."

"I'm not afraid of a little competition, mind you."

"Sam . . ." She put a hand on his arm. "Logan Powell is no competition for you."

"That's good to hear. I don't reckon he's tasted those muffins yet, though. That might get him even more interested."

"He's not interested. He has a lovely wife. But he *will* get a chance to try those muffins tomorrow. I suppose we'll see what happens then."

Chapter 8

🧁

$\mathcal{P}$hyllis had made the pumpkin muffins a couple of times before. This batch turned out to be just as good as the others, maybe even better. Eve and Sam raved about them when they tried them after supper. Carolyn just said, "I can't comment. It wouldn't be proper, me being a judge in the contest tomorrow and all."

Phyllis noticed that she ate two of the muffins, though.

Sam had noticed that there was an empty place in the muffin tin. "Looks like a little thief snuck in and helped himself before supper," he said with a grin as he looked at the little boy.

"It was Gran'mama's idea, I swear!" Bobby said. "And she ate half of it!"

Phyllis laughed. "I might not have given in if I'd known you were going to throw me under the bus that way. Sam didn't even have to tickle you first to get the truth out of you."

"I could tickle him now," Sam offered.

Bobby bolted out of his chair and ran laughing into the living room.

Carolyn stood up and said, "You've done all the cooking today, Phyllis, so Eve and I will clean up."

"We will?" Eve said.

Carolyn began gathering up the plates. "Yes, we will. Come on."

Phyllis didn't argue. What with looking after Bobby for the past few days and now helping with the preparations for the festival, she was a little weary tonight and didn't mind admitting it.

Sam lingered at the table with her. "Bobby got a real kick out of workin' with me this afternoon," he said. "And he didn't even cut any fingers off."

"How could he? You didn't let him use the tools, remember?"

"Yeah, that's right. When the time comes, though, I reckon he'll be good at it."

"I appreciate you mentioning Kenny the way you did. Even though Bobby never met him, I want to make sure he knows about his grandfather. I think it's important for people to have a sense of—I don't know—continuity with the generations that came before them."

Sam nodded. "I couldn't agree more. Got to know where you came from to really know where you're goin'."

Before either of them could say anything else, the doorbell rang. Since Carolyn and Eve were in the kitchen, Phyllis called out, "I'll get it," as she stood up from the dining room table. She hoped Bobby wouldn't open the door before she could get there. Surely Mike and Sarah had taught him not to do such a thing.

She didn't have to worry about that, she saw. He came running back down the hall from the living room, and when he saw her, he said, "Somebody's here, Gran'mama!"

"Yes, I know," Phyllis said with a nod. "We'll see who it is."

Sam trailed behind her as she went to the front door, and she was glad he was there. She wasn't really nervous about answering the door like this after dark—this was a nice, safe neighborhood, after all—but she couldn't help but remember how she had been assaulted and a murder had taken place right next door a couple of years earlier.

When Phyllis reached the front door, she parted the curtain over the narrow window next to it. The porch light was equipped with a motion detector, so it was already turned on. Phyllis frowned in surprise as she saw Dana Powell standing on the porch with an upset, impatient look on her face. She appeared to be alone.

Phyllis opened the wooden door, then the screen. "Hello, Dana," she said. "I didn't expect to see you again so soon."

"Mrs. Newsom," Dana said, "did you and Carolyn take my keys back to the office at school?"

Phyllis was taken even more aback by the abrupt question. She glanced past Dana toward the curb at the edge of the street and saw the red SUV parked there.

"Of course we took them back," Phyllis said. "Or rather, I did. I gave them to Katherine Felton myself."

Dana's shoulders suddenly sagged, and a look of contrition mixed with exhaustion came over her face. "I'm sorry," she said. "I didn't mean to sound like I was accusing you of anything. I'm just ... I don't know what...."

A wave of sympathy went through Phyllis. She stepped back, holding the door. "Come in," she said. "You look like you ought to sit down and take it easy for a minute."

"I really don't have time—"

"I have some nice herbal tea already brewed. And some pumpkin muffins," Phyllis said.

Over her shoulder, Sam added, "They're really good muffins, too."

"I ... I guess it wouldn't hurt to ..."

Phyllis wanted to find out what had happened with the keys, and she wasn't sure it was a good idea for Dana to be driving around while she was so upset. She needed to calm down and revitalize a little first. Phyllis reached out, put a hand on the younger woman's arm, and said, "Come in for a few minutes. Please."

"All right." Dana sighed. "Thank you."

Phyllis ushered her into the living room, where they both sat down on the sofa, Dana putting her purse at her feet. Phyllis looked up at Sam and asked, "Could you go get a cup of tea and one of those muffins?"

"Sure," he said. "Be glad to."

"Don't go to any trouble," Dana said.

"It's no trouble at all," Phyllis assured her. As Dana sat back and sighed, Phyllis went on, "What's this about your car keys? I saw that you came here in your SUV."

Dana nodded. "I have a spare key. It doesn't have the remote on it, of course. So I was able to get in and start it. I'm worried about the others, though. My house keys are on there."

Phyllis wasn't surprised that Dana kept a second set of keys. She did the same herself in case she accidentally locked her keys in her car. She asked, "Katherine didn't give them back to you?"

"They weren't in the office," Dana replied with a shake of her head. "Or at least Katherine couldn't find them. She said she thought you brought them back, but things got really busy in the office, and she couldn't be sure."

"I did bring them back," Phyllis said. "Barbara Loomis and Jenna Grantham were even in there when I gave them to Katherine. They can tell you what happened."

"They were already gone when I left the school. I haven't seen them since then." Dana sighed again. "Now I don't know whether to be relieved or even more worried. The keys could still be in the office somewhere. To tell you the truth, Katherine's gotten so absentminded, she could have put them somewhere and forgotten where." Dana hesitated. "Or she could have set them down on the counter and someone could have walked off with them without her noticing."

Phyllis shook her head. "Surely not. They'll probably turn up in a day or two."

"I hope so. It's a scary feeling, knowing that the keys to your house and car could be floating around out there somewhere, in the hands of God knows who."

Sam came back into the living room then, carrying a couple of saucers, one with a teacup on it, the other with a pumpkin muffin. He placed them on the coffee table in front of the sofa where Phyllis and Dana sat, saying, "There you go."

Phyllis realized she had neglected to introduce Dana and Sam. "Mrs. Powell, this is my friend Sam Fletcher. Sam, Dana Powell."

Sam gave the visitor a polite nod. "I'm pleased to meet you," he said. "Heard quite a bit about you the past few days, what with this Harvest Festival comin' up. I understand you've been doin' a lot to make it successful."

"I hope so," Dana said. She picked up the tea and took a sip, and she seemed to calm down a little right before Phyllis's eyes. "It's for a good cause, but it's certainly been a lot of work. I have to go back to the park tonight and make sure that everything is set up like it's supposed to be. I'll head over there as soon as I've gone home and changed clothes." She was still wearing the dress she'd worn to school that day.

"Maybe you should skip it, since you're tired and upset," Phyllis suggested. "I'm sure the other volunteers can take care of things."

Dana shook her head. "No, I'll be fine. I know Carolyn's going over there, and my husband is, too, along with several of my other friends. I can't let them down."

"Have you even had supper yet?"

Dana reached for the muffin and smiled. "This will tide me over," she said. She took a bite, chewed it, and let her eyes widen in appreciation. "Oh, that's so good!"

"And sweet enough to keep you goin'," Sam said.

"That's exactly what I need."

Dana seemed to feel a lot better by the time she finished the muffin and the tea. She thanked Phyllis, who said, "Let me get you another muffin. You can take it with you, in case you run out of steam later tonight and need something else to eat."

"Oh, that's not necessary—"

"I insist. I can always make plenty more. In fact, I plan to, because they're going to be my entry in the contest tomorrow."

Dana laughed. "I think you have a good chance of winning, then. That muffin was delicious."

Phyllis went to the kitchen to get the muffin. Carolyn

and Eve were just finishing up with the dishes. "Sam mentioned that was Dana at the door," Carolyn said. "Is she still here?"

Phyllis nodded as she wrapped one of the muffins in a paper towel. "Yes, but she's on her way home to change; then she insists she's going to the park to help with the last-minute preparations."

"That and to keep an eye on her husband," Carolyn said, keeping her voice quiet enough so that it couldn't be heard in the living room.

"What do you mean by that?" Phyllis asked.

"You saw the way Logan was flirting with you today. I don't think he meant anything by it, but if he does that with all the women he meets, sometimes he's bound to be serious about it."

Eve looked interested. "What's this about some man flirting with Phyllis?"

"It was nothing," Phyllis insisted. "I'm still convinced that Carolyn was mistaken."

Carolyn looked at Eve and said, "I'll tell you all about it later." She hung the damp dish towel over its rack. "Right now, though, I have to get to the park myself. I may be over there late, so don't wait up for me."

"I wasn't planning to, dear," Eve said.

Phyllis took the muffin back to the living room and handed it to Dana, who stood up. "Thank you so much," the younger woman said. "And again, I'm sorry I sounded like I was accusing you of something. I just wanted to make sure that Katherine hadn't gotten mixed up. Actually, I was sort of hoping that she had, because that would mean you still had my keys."

Phyllis shook her head. "No, I'm sorry. I wish I knew what happened to them."

"Well, like you said, maybe they'll turn up." She went to the door and turned to smile at Phyllis and Sam. "I'll see you tomorrow at the festival, I hope."

"We'll be there," Phyllis promised. "Wouldn't miss it."

Chapter 9

Phyllis was up early the next morning, getting two dozen more muffins in the oven. That would give her plenty for the contest judges, as well as small samples that visitors to the festival could pick up and try once the contest was over.

True to Carolyn's word, she had been at the park late the night before. In fact, Phyllis wasn't even sure when Carolyn had come in. She had been asleep by then.

Bobby had slept through the night without any problem, and he was still asleep this morning as Phyllis worked on the muffins. She had just put the first batch in the oven when Sam came into the kitchen, wearing his bathrobe and pajamas and holding a hand over his mouth as he yawned.

"Just heard the weather forecast on the radio," he said. "Cool front's still supposed to come through this mornin'. We're lookin' at sunny and dry, with a high in the upper fifties."

"Perfect weather, in other words," Phyllis said as she closed the oven door. "That ought to ensure that there's a fine turnout for the festival."

"I'm sure there will be. There's signs all over town advertisin' it." Sam got a cup out of the cabinet and reached for the coffeepot.

Carolyn came in a few minutes later. Eve tended to

sleep in most mornings, so Phyllis knew they wouldn't see her for a while. Carolyn helped herself to coffee.

"Late night?" Phyllis asked. "I didn't hear you come in."

"It was after midnight," Carolyn said as she sat down at the table. "That's all right; I don't sleep as much as I used to, anyway."

"That's one of the perils of gettin' old," Sam said. "Sleep gets harder and harder to come by."

Carolyn nodded in agreement. "It certainly does. I wasn't the only volunteer there, though, by any means. In fact, a few people were still there when I left."

"What about Dana?" Phyllis asked as she added some more coffee to her own cup to heat up what was already there.

Carolyn frowned and shook her head. "No, Logan was still there, but Dana left earlier. It looked to me like she was upset."

"Oh, no," Phyllis said. "I hoped that when she left here, she had calmed down. I know it's upsetting to lose your keys, but . . ." Her voice trailed off as she saw Carolyn shaking her head again. "It wasn't about the keys?"

"I don't know. I couldn't hear what they were saying. But it looked like they were arguing. They walked out onto that bridge over the drainage ditch leading into the lake, and Logan was waving his hands around and almost shouting. Then Dana stormed off and left a few minutes later."

"I hate to hear that."

"Mark my words: It was about another woman," Carolyn said. "Logan just has that look about him."

Sam said, "You can tell by lookin' if a fella's liable to cheat on his wife?"

"Of course," Carolyn answered.

"That doesn't seem possible," Phyllis said.

"Oh, no? Think about the famous celebrities and politicians who were philanderers. Once the scandals broke, didn't you feel like you should have known, just by the way they looked and acted in public?"

"Maybe, but it still seems far-fetched to me," Phyllis insisted. "And Logan Powell isn't a celebrity or a politician. He's a real estate agent."

"Who's a self-styled big shot in the chamber of commerce. That brings him into contact with a lot of professional women, not to mention the ones who are involved in his own business. Did you ever see a woman selling real estate who *wasn't* attractive? They're almost as good-looking as those pharmaceutical reps who go in and out of doctors' offices all the time!"

"I suppose Logan probably has some temptations," Phyllis said. "You can't be sure that he ever gives in to them, though."

"I know what I know," Carolyn said.

"It does seem like you ladies have a way of lookin' right through a fella and seein' what he's up to," Sam said.

Phyllis frowned at him. "So you agree with Carolyn?"

"All I'm sayin' is that fellas who run around on their wives usually get caught at it sooner or later. I don't know Logan Powell myself, so I couldn't tell you whether he's that sort or not."

"He is," Carolyn said. "Take my word for it."

Phyllis wasn't prepared to do that, but at the same time, for all she really knew, her friend was right. And it was none of her business either way. She just hated to see anyone unhappy, and from the sound of it, Dana Powell certainly had been when she left the park the night before.

There was nothing she could do about it, though, so she turned her attention back to her baking. "There are still muffins left from the batch I made yesterday, and you're welcome to those," she told Sam and Carolyn. "Otherwise you're on your own for breakfast this morning."

"A couple of those muffins'll do me just fine," Sam said with a smile.

"I believe I just want coffee," Carolyn said. "I'll be sampling a lot of baked goods later on this morning. We'll be doing the judging at eleven o'clock, and the results will be announced at eleven thirty."

When Bobby got up, he was satisfied with a muffin for breakfast, too. Maybe that wasn't the healthiest breakfast in the world, Phyllis thought—all right, it definitely wasn't the healthiest breakfast for a growing four-year-old—but for one morning it wouldn't hurt him. And she was a grandparent, after all. It was her job to spoil her grandson just a little.

The morning's preparations went by in a blur. The festival opened at ten o'clock, and the entries for the contest had to be on hand by ten thirty. Phyllis got Bobby and herself dressed in comfortable clothes that would be warm enough in the cool breeze out of the north, then put him and the muffins in the backseat of her car. Carolyn had already left, and Eve was going to ride with Phyllis. Sam intended to take his own pickup. The two of them came out of the house, and Phyllis said, "All right, I believe we're all ready to go."

Sam lifted a hand. "See you at the park."

Phyllis and Eve got into the car. "Do you have the canned goods?" Eve asked.

"Two big bags in the trunk," Phyllis answered, "and Sam has two more in his pickup. That's more than we have to donate, but it's such a good cause."

All of them had chipped in to buy the food, which Sam had generously offered to pick up the day before. Carolyn's story about growing up poor had touched Phyllis, and she wanted to do whatever she could to help make this Thanksgiving season memorable and happy for the families in town who hadn't been as blessed as she was.

It was barely ten o'clock, but the parking lots on both sides of the lake, neither of which was very big, were already full, as was the lot at the complex of softball fields next to the park. Cars also lined the sides of the roads leading to the park.

"We're going to have to walk quite a way, it looks like," Eve said. "It's a good thing I wore comfortable shoes today."

Phyllis tried to wear comfortable shoes just about every day, but she knew what Eve meant. She found a place to park her car, and as they all climbed out, she said, "I'm going to trust you to carry the muffins, Bobby, while Mrs. Turner and I carry the bags of canned goods. Can you do that?"

"Sure, Gran'mama," the little boy answered. "I'll be really careful with 'em, too."

"I'm sure you will," Phyllis said as she placed the two plastic containers in Bobby's outstretched arms. The muffins didn't weigh much, relatively speaking, and she thought he could handle them all right.

The bags of canned goods were much heavier, heavy enough so that she and Eve both had tired arms before they reached the booth at the end of the long line of people going into the park. Sawhorses had been set up to funnel visitors through a single entrance on each side of the lake. When each family reached the booth, they handed over their bag, or bags, of canned goods to volunteers, who placed them into the back of a truck parked next to the booth. Then every visitor received a little ink stamp on the back of the hand to prove that he or she had made the appropriate donation.

Bobby giggled as one of the volunteers stamped the back of his hand. "Look, Gran'mama!" he said as he held it up so that Phyllis could see. "It's a duck!"

Indeed it was. The rubber stamp was made in the shape of a duck, like the ones who made the little lake their home for much of the year. There were no ducks swimming around on the water or waddling along the banks today, though. Even if any of them had been flying over and considered stopping in their southward migration, the commotion in the park would have scared them off. A local band set up in front of one of the log cabins was playing country music, and the sounds of talk and laughter and happy shouts of children filled the air as well. Phyllis loved events like this. They were so full of life.

"I can take those muffins now, Bobby," she offered as they walked between two of the bales of hay with scarecrows propped up on them and started toward the other log cabin, where the cooking contest would take place in the covered dogtrot.

"I got 'em," he said proudly. "No problem."

Phyllis smiled. "All right."

Eve touched her shoulder and said, "I'll see you later, Phyllis. I'm going to check out the craft displays."

"All right."

When they reached the cabin, Carolyn was sitting behind a table at the front of the dogtrot with the other four judges. At the back of the dogtrot, under the connecting roof, was one of the hay bales, with a scarecrow leaned against the wall of the cabin. The other judges were the editor of the local newspaper, the owner of an auto dealership who was also the president of the chamber of commerce, a professor from the junior college, and the retired but still much-beloved superintendent of schools, Dolly Williamson. Phyllis knew all of them fairly well, especially Dolly, and they all greeted her with smiles.

"Whatever you've got there, Phyllis, I know it'll be delicious," Dolly said.

"It always is," the editor agreed. "You're one of the best contestants we have in these things, Phyllis." He glanced over at Carolyn. "No offense to my distinguished fellow judge."

"Oh, I'm not worried about that," Carolyn said with a casual wave of her hand. "Phyllis is one of the best bakers I've ever seen, no doubt about it."

"You can flatter me all you want," Phyllis said, "but all that counts is right here." She motioned for Bobby to put the containers of muffins on the table.

The professor was handling the contest paperwork. "We'll get these logged in for you, Phyllis."

"Thanks." Phyllis put her hand on Bobby's shoulder. "Now, I think I know someone who wants to see what else the festival has to offer."

"Yeah!" he said as he looked up at her.

They turned to walk around the rest of the park, but Phyllis stopped short when she saw Dana Powell standing there with a frightened look on her face and tears shining in her eyes.

Chapter 10

"Dana, what's wrong?" Phyllis exclaimed. Then something occurred to her, and she went on. "Oh, no! Someone really did get hold of your keys and broke into your house!"

"What?" Dana said. "No. No, that's not it. Have you seen Logan?" She looked past Phyllis at the judges seated at the table. "Have any of you seen Logan?"

"Come to think of it, I haven't," the president of the chamber of commerce responded. "And I figured he'd be here bright and early this morning."

The other judges shook their heads, and Phyllis said, "I just got here, but I don't recall seeing him on the way into the park."

Carolyn stood up and came around the table. "I'm sure he's fine, Dana. He's bound to be around here somewhere. What time did he leave home this morning?"

"That's just it." Dana drew in a deep, shaky breath. "He didn't leave home this morning. He never came home last night."

Phyllis and Carolyn exchanged a glance. Then Carolyn suggested, "Why don't we go somewhere a little quieter and talk?"

Phyllis would have liked to take part in that conversation, but she had Bobby to look after, and she didn't want to drag him along and make him listen to what might well be a pretty frank discussion.

Then she saw Sam ambling toward them in the loose-jointed way that all tall, athletic men have about them, and she said, "Sam, would you mind watching Bobby for a little while?"

Sam came to a halt and tucked his hands into the back pockets of his jeans as he shook his head. "Nope, wouldn't mind at all," he said. He grinned down at Bobby. "You want to see part of the festival with me, sport?"

"Sure!" Bobby said. "Can I get my face painted?"

Distracted by concern about the emotional state Dana was in, Phyllis nodded. "That's fine."

"Maybe I'll have 'em paint a daisy on my face," Sam told Bobby as they walked away.

Phyllis turned back to Carolyn and Dana. Carolyn had a hand on the younger woman's arm. "Let's go over there," she said, pointing with her other hand.

With fallen leaves crunching underfoot, they followed one of the sidewalks to an area where no booths had been set up, creating a small zone of privacy. Phyllis, Carolyn, and Dana stopped under the trees.

"Are you *sure* that Logan didn't come home last night?" Carolyn asked.

Dana nodded. "Don't you think I'd know something like that?"

"Well . . . maybe he was home but just didn't come to bed. He could have slept on the sofa, or in the guest room if you have one."

"He didn't," Dana insisted. "The bed in the guest room hadn't been touched, and Logan won't sleep on the sofa. The one time he tried to, after one of our . . . fights . . . it wrecked his back and he couldn't straighten up for a week. He won't hardly sit on it now, let alone sleep on it."

"Maybe he pulled into the garage and slept in his car," Phyllis said. "Men do really silly things like that sometimes when they're upset."

"I suppose it's possible . . . ," Dana said, but her tone

of voice made it clear she didn't really believe that was what had happened. "But even if he did, where is he this morning? He would have been here unless . . . unless something had happened to him."

Carolyn said, "Maybe something came up with his work."

"That's right," Phyllis said. "He was working on some sort of big deal, wasn't he? NorCenTex Development, or something like that?"

"That was it," Dana said with a nod. "But anything to do with business could have waited until Monday. I realize that Logan . . . that, well, he put on a show, I guess you'd say, about how much work he was doing to get ready for the festival, but it really was important to him. I believe that."

"You know him better than anyone else, I suppose," Carolyn said.

Dana smiled, but there was no humor in the expression. "You'd think so, wouldn't you? But I'm not so sure. If he decided to . . . sleep somewhere else last night . . . he probably didn't have much trouble finding a place."

"What are you saying?"

"You know what I'm saying, Carolyn," Dana answered heavily. "You must have seen us arguing last night. Logan was having an affair. For all I know, more than one. I'm sure of it."

"Did he admit it?" Phyllis asked.

"He practically threw it in my face. Told me not to ask questions that I didn't want to know the answers to. He said that he . . . that he would do whatever it took to make himself happy." Dana sighed. "I've known for years that he was probably fooling around on me. Whoever the woman is now, she's not the first one. But I stayed with him anyway, because in some ways we're really well matched. We're both devoted to our careers, and . . . and Logan was fine with the fact that I can't have children."

Carolyn murmured, "I didn't know that."

"It's true. We talked about adopting but never got around to doing anything about it. I had the kids at school, and I guess that . . . filled whatever need I have. I was never that maternal to start with." She wiped tears away from her eyes. "But all that doesn't change what I'm really worried about now. Logan should be here, and if he's not, then something must have happened to him."

"You checked with the volunteers at the entrance to find out if any of them had seen him?" Phyllis asked. "I'm sure they all know him."

"Yes, they do. But none of them recalled seeing him this morning."

"Wait a minute," Phyllis said. "I know he has a cell phone. I saw him using it. Surely you've tried calling it?"

"Of course. I did that the first thing when I realized he hadn't been home last night. But it goes straight to voice mail, which means the phone is turned off." Dana's tone grew a little more animated, though, as she went on. "But that's a good thought. Don't all those phones have chips in them now, so the police can trace them and find out where they are?"

"I think so, although all that sort of thing is a little beyond me. The police can't do anything, though, until you file a missing persons report, and you can't do that when Logan hasn't even been gone twenty-four hours yet. I think someone has to be missing for at least forty-eight hours before the police can get involved."

"That's crazy!" Dana said. "He's missing now."

Phyllis made her voice as sympathetic as possible as she said, "That's true, but you have to look at it the same way the police would. The first thing they'd ask you is if you and Logan quarreled recently. When you told them about your argument with him last night, they'd naturally assume that he didn't come home because of that."

"Well, what about today?" Dana demanded. "Why isn't he here at the festival?"

Phyllis hesitated. She didn't want to tell Dana what the police would say to that. Their theory would be that Logan was either shacked up with a girlfriend or had gotten drunk and was sleeping it off . . . or both.

Always the practical one, Carolyn stepped in just

then and said, "Why are we standing here talking when we could be walking around looking for him? Logan could be here, Dana, and you just haven't spotted him yet. Why, there are a lot of people in the park already. You can't just say he's not here."

Dana thought about it for a second and then nodded. "I suppose you're right."

Carolyn took hold of her arm. "Phyllis and I will come with you. We'll find him if he's here to be found."

"That's just it. I'm afraid he isn't."

"Well, we won't know until we look."

They spent the next twenty minutes doing that, making their way through the crowd and looking everywhere they could think of for Logan Powell. They didn't see any sign of him, although they did run into Sam and Bobby twice, and Eve once. Phyllis was glad to see that Bobby seemed to be having a great time. He had a turkey painted on one cheek and a pumpkin on the other. He pointed at the turkey and said, "Gobble, gobble, Gran'mama!"

"Gobble, gobble to you, too," Phyllis said as she paused for a second.

"Everything all right?" Sam asked.

"Of course," she said, but the look in her eyes made it quite clear that she didn't know if that was the case or not.

Sam must have picked up on that, because he asked, "Anything I can do?"

"You're doing it," Phyllis told him with a little nod toward Bobby. Sam nodded in understanding and put a protective hand on the little boy's shoulder.

"Come on, Bobby. Let's see what other mischief we can get into."

Phyllis caught up with Carolyn and Dana. "Your son is a police officer, isn't he, Phyllis?" Dana asked. "Do you think he could do something to get around that forty-eight-hours business?"

"He's a deputy sheriff, not a member of the Weatherford police," Phyllis explained. "Anyway, he's out of town right now and won't be back until after Thanksgiving."

"But maybe you know someone there ...?"

"I'm sorry," Phyllis said, and meant it. "They wouldn't listen to me any more than they would to you."

Carolyn checked her watch. "I'm sorry, too, Dana, but I have to get back to the cooking contest. The judging is about to start."

"I didn't mean to take the two of you away from the festival. I'm just at my wit's end."

"I know. But you have to remember, Logan's a grown man, and he can take care of himself. I'm sure he'll either show up here at the festival later on, or he'll be at your house when you go home."

"I hope so," Dana said. She made a visible effort to brighten her attitude. "Oh, well, maybe I'll go see how the contest turns out. I haven't had anything to eat yet this morning, so maybe I can sample the goodies after the winners have been announced."

"That's the plan," Phyllis told her, smiling.

They returned to the cabin. The table at the front of the dogtrot was crowded with contest entries now, and a lot of people were standing around to watch the judging and then hear the results. Many of them were probably contestants, Phyllis thought, but there were plenty of hungry festival-goers, too. Dana joined them, but she still looked worried.

As Carolyn went into the dogtrot, she frowned at the bale of hay and the scarecrow. "That shouldn't be back there," she said. "No one can really see it that well. I don't know who put that scarecrow right there, but it's been bothering me all morning."

"I suppose we could move it," Phyllis said.

"Good idea. There's still a few minutes before the judging starts. You grab the scarecrow, and I'll drag the bale of hay out into the open where it's more visible."

They went around the table and walked across the dogtrot. Phyllis looked for the stake that was supposed to hold up the scarecrow, but she didn't see one at the back of the figure's overalls. The way it was propped against the cabin wall supported it enough for it to stay upright, she supposed. She reached for the scarecrow's shoulders, then suddenly drew back as her hands closed over the flannel shirt.

"What's the matter?" Carolyn asked.

"That scarecrow doesn't . . . feel right," Phyllis said.

"What do you mean, it doesn't feel right?"

"It's too heavy. Too solid. Like it's stuffed with something besides paper and dried weeds."

"That's impossible," Carolyn said. "Let me get it."

She stepped past Phyllis, grabbed the scarecrow under the arms, and started to haul it upright. Then she gave a startled yelp, let go of the scarecrow, and stepped back so fast she almost lost her balance. The scarecrow dropped onto the hay bale, tilted to one side, and toppled to the cement floor of the dogtrot, landing with a solid thud.

"Phyllis, that . . . that's not right!" Carolyn said.

Phyllis swallowed hard. "I know." The scarecrow's straw hat had fallen off when it landed, and the burlap bag that was supposed to form its head had pulled away from the shirt, revealing a narrow strip of what looked like human flesh. "There's someone in that costume."

"Oh, my God!" Carolyn leaned over, and before Phyllis could stop her, she took hold of the burlap bag and pulled it off. Then she dropped the sack, stumbled backward, and cried out in shock.

Staring up at them from a twisted, agonized face were the lifeless eyes of Logan Powell.

Chapter 11

$\mathcal{P}$hyllis knew all too well that evidence at a crime scene should never be disturbed. If she'd had time, she would have warned Carolyn to leave the body alone. They had already disturbed it enough.

But it was too late for that. Logan's corpse was lying there in plain sight, where scores, if not hundreds, of festival-goers passing by could see it, and Carolyn's startled cry had drawn plenty of attention. Several women screamed, men shouted questions, and Dana Powell suddenly shrieked, "Logan! Oh, my God! Logan!"

She rushed past the judge's table, ran through the dogtrot, and tried to reach her husband's side. Phyllis got in her way and grabbed her by both arms.

"Dana, no!" she said. "We have to stay back. . . . Everyone has to stay back until the police get here."

"That's my husband!" she cried as she struggled against Phyllis's grip. "Let me go! Is he alive? Somebody help him!"

Logan was beyond help. Although Phyllis wished it weren't the case, she had seen enough bodies to know when someone was dead. As she tried to hang on to Dana, she looked over her shoulder at Carolyn and said, "Call the police!"

That wasn't necessary. Even while Carolyn was trying to get her cell phone out of her purse, a couple of the officers who were on duty at the festival came trotting up, drawn by the sudden commotion. They took one look at Logan's body garbed in the bizarre scarecrow costume and knew they were going to need help. One of the cops grabbed the walkie-talkie that was clipped to his belt and started trying to raise his superior.

The other officer stood beside the body and started waving everybody back. When Dana cried again, "He's my husband!" the cop pointed a finger at her and ordered sternly, "Stay right there, ma'am! There'll be an ambulance here shortly. Are you injured?"

He had to ask the question again before Dana managed to shake her head. Tears streaked her face. She wasn't trying to pull away from Phyllis anymore. Instead she stood there shaking as Phyllis put an arm around her shoulders and tried to comfort her.

Suddenly, Dana's knees unhinged, and she would have fallen if Phyllis hadn't been there to hold her up. Even though Dana was slender, having her turn abruptly into deadweight put a strain on Phyllis's muscles.

Then Sam was there at her side, saying in his deep voice, "Let me give you a hand." He got his arms around Dana, who turned and buried her face against his chest as she sobbed. Sam leaned against the cabin wall as he held her and awkwardly patted one big hand on her back.

The cop who had called for help on his walkie-talkie came over to Phyllis and asked, "Do you know who that man is?" He gestured at the corpse.

"His name is Logan Powell," Phyllis told him. "He's a member of the chamber of commerce, and he was one of the organizers of this festival."

"What the heck happened to him? How'd he wind up dressed like a scarecrow?"

"I have no idea," Phyllis said honestly.

"What'd he die of?"

"You're asking the wrong person," Phyllis pointed out.

Now that she thought about it, though, she hadn't noticed any blood on the clothing that made up the scarecrow costume. She looked at it again, as best she could with Logan lying there on his side, and still couldn't see any bloodstains on the overalls and flannel shirt. There weren't any on the burlap bag that had been placed over Logan's head, either. It still lay there on the ground near the body where Carolyn had dropped it.

Lines of pain and stress were etched into Logan's face, but Phyllis didn't see any actual injuries on it. He didn't appear to have been attacked. In fact, as far as she could see, he looked like a man who had died of natural causes.

Other than the fact that he was dressed like a scarecrow, of course. That was about as *un*natural as you could get.

She looked over at Sam, who was still holding Dana Powell, and asked quietly, "Where's Bobby?"

"Over yonder with Eve."

He nodded, and Phyllis looked in the direction he indicated. She saw Eve and Bobby standing in the crowd of curious festival-goers. Eve had a firm grip on one of Bobby's hands. Phyllis gave her a quick nod of thanks. At least she didn't have to worry about Bobby while all this commotion was going on. Not his physical well-being, anyway. He looked a little confused and upset, probably because so many of the adults around him felt the same way.

Carolyn came up beside Phyllis and murmured, "This is awful, just awful. Poor Dana."

"How do you think Logan wound up in that costume?"

"I have no idea," Carolyn said, echoing what Phyllis had told the police officer a few minutes earlier. "The very idea is just . . . weird."

That was a good word to describe it, all right, Phyllis thought. And she wondered, not for the first time, why these weird, awful things always seemed to happen while she was around.

The crowd parted, and several more uniformed police officers came through the gap, followed by a stocky man in blue jeans and a Weatherford Kangaroos sweatshirt. Phyllis recognized him as Ralph Whitmire, the chief of police. From the looks of the chief's clothes, he had been attending the festival, not working at it as part of his duties. That had certainly changed now. He stopped short and looked at Phyllis over Logan Powell's body.

"Mrs. Newsom," Chief Whitmire said.

"Hello, Chief."

Whitmire frowned. "You found the body?"

"Well, as a matter of fact, Mrs. Wilbarger and I did."

Whitmire looked over at Carolyn, nodded, and said, "Mrs. Wilbarger."

Carolyn just said, "Hmmph." She hadn't forgotten that both she and her daughter had been suspects in a murder several years earlier. Probably she never would.

Whitmire turned to his men and went on, "All right, secure the area. Crime Scene's already on the way, along with an ambulance."

"Do we close down the festival, Chief?" one of the officers asked.

Whitmire looked around at the park and at all the people already crowded into it. He sighed and said, "No, just get some crime-scene tape and string it around these trees." He waved a hand at the oaks surrounding the two cabins. "We'll keep everybody away from this part of the park as much as we can, but let them go on and enjoy the rest of the festival."

"What about a canvass?"

"With this many people, and the manpower we have?" Whitmire shook his head. "Impossible. Anyway, we don't even know for sure that there's been a crime here." He glanced at the corpse. "Something weird, for sure, but maybe not a crime."

One of the officers who was first on the scene pointed at Dana, who wasn't crying anymore but still stood huddled in Sam's arms. "That's the dead guy's wife, Chief."

Whitmire nodded. "Thanks." He looked at Phyllis. "Who was close by here when you found the body?"

She half turned and held out a hand to indicate the judges from the cooking contest, which surely wouldn't be going on now since all the entries were sitting smack-dab in a possible crime scene.

"Okay, folks," Whitmire told them, "I'm going to

need you to stay right here until we have a chance to talk to you."

"Is the contest canceled?" Dolly Williamson asked.

Whitmire managed a tired smile. "I'm afraid so."

"Then should we let all the people who brought food for it take their entries?"

"No!" Whitmire said. "Nothing and nobody who was in this area when the body was found leaves until we figure out what happened here."

Dolly looked a little surprised at the chief's vehemence, but she nodded and said, "All right."

Whitmire hunkered on his heels next to the body, studying it without touching it, and asked, "Who is he?"

The officer who had asked Phyllis the same question said, "Name's Logan Powell, Chief."

Whitmire looked up. "The real estate guy?"

"I don't know, Chief. I just got his name."

"Yes, that's him, Chief," the president of the chamber of commerce said. "We all knew him."

"You have any idea what happened to him?"

All Whitmire got in response to that question were shaking heads.

A siren wailed. The music from the other cabin had stopped, but there was still a lot of hubbub in the air. It went silent for a moment at the sound of the approaching siren. When the wail cut off, the noise came back up, only to die down again as a team of EMTs wheeling a gurney over the rough ground made their way from the parking lot to the cabin where Logan's body lay.

Everyone gave the paramedics room as they gathered around the body. One of them took out a stethoscope and listened for a heartbeat. Not finding one, he searched for a pulse in Logan's neck and failed to locate that, too. He looked up at Whitmire and said, "We're gonna have to declare him dead on the scene, Chief."

Whitmire nodded. "Got any idea what killed him?"

The EMT looked over the body. "No visible sign of wounds. I think COD's gonna have to wait for the medical examiner.... Wait a minute."

Whitmire leaned forward tensely. "You see something after all?"

"I think there's something in his mouth," the man said as he bent closer to peer between Logan's lips, which were parted slightly. Carefully using a couple of gloved fingers, he opened Logan's mouth a little wider and put his face close enough that he could sniff. Phyllis shuddered as she looked away. There was something so intimate and yet so grotesque about the scene that she had a hard time looking at it. She was glad that Sam had Dana turned so that she couldn't see what was going on. It was bad enough that she had to hear it, although Phyllis thought she might be in such a state of shock that she wouldn't actually understand what she was hearing.

"Chief, I'd better not mess with this anymore," the EMT said as he straightened from the body. "I'm not trained in forensics. But there's definitely some sort of ... brown slime in his mouth. You'll want to have your crime-scene people check it out, and of course the ME will, too."

"Brown slime," Whitmire repeated. "Like poison of some sort?"

The EMT shrugged. "Could be."

Whitmire lowered his voice and asked, "Maybe some sort of biological weapon?" As always these days, terrorism was one of the first things the authorities considered whenever something mysterious happened.

"Oh, Lord, Chief, don't ask me. All I know is that it had sort of a familiar smell, kind of sweet and doughy and almost like ... pumpkin, maybe?"

"Oh, my God, Phyllis!" Carolyn exclaimed. "Your pumpkin muffins!"

Phyllis felt all the pairs of eyes as they turned to look at her, and as she felt the weight of the stares, she burst out, "Oh, come on, people! What are the odds that a ... a dead man would have one of my pumpkin muffins in his mouth? That's crazy!"

But even as the words left her lips, she wished that she wasn't wondering the exact same thing as everybody else here. She really did.

Chapter 12

$\mathcal{B}$y this time, the police had moved all the festival-goers well back, away from the cabin and the dogtrot where Logan's body lay. They unrolled bright yellow crime-scene tape and strung it from tree to tree to close off the area, leaving only a gap where they could come and go and where the body could be wheeled out once it was placed on the gurney that had been brought from the ambulance.

The body couldn't be moved, though, until the photographer and the forensics team arrived and did their work. Phyllis knew this because of Mike's involvement with police work and her own brushes with murder over the past few years; plus, like everyone else, she watched TV and movies and had such things ingrained in her knowledge now.

She had never forgotten what Mike had once told her about police procedure and forensics science as they were presented on television, though: Part of what went on was realistic; a larger part was far-fetched but barely plausible; the biggest part of all was pure fantasy.

Following Chief Whitmire's orders, several cops herded Phyllis, Sam, Dana, Carolyn, and the other judges from the contest into the area in front of the cabin, gathering them around a circular rock wall that was supposed to look like a well, even though there was nothing inside it but more dirt. "Wait right here," one of the officers told them. "Either the chief or a detective will be talking to you in a little while."

Dana was able to stand up on her own now, but Phyllis and Sam both stayed close to her in case everything overwhelmed her and she started to collapse again. She wiped at eyes that were red rimmed from crying and said, "I . . . I just don't understand. How can he be dead? I . . . I saw him just last night."

"It's a terrible thing, Dana," Carolyn told her. "But remember that you have plenty of friends ready to stand by you and do whatever you need to help you get through this."

As if to prove that, someone called Dana's name from beyond the crime-scene tape. Phyllis looked in that direction and saw four women standing there with worried expressions on their faces. She recognized Barbara Loomis and Jenna Grantham from the day before at Loving Elementary. She was acquainted with the other two women as well. The one with curly brown hair falling around her shoulders was Taryn Marshall, the art teacher at the elementary school, and the woman with short blond hair and glasses was Kendra Neville, the librarian.

Dana started to cry again as she saw them. Jenna got a determined look on her face and suddenly lifted the crime-scene tape, ducking under it and starting toward Dana. The other three women hesitated for a second, then followed her.

One of the officers moved swiftly to get in their way. He held up both hands, palms out, and ordered, "Hold it, ladies. You need to get back on the other side of that tape *right now*. This area is off-limits."

"That's our friend over there," Jenna said angrily, "and she's in pain. We're going to do whatever we can to help her."

"Not now you're not," the cop insisted.

Jenna glared at him. She was tall and athletic enough that she looked like she might be able to take the officer, if it came to that, Phyllis thought, although in reality that was highly unlikely.

But then Jenna sighed and nodded. "All right," she said in a surly voice. "But I don't have to like it." As the officer began herding the four of them back toward the yellow tape, Jenna called over the man's shoulder, "If there's anything we can do for you, Dana, just let us know!"

Carolyn patted Dana on the back and said, "See, I told you that you have lots of friends. We'll get you through this, Dana."

"I'm not ..." Dana swallowed hard. "I'm not sure I *want* to get through it. I never even thought about what it would be like to ... live without Logan. Even with all the problems we had, I ... I just can't imagine. ..."

Her shoulders started to shake, and once again tears welled from her eyes. This time it was Carolyn who embraced her in an attempt to bring her whatever meager comfort was possible at this terrible moment.

The forensics team arrived, prompting the ambulance crew to step aside from the body. If they didn't get any other calls, they would wait until the police were finished, then transport Logan's remains to the morgue at the hospital a couple of miles away. Phyllis watched as the investigators photographed the body and all the area around it, then set about gathering whatever evidence they could find. They put the straw hat Logan had been wearing into a plastic bag and sealed it. The burlap bag that had been pulled over his head was treated the same way. One of the technicians swabbed some of the brown slime out of Logan's mouth and dropped that swab in an evidence bag. Phyllis couldn't see it very well, but she could tell it was about the same color as one of her pumpkin muffins.

But that still made no sense at all, she thought. All the muffins she had brought to the park for the contest were still in their plastic containers, sitting on the table at the front of the dogtrot. They hadn't been touched since Bobby had placed them there. Whatever it was in Logan's mouth had to be something else. He couldn't possibly have been eating one of Phyllis's muffins when he died.

Then every muscle in her body suddenly stiffened as

she recalled that Dana had taken one of the muffins with her the night before when she left Phyllis's house.

Phyllis looked over at Dana, who stood there with Carolyn's arm around her shoulders looking as pale and haggard and grief stricken as ever. She had said that Logan never came home from the park the night before, and Phyllis had no reason to think that she was lying. According to Carolyn, Dana had left the park before Logan, so if she'd given him part of the muffin she'd brought from Phyllis's house, or even the whole muffin, it wouldn't have still been in his mouth when he died later. Therefore, Phyllis reasoned, the brown slime in his mouth couldn't be from her muffin.

Unless Dana had come back to the park while Logan was still here but everybody else was gone . . .

That still wouldn't explain how Logan had died. Phyllis had once been accused, briefly, of baking something that had killed someone when they ate it, but she knew perfectly well that wasn't the case here. There was nothing in those muffins that would hurt anybody. As far as she knew, there wasn't even anything that could have caused a dangerous allergic reaction in someone who was hypersensitive to certain foods.

She told herself to stop worrying about the muffins and concentrate on the tragic loss Dana had suffered instead. But there was nothing else any of them could do to help with that right now. They were stuck here until the police were through with them.

Phyllis saw Chief Whitmire talking to an attractive woman with short, midnight black hair and olive skin who was wearing black slacks and a black jacket over a white blouse. She recognized the woman as Detective Isabel Largo. Detective Largo had investigated one of the crimes in which Phyllis had found herself unwillingly involved.

That didn't necessarily mean that the police already considered Logan's death a homicide, though. It was much too early for anyone to draw such a conclusion. But any mysterious death would be investigated thoroughly, Phyllis knew, and she supposed that Detective Largo had been assigned to this case.

A few minutes later, Detective Largo nodded to the chief, then walked through the dogtrot and came over to where the witnesses were gathered. She nodded to Phyllis and said, "Mrs. Newsom."

"Hello, Detective."

"Chief Whitmire tells me that you discovered the body."

Carolyn said, "Actually, Phyllis and I both did."

"Hello, Mrs. Wilbarger," Detective Largo said with another nod. "I'll be talking to you, too, in a few minutes." She turned back to Phyllis. "But right now, Mrs. Newsom, I'd like for you to come with me."

Phyllis looked around. Even though the crowd had been moved back, she didn't have any trouble spotting Eve and Bobby. Many of the festival-goers had drifted away, determined to enjoy their day at the park, but quite a few still stood behind the yellow tape watching the scene around the old cabin, and Eve and Bobby were in the forefront of that group.

"My grandson is here," Phyllis told Detective Largo. She gestured toward Eve and Bobby. "My friend is watching him right now, but I need to talk to her for a minute before I go anywhere."

The detective considered Phyllis's request for a few seconds, then nodded. "All right. You can go over there and talk to them. But come right back."

"I will," Phyllis promised.

She walked up to the crime-scene tape that was holding back the onlookers. Bobby asked anxiously, "Gran'mama, are you all right?"

She smiled at him. "I'm fine, Bobby, but I may be busy here for a while. Maybe most of the day. Do you mind seeing the festival with Mrs. Turner?" She glanced at Eve. "If that's all right?"

"Of course it's all right," Eve answered without hesitation. "You know me, Phyllis. I'd absolutely love to spend the day with a handsome young man, and Bobby certainly qualifies."

"Thank you." Phyllis looked down at her grandson. "Okay, Bobby?"

"I guess. I wish I could have one of those punkin muffins we brought, though."

"I'm not sure anybody's going to get them," Phyllis told him. "But we can always make more when we get home, can't we?"

That brought a smile to Bobby's face. "Yeah!"

Phyllis looked at Eve again and said, "I'll give you the key to my car. You can use it to take Bobby home whenever the two of you are ready to go."

"How will you get back?"

"I'll catch a ride with Sam or Carolyn," Phyllis said as she took the key ring from her purse and handed it over.

Eve nodded. "All right. Is there anything else I can do to help?"

"No, I don't think so. I'm just glad you were here, Eve, and you didn't get caught in this mess like the rest of us did."

"What if Mike calls? Do I tell him—?"

"Good Lord, no." The last thing Mike needed to hear while he was out there in California with his wife and his dying father-in-law was that his mother was mixed up in another murder back home. She added, "There's nothing he could do, anyway."

Phyllis glanced back and saw that Detective Largo was watching her with a particularly intense stare. She knew she had probably already stretched the detective's patience as far as she ought to. She bent down under the crime-scene tape and hugged Bobby, then said quickly, "I'll see you later," and walked back over to Detective Largo.

"Why did you give Mrs. Turner your keys?" the detective asked.

"So she could take Bobby home," Phyllis explained. "Eve didn't bring her car."

Detective Largo considered that answer for a moment, then nodded, apparently accepting it. "Follow me," she said.

She led Phyllis away from the taped-off scene, through the park, and back to the parking lot. She opened the passenger door of a nondescript sedan that was either her personal car or an unmarked police vehicle.

"Have a seat," Detective Largo said. It was an order as much as an invitation, Phyllis knew.

"Are you taking me to police headquarters?"

The detective shook her head. "No, I just thought this would be a good place for us to talk."

That relieved Phyllis's mind a little. She slid into the car. Detective Largo closed the door and went around to get in behind the wheel. It was warmer and quieter in there.

Detective Largo took a small digital recorder from the pocket of her jacket, switched it on, gave the time, and identified herself and Phyllis. She said, "You're not under arrest, Mrs. Newsom, and you don't have to talk to me if you don't want to."

"That's all right," Phyllis said with a shake of her head. "I don't mind answering your questions. I want to help. I want to find out what happened to Logan Powell as much as you do."

"Fine," Detective Largo said. "Tell me how it happens that you discovered a body under mysterious circumstances ... again."

Chapter 13

Phyllis felt a brief surge of annoyance at the detective's tone, but she told herself to be reasonable. Most people went through their entire lives without ever finding even a single dead body, if they were lucky. There was no denying that she had stumbled onto more than her fair share of them over the past few years.

She made herself reply in a calm voice, "I delivered my entry for the cooking contest to the dogtrot when I got here to the park with my grandson and my friend Eve Turner."

She didn't mention that her entry was pumpkin muffins. Let Detective Largo find out if there was any connection between those muffins and the unidentified brown substance found in Logan Powell's mouth.

"From there, Carolyn—Mrs. Wilbarger—and I walked around the park for a while with Mrs. Powell, who was looking for her husband," she went on.

"Wait a minute. That's the dead man, right?"

Phyllis nodded. "Logan Powell, yes."

"So his wife was looking for him?"

"That's right. She said he hadn't come home last night, and she was worried about him."

"Did you believe her?"

"I didn't have any reason not to," Phyllis said. "And

Mrs. Powell certainly looked and sounded like she was sincere about the way she felt."

"But you didn't find Mr. Powell anywhere else in the park, of course, because all the time he was sitting on that hay bale dressed like a scarecrow."

"That's right," Phyllis said again, thinking that the situation sounded even more bizarre when summed up in Detective Largo's flat, emotionless voice.

"I noticed some other scarecrows sitting on bales of hay when I was walking into the park," the detective said. "Are they just for decoration?"

Phyllis nodded. "Yes, volunteers made them this week and then put them out because they fit in with the Harvest Festival theme. In fact, I was one of the people who put them out on display yesterday."

"That's interesting. Who was responsible for placing the one in the dogtrot, there between the two halves of the cabin?"

"That's just it," Phyllis replied with a shake of her head. "There wasn't supposed to be a scarecrow there. There wasn't when I left the park yesterday. They were scattered around all over, but not in the dogtrot."

"So someone moved that hay bale, dressed Mr. Powell in the scarecrow costume, and propped him up on it?"

Again, Detective Largo's description of the event made it sound even more far-fetched. But Phyllis could only nod and say, "Yes, that must be what happened. It's the only explanation." Something occurred to her. "Unless . . ."

A spark of interest flared in the detective's dark eyes. "Unless what?"

"Unless Logan moved the hay bale and put the costume on himself," Phyllis said. "I suppose he could have done that."

"Why would he do such a thing?"

Phyllis had to respond with the answer that was cropping up a lot this morning. "I have no idea."

"But if he did, then he sat down there and died."

"Maybe he had a heart attack, or something like that." Phyllis nodded, seeing how the theory fit together.

"In fact, I saw his face, and it looked like he was in pain before he died. It could have happened just that way, Detective."

"Maybe it could have," Detective Largo said. "But that doesn't explain why he moved the hay bale or put on that scarecrow costume."

"No," Phyllis admitted. "No, it doesn't."

"Let's get back to when you found the body. You and Mrs. Powell and Mrs. Wilbarger walked around the park looking for Mr. Powell, and when you didn't find him, what then?"

"We went back to the cabin. The judging for the contest was going to be starting soon. Carolyn had to be there because she was one of the judges, and of course I wanted to be on hand because I had an entry in the contest."

"And Mrs. Powell came with you?"

"That's right. She was still worried and upset, of course, but Carolyn and I had tried to convince her that Logan would turn up sooner or later."

"Well, he did, didn't he?"

Phyllis caught her lower lip between her teeth for a moment. She hadn't thought about it like that, but Detective Largo was right. She sighed and nodded.

"Yes, he did."

"Why did you and Mrs. Wilbarger go over to the scarecrow?"

"I told you, we helped put them out on display yesterday. We knew there wasn't supposed to be one there in the dogtrot. Carolyn said it had been bothering her all morning, so she suggested that we move it, since there were still a few minutes until the contest judging began."

"So it was Mrs. Wilbarger's idea to move the scarecrow?"

"Yes, but that doesn't mean anything."

"I think it'll be up to the investigation to determine what means something and what doesn't, Mrs. Newsom."

This time Phyllis couldn't keep a slight edge out of her voice as she said, "If you think Carolyn had anything to do with Logan's death, you're wrong, Detective."

"I didn't say that," Detective Largo replied smoothly, unperturbed. "Go on with your story."

"Well, Carolyn said she would move the hay bale, and I could move the scarecrow. They don't weigh much. But as soon as I took hold of it, I knew something was wrong."

"How did you know?"

"It didn't feel right. It was too heavy. It felt like there was something solid in it, not just some paper stuffing."

"Then what happened?"

"I stepped back and said there was something wrong. Carolyn took hold of the scarecrow and started to lift it; then she let go, and it fell back on the bale, and . . . then it fell off onto the ground and made this noise. . . ."

"A noise like a body landing on concrete?" the detective suggested.

"Yes," Phyllis said. "That was exactly what it sounded like."

"So you knew then what you'd found." Detective Largo didn't bother making it sound like a question this time.

Phyllis nodded. "I had a pretty good idea. The scarecrow's hat had come off when it fell, and the burlap bag over the head had slipped some. I could see what looked like skin between the bottom of the bag and the shirt collar."

"What did you do?"

"I was about to tell Carolyn to get away from it and not disturb it anymore—"

"Because you know how evidence is supposed to be handled."

"Well, yes. But I was still a little shocked, and before I could say anything, Carolyn reached down and pulled the burlap bag off, and . . . there was Logan." Phyllis shrugged. "Then there was all sorts of commotion, of course, and two of the officers who were on duty here at the festival showed up, and I expect you know everything after that from talking to Chief Whitmire."

Detective Largo flicked off the recorder and smiled politely. "Thank you, Mrs. Newsom."

"That's all?"

"Yes. I think you've provided all the information you can, based on your own direct knowledge."

That was true enough, Phyllis supposed. She opened the car door and stepped out. So did Detective Largo. Without saying anything else, they walked back across the park to the cabin.

"Mrs. Wilbarger, would you come with me?" Detective Largo asked when they got there.

Carolyn frowned suspiciously. "Why?"

"I just want to find out what you can tell me about discovering the body."

"You mean you want to see if my story matches what Phyllis told you."

"It'll only take a few minutes."

Carolyn went with the detective, grudgingly. She would never fully trust the police after that earlier case, Phyllis supposed. She wasn't sure she could blame her friend for feeling that way, either. The very idea that Carolyn Wilbarger could ever murder anybody was ludicrous.

Phyllis looked around, curious to know how Dana was doing, but she didn't see her right away. Then she spotted Dana sitting on one of the folding chairs that the judges would have been using during the contest if it had taken place as scheduled. Someone had taken it from behind the table and brought it out here in front of the cabin so that Dana could sit down, and Phyllis had a pretty good idea who that someone was, since Sam was still standing near Dana as if he were watching over her.

She went up to him and asked quietly, "You got that chair for Dana, didn't you?"

"She's had a mighty hard time of it," Sam replied with a shrug. "I didn't want to have to try to catch her if she fainted."

"How's she doing?"

"Hangin' in there, I reckon. It's got to be pretty bad for her. She must feel like her whole world's been yanked right out from under her."

Phyllis put a hand on his arm and squeezed for a second. "You're a nice man, Sam Fletcher," she said. "Looking out for Dana like this when you barely even know her."

He shrugged. "I figure she must be all right if you and Carolyn are her friends."

As a matter of fact, though, Phyllis thought, she and Dana weren't really all that close. They were acquaintances more than friends, the way it was with Phyllis and those other teachers from that little circle at Loving Elementary. Sam didn't know that, though, so he was doing what he assumed Phyllis would want him to do.

Phyllis stood there for a moment looking at Dana, who was gazing at the dogtrot and the crowd of police in it with what could only be termed stark horror on her face. She probably couldn't see Logan's body from where she was—all the police standing around blocked the sight—but she had to know it was there. If Dana had really had anything to do with Logan's death, she was one of the best actors in the world, Phyllis told herself. Of course, anything was possible. People had fooled Phyllis before . . . but not for long.

"That detective get through askin' all her questions?"

Phyllis looked over at Sam. "What? Oh, yes. I wouldn't be surprised if she has more later on, though."

"Detectives never run out of questions until they have the answers they're lookin' for," Sam said. "I know that from bein' around you."

"Well, I won't be investigating this case," she said. "We don't even know that there's a case to be investigated. Logan may have died of natural causes. Just because he was found in odd circumstances doesn't mean he was murdered."

A grim chuckle came from Sam. "Maybe so . . . but I wouldn't count on it."

Neither would she, Phyllis thought.

Neither would she.

Chapter 14

A few minutes later, there was a flurry of activity inside the dogtrot. Phyllis thought she knew what would happen next, and she was right. The ambulance crew loaded Logan Powell's body, now zipped up in a black body bag, onto the gurney and wheeled it out through a passage that the police opened up in the crowd. They took it out of the park and put it into the back of the ambulance.

Dana had shot to her feet at the first sight of the body bag. Phyllis and Sam both went to her, standing on either side of her as she watched Logan being taken away. The look on her face was so grief stricken that Phyllis's heart broke for her.

No woman who looked like that could have had anything to do with her husband's death, Phyllis thought. She just didn't believe it was possible.

"I . . . I suppose I should go," Dana said in a halting voice. "I have to . . . make arrangements."

Phyllis put a hand on her arm. "I think you should sit down and stay here right now," she said. "Everything else can wait."

She didn't want to put into words the fact that the police wouldn't *let* Dana leave the park at this point. Not until they had questioned her, and obviously Detective Largo intended to get all the background in place first, before she talked to Dana.

In any death without an obvious explanation, the deceased's spouse was always going to be the first person the police looked at as having some possible involvement. There was a *lot* about Logan Powell's death that didn't have an obvious explanation. Dana wasn't thinking straight right now, or she would realize that. She would be doing good if the police were through with her before the day was over, Phyllis knew . . . unless, of course, she called a lawyer and forced them to either arrest her or let her go.

And that was a tactic that wouldn't look good at all.

Dana clearly didn't understand that, however, because she pulled away from Phyllis and said, "No, I have to *go*. I have to take care of things. Logan will be depending on me."

There was a shaky edge in her voice that told Phyllis she was bordering on hysteria. "Wait right here," Phyllis told her. "I'll go talk to Chief Whitmire and see if it's all right for you to leave."

"It has to be," Dana said. "I have things to *do*."

Phyllis knew what was going on. Dana wanted to deal with the mundane aspects of Logan's death because that gave her something to hang on to, tasks to distract her from the terrible loss she had suffered. It was a way of fooling her brain into not thinking about what had actually happened. Unfortunately, Phyllis had a hunch that the police weren't going to cooperate in that emotional defense mechanism Dana was trying to set up.

Chief Whitmire stood talking to several officers from his forensics team. He saw Phyllis coming toward him and turned to face her as the other officers went on about their business of gathering and evaluating evidence.

"What can I do for you, Mrs. Newsom?" Whitmire asked. "If Detective Largo has already talked to you, I suppose you're free to go."

"It's not me I'm worried about, Chief," Phyllis said. "Mrs. Powell wants to leave so she can make arrangements for her husband's funeral."

Whitmire's forehead creased in a frown. He shook his head. "She can't do that. We haven't questioned her yet. Anyway, right now there's no way of knowing when Powell's body will be released. The ME hasn't even looked at it yet."

Phyllis nodded. "I understand. There'll have to be an autopsy. I believe Mrs. Powell just wants to stay busy so she won't have to think too much about what happened here."

Whitmire grunted and said, "Maybe that's what she wants you to believe. Maybe that's what she wants all of us to believe."

"Chief, you can't seriously think that that poor woman had anything to do with what happened to her husband. She's devastated! Anyway, you don't even know yet how Logan died."

"And until we do, everything else can wait," Whitmire said. "Sorry, but that's the way it's gotta be."

Phyllis could tell that he wasn't going to budge. That came as no surprise. She had known she was probably wasting her time before she ever came over here to talk to the chief. She nodded and said, "All right. But this is one time you're wrong to be suspicious of the spouse."

Detective Isabel Largo asked from behind Phyllis, "Is that so, Mrs. Newsom?"

Phyllis tried not to jump a little. She hadn't heard the detective come up behind her. As she turned to face her, Detective Largo went on, "Is that why you didn't tell me about the argument between Mr. Powell and his wife last night, or her belief that he was cheating on her? Because you believe she didn't have anything to do with his death?"

There was a sharp undertone of accusation in the younger woman's voice. Phyllis kept a tight grip on her temper and said, "You didn't ask me about any of that, Detective. If you had, I would have told you what I know, which is all hearsay, anyway."

"That's all right," Detective Largo said. "Mrs. Wilbarger told me all about it."

Phyllis glanced toward the old well and saw Carolyn

standing there with Sam and Dana. She and Detective Largo must have returned from the parking lot while Phyllis was talking to Chief Whitmire.

The chief said, "So the two of them argued last night, did they, Detective?"

"That's right. Mrs. Wilbarger witnessed it, and Mrs. Powell told her about believing that Mr. Powell was cheating."

Whitmire looked at Phyllis. "You should have mentioned that when you were talking to Detective Largo, Mrs. Newsom."

"With all due respect, Chief, it's not my responsibility to volunteer information," Phyllis said. "It's your detective's job to ask the right questions."

She saw the way Detective Largo's jaw tightened and anger glittered in her dark eyes, and she knew she had just made an enemy by pointing out that Largo had dropped the ball. At the moment, she didn't really care. She was a lot more worried about how the suspicions surrounding Dana were growing stronger.

"You have a duty as a citizen to cooperate with the police," Whitmire began, but then he shook his head and gave a dismissive wave of his hand. "But we'll let that go. I'll ask you straight out: What do you know about the Powells' marital troubles?"

"I was there when Dana said she thought Logan had been cheating on her," Phyllis admitted. "And Carolyn told me that she saw them arguing last night, over there on the bridge over the drainage ditch."

She pointed at the wooden bridge, which was visible through the trees.

"You don't know anything else about Powell's affair?"

"I don't know that he was having one. Like I told you, Chief, all I know about this subject is hearsay."

"Well, we'll see what the lady herself has to say about it," Whitmire said heavily. He looked at Detective Largo. "I think you should take Mrs. Powell back to the office to question her, Detective."

Largo nodded. "Of course, Chief."

Phyllis wanted to try to talk them out of it, but she knew it wouldn't do any good. She watched helplessly as Detective Largo turned and strode over to where Dana, Sam, and Carolyn were standing. In a loud, clear voice, the detective said, "Mrs. Powell, I'd like for you to come with me."

Dana looked confused. "What? Come with you? Where? I can't go. I . . . I have to make arrangements. . . ."

"There'll be plenty of time for that later," Detective Largo said. She put a hand on Dana's arm. "Come with me, please."

Dana pulled away. "No!"

"You ought to leave her alone," Carolyn said. "She's suffered a terrible shock."

"Yes, ma'am," Largo said, "but we still have to question her."

"Question me?" Dana repeated. "Why do you need to question me?" Her voice rose, became more shrill. "You need to be trying to find out what happened to Logan!"

"That's what we're doing, ma'am." Detective Largo gestured to a couple of uniformed officers who stood nearby. "That's why you need to come with me, so I can talk to you about it."

Dana shook her head. "But I don't know anything. He . . . he never came home last night. I was so worried. I was afraid something had happened to him, and . . . and it has." Her hands came up and covered her face. "He's dead!"

The words came out of her in a wail. She shook from the depth of the terrible emotions coursing through her. Detective Largo jerked her hand at the cops, and they hurried forward and reached for Dana. Before they could take hold of her, though, she crumpled. She hit the ground hard and sprawled there, senseless.

"Oh, dear Lord!" Carolyn said. She started to kneel next to Dana, but Detective Largo got in her way.

"Everyone stay back!" the detective snapped.

"But she fainted! She may be hurt."

Largo ignored Carolyn's protests. She called, "Chief,

we need another ambulance." Whitmire started talking emphatically into his radio.

Phyllis, Carolyn, and Sam couldn't do anything but stand there, shocked at this sudden turn of events. Phyllis wasn't too shocked, though, because she had been able to see that Dana was on the verge of collapse ever since the discovery of Logan's body. At some level, Dana must have realized that the police considered her a suspect in his death, if it turned out that he had died from foul play. The burden of that knowledge, along with everything else, had been too much for her to bear any longer.

"I hope you're satisfied with yourself," Carolyn said in scathing tones to Detective Largo.

"I'll be satisfied when I know for sure what happened here, Mrs. Wilbarger," the detective replied. "But not until then."

Dana's collapse and the arrival a few minutes later of another ambulance with screaming siren got the attention of everyone in the park again. Phyllis wasn't sure the Harvest Festival could continue after this second disruption. She hoped it would, though, because despite everything else, it was still important to collect as much food as possible for the people who needed it. Hard though it was to believe after everything that had happened, it wasn't quite noon yet. The festival still had a lot of hours to run, and a lot more food could be collected in that time. Things would settle down once the police were through here, she told herself.

The EMTs with this ambulance were able to revive Dana after checking her out and making sure her vital signs were stable. "Take her to the hospital," Chief Whitmire ordered. He added to Detective Largo, "You go with them, and don't let her out of your sight. As soon as a doctor gives the okay, go ahead and question her."

"Right, Chief."

From the stony look on the detective's face, Phyllis knew that Largo was determined to make up for any perceived shortcomings in her earlier questioning. Dana was going to be in for a rough time of it. She couldn't expect much sympathy from Isabel Largo.

All of which was ridiculous, Phyllis thought, because they didn't even know for sure that Logan Powell had been murdered. The cause of death was still up in the air. But just in case it turned out that someone had deliberately caused it, the police didn't want to let that slip past them. The problem for Phyllis was that she didn't believe Dana could have done anything to harm her husband, or anyone else, for that matter.

She hadn't believed that about some other murderers she had encountered, she reminded herself. But logic was one thing, and belief something else entirely.

The ambulance crew insisted on putting Dana on a gurney and wheeling her out of the park. She didn't protest. She wore a stunned, almost uncomprehending look now, as if she could no longer quite grasp what was happening to her. Phyllis's heart went out to her, and as the siren receded in the distance as it headed toward the hospital, she couldn't help but think how much it sounded like the wail of a dispossessed soul.

Chapter 15

🧁

$\mathcal{D}$etective Largo followed the ambulance, while Chief Whitmire stayed at the park to continue supervising the investigation there. He took over the questioning of the other witnesses, primarily Carolyn's fellow judges in the cooking contest, who had been at the other end of the dogtrot when Logan's body was discovered. Phyllis didn't imagine any of them would be able to tell the chief anything he didn't already know.

The questioning did clear up the problem of what to do about the baked goods that had been entered in the contest, though. Phyllis had a feeling that Whitmire had considered impounding all of them as possible evidence, since the cause of Logan's death was still unknown, but after talking to Dolly Williamson and the other judges, all of whom confirmed that the entries had been brought to the park that morning, after Logan's body was dressed in the scarecrow costume and placed on the hay bale, the chief decided to allow the contestants to claim their entries.

Sam hung on to the two containers of pumpkin muffins for Phyllis. "Would've been a dang shame to have all those goodies go to waste," he said as he gave the top container an affectionate pat. "At least this way folks will get to eat them."

"If anyone wants food that was sitting in the same place where a corpse was discovered," Carolyn said.

"Well, it looked like it was all sealed up good," Sam pointed out.

Finally all the photographs had been taken and the entire dogtrot, as well as the surrounding area, had been combed for evidence by the forensics team. Phyllis thought it was unlikely they had found anything important. Even though the festival had been going on for less than two hours when Logan's body was found, scores of people had already trampled all over the place, destroying any potential evidence.

Phyllis wondered whether the person who had put him on the bale of hay had been counting on that happening.

Then she thought that she was getting ahead of herself. Again, it was hard to ascribe motives to a murderer when she didn't even know that a murder had taken place.

Chief Whitmire issued orders for the crime-scene tape to be taken down. He came over to Phyllis and the others and said, "You folks can go home, or stay and enjoy the rest of the festival—whatever you want. Thank you for your cooperation."

"You're going to let the festival continue as planned?" Phyllis asked.

The chief shrugged. "It's been going on all day so far. No reason to stop it now. And it's for a good cause, after all."

Phyllis couldn't argue with that. Once all the crime-scene tape was down, another local band began playing on the temporary bandstand in front of the other log cabin. People still thronged the park, enjoying the beautiful weather of this crisp autumn day. The ones who were just now arriving might not even know that a body had been found here earlier, although they would probably hear the gossip about it if they were here for very long. Phyllis heard quite a few people talking about the incident as she and Sam and Carolyn walked away from the log cabin.

A minute later, they spotted Eve and Bobby in front of them. Bobby was eating a corn dog and looked like he was really enjoying it. When he saw Phyllis, he ran toward her, grinning as he called, "Gran'mama!"

"Slow down, Bobby," she told him. "You know it's not safe to run while you're holding a stick, even if there is part of a corn dog still on it."

"That reminds me," Sam said. "I'm a little hungry."

"You've got the punkin muffins!" Bobby said. "Do we get to eat 'em after all?"

"I suppose so," Phyllis told him. "If you want them."

Bobby licked his lips. "What do you think?"

The little boy's enthusiasm brought a smile to Phyllis's lips. It was very welcome after the grim events of the past couple of hours, too.

"We'll take the muffins home and have them there later," she said. "Right now, why don't you show us where you got that corn dog?"

Sam said, "That's what I was just about to suggest."

While they followed Bobby toward the booth where the corn dogs were being sold, Eve dropped back behind with Phyllis and said quietly, "I was trying to keep an eye on what was going on while keeping Bobby away from it. Did you really find Logan Powell's body?"

"I'm afraid so."

"How terrible! Poor Dana must be devastated. Didn't I see them taking her away in an ambulance? Did she faint?"

Phyllis nodded. "But only after the police started talking about questioning her. I guess that pushed her over the edge."

"Questioning . . . ," Eve repeated. Her eyebrows rose. "You don't mean they think she had something to do with her husband's death, do you? Seriously?"

"It looked pretty serious to me," Phyllis said. "I'm not convinced, though. For one thing, we don't know how Logan died. It might have been natural causes."

"But then why was he dressed like a scarecrow?"

That was the question everyone kept coming back to, Phyllis thought. And it still didn't have an answer.

"I'm sure all the facts will come out eventually," she said, knowing even as she spoke that the comment was pretty lame.

"You're going to find out what happened, aren't you?" Eve asked.

"I don't see how, unless I read it in the paper or see it on the news like anyone else."

Eve gave Phyllis a long, skeptical look. "All those murders you've solved, and you're not even the least bit curious about what happened here?"

"I didn't say that. I'm as curious as anybody else. But I'm not a detective, Eve. I never have been. I'm a retired schoolteacher."

"I'd say that anyone who solves crimes is a detective, even a retired schoolteacher," Eve insisted. "I know that if I was ever in trouble with the law, Phyllis, I'd want you on the case."

That sounded crazy to Phyllis, but she didn't say so.

They reached the corn dog booth and had lunch there, then spent the next couple of hours taking in all the other attractions at the festival. By the middle of the afternoon, Bobby was obviously exhausted.

"I think we've seen everything there is to see," Phyllis told him. "Are you ready to go home, Bobby?"

"Yeah, I guess. Can I have a punkin muffin when we get there?"

"I don't see why not." She had already let him have way too much sugar since he'd been staying with her, Phyllis thought . . . so a little more probably wouldn't do any harm.

The hay bale was still sitting in the dogtrot, she noticed as they walked past the cabin. The sight of it made her frown as she thought of something.

"Sam, would you mind taking Bobby and Eve back to the house?" she asked him. "Eve still has my keys and can get Bobby's booster seat. Be sure and put it in the backseat of the cab. I have another set of keys in my purse that I can use. Carolyn and I have something we need to do."

"We do?" Carolyn said.

Phyllis nodded. "Yes, we do."

"Sure, I don't mind," Sam said. He handed the muffin containers to Bobby. "You can carry these. Unless you'd rather drive the pickup, in which case I'll hang on to 'em."

Bobby giggled. "No, I'll take 'em."

"We'll be there in just a little while," Phyllis said.

She and Carolyn waited until the other three were gone; then Carolyn said, "What in the world is this all about? It's been a long, hard day, Phyllis."

"I know, but I need to pick your brain. We put out all the scarecrows yesterday, right?"

Carolyn nodded. "That's right."

"I think I remember where all the hay bales were for the ones I put out. Do you recall where the others were?"

Carolyn frowned as she thought about the question. "Maybe," she said. "Why?"

"The bale where Logan was sitting is still in the dog-trot. That means it's *not* where it was when one of us put a scarecrow on it yesterday."

Understanding dawned on Carolyn's face. "You want to figure out which bale it is."

"That's right."

"Why is that important?"

"I don't know. Maybe it's not. But I'm curious, and I'd like to know."

Carolyn put her hands on her hips and peered around the park. "Hay bales are heavy," she said. "You'd think that whoever dragged it into the dogtrot, whether it was Logan or someone else, wouldn't have wanted to lug it too far."

"That's what I was thinking," Phyllis agreed with a nod. "Let's start with the ones that are closest to the cabin."

It didn't take them long. The ground sloped slightly from the parking lot down to the lake, and one of the scarecrows had been placed about halfway between the cabins and the lot, next to one of the paths that led through the park. There was a clump of yucca plants on the other side of the path, surrounded by a ring of rocks.

"I know there was one right here," Carolyn declared as she pointed at the now-empty spot. "The bale was sitting there, and I set the first scarecrow I carried into the park on it. I remember it distinctly."

Now that Carolyn had pointed it out, Phyllis remembered seeing the scarecrow and the bale of hay as she entered the park the day before. "Then it must have been this bale that wound up down there in the dogtrot," she said. "We should check the others, though, just to make sure."

That took a little longer because of the crowd that had filled the park, but within fifteen minutes they had accounted for the other eleven bales of hay. Each bale was in its proper place.

Phyllis and Carolyn headed back to the spot where the hay bale had been moved. "All right, we're sure," Carolyn said. "What does that tell us?"

Phyllis thought hard, trying to figure out why her instincts told her this could be important. After a moment, something came to her.

"The stake," she said.

"What stake?"

"The one that was supposed to hold the scarecrow up. All the others have a stake down the back of the overalls that was pushed into the hay to keep it in place. Where's the stake from this scarecrow and this bale?"

Carolyn shook her head. "I don't know. Whoever moved the bale and the scarecrow must have pulled it out, though. Otherwise they couldn't have put those clothes on Logan."

"And even if he did it himself, he still would have had to pull the stake out first," Phyllis said. "So where is it?"

She started to look around. The object of her search was just a simple piece of wood, a section of a one-by-two board about three feet long, with one end cut at angles so that it formed a sharp point.

Careful. You could kill a guy with that thing.

She seemed to hear Logan Powell's voice telling her the same thing he had said to her the day before. He'd been right, too. The stake was sharp enough that someone with enough strength could drive it into a body, yet small enough that it wouldn't leave a very big wound. If that wound was in the right place, it might not even bleed much. If Logan had been murdered, it was possible that the missing stake was the murder weapon.

But in that case, wouldn't the killer have taken it away? Even if the stake had been discarded somewhere here in the park, somebody else could have picked it up and carried it off without having any idea that it had been used to end someone's life. Phyllis knew that finding it was a long shot. . . .

Those thoughts were going through Phyllis's head when her gaze slid over the clump of yuccas on the other side of the path, then jerked back suddenly to the long-leafed plants. She stepped closer to them and bent over.

"Be careful, Phyllis," Carolyn urged. "Do you see something over there?"

"Yes," Phyllis said. The stake was there, lying on the ground, nestled in the middle of the plants, almost invisible if a person wasn't looking for it. No one would be likely to stumble over it, either.

Phyllis took her phone out of her purse.

"What are you doing?" Carolyn asked.

"Calling the police. They have some more evidence to come and collect."

Chapter 16

The 911 operator Phyllis talked to instructed her to stay right where she was. That was fine, because Phyllis didn't intend to budge from the spot until the stake she had found was in the custody of the police. She didn't know if it was important evidence or not, but it certainly could be. She wondered if it was possible to get finger-prints off a piece of wood.

Carolyn offered to stay with her until the police arrived. "I don't think anyone is going to go wandering out into those plants," Carolyn said as she crossed her arms and planted herself beside the path, "but we'll guard it just to make sure."

That sounded like a good idea to Phyllis. She took up her position next to them.

They didn't have to wait very long before a police van pulled up in the parking lot. Somewhat to Phyllis's surprise, an unmarked car stopped behind it, and Chief Whitmire got out. Whitmire followed the two officers in Crime Scene Windbreakers who came down the path.

"What is it you've found, Mrs. Newsom?" the chief asked as he came up to Phyllis.

She pointed into the clump of yuccas. "Do you see that wooden stake, Chief?"

Whitmire leaned toward the plants and looked at the almost-hidden stake. "Yeah," he said. "What about it?"

"I'm reasonably sure it was used to hold up the scarecrow that should have been sitting on that bale of hay instead of Logan Powell."

Quickly, Phyllis explained how the scarecrows had been set up and how she and Carolyn had used a process of elimination to determine which of the bales was now sitting inside the dogtrot.

"I just got to thinking about that and wondered which bale it was," she said. "Then I asked myself what had happened to the stake. I noticed that it wasn't there when Carolyn and I approached the scarecrow in the dogtrot this morning, but then, what with finding Logan's body and all, I didn't think about it again until just a little while ago."

Whitmire nodded. "I suppose that makes sense. You think whoever put him in that scarecrow outfit pulled out the stake and tossed it in among those plants."

"That's right."

The chief turned to his officers. "All right, get that stake out of there. Be careful with it."

While the officers were retrieving the stake carefully to preserve any evidence on it, Chief Whitmire turned to Phyllis and said, "I hope this doesn't mean you've decided to investigate this case on your own, Mrs. Newsom."

"Don't you mean 'play detective,' Chief?" Phyllis asked.

Whitmire shrugged his burly shoulders. "Call it what you want. It's not something civilians need to be doing."

"I'm well aware of that. Like you said earlier, though, we have a duty as citizens to assist the police when we can. I happened to think about that stake and thought you should know."

"And I appreciate that. It could turn out to be an important piece of evidence. If you think of anything else, I'm sure you'll let us know."

"Of course."

"But that'll be the end of it."

Carolyn said, "You just don't want Phyllis solving this murder before you do."

Whitmire's face hardened with anger for a second before he controlled the reaction. "I know you don't think much of the police department, Mrs. Wilbarger, and it may surprise you to know that I understand why you feel that way. But we don't know that Logan Powell was murdered, and until we do, I'd appreciate it if you wouldn't go around saying that he was. That might compromise our investigation. Which we *will* be carrying out to the best of our ability. I assure you, we'll get to the bottom of Mr. Powell's death."

"By dragging his wife off to be questioned? Whatever happened to Logan, Dana didn't have anything to do with it."

"If that's true, then that's what our investigation will show."

Phyllis wished that Carolyn would quit arguing with the chief. She was about to say something in an attempt to smooth things over, when she saw one of the Windbreaker-clad officers lifting the stake from the middle of the plants. She could see the sharpened tip now. Her eyes searched keenly for any sign of bloodstains on it.

The stake looked perfectly normal, though. Phyllis didn't see any blood on the wood. She felt a brief pang of disappointment, then instantly was ashamed of herself for feeling that way. She supposed she had hoped that the stake would turn out to be the murder weapon, because that would have answered one question and brought them that much closer to a full explanation of Logan Powell's death.

Handling the stake with rubber gloves, the officers put it into a clear evidence bag the size of a kitchen garbage bag and sealed it shut for the time being. Phyllis knew they would take it back to their lab and test it for fingerprints and any foreign substances, including blood. Getting the full results would take a while, but Phyllis thought they would be able to determine pretty quickly whether there was any blood on the wood—and whether it had played any role in Logan's death.

Carolyn and Chief Whitmire had been distracted by the stake, too, and their brief clash seemed to be over. The chief nodded to Phyllis and said, "Thanks again for your help, Mrs. Newsom," then turned his head and nodded to Carolyn, "Mrs. Wilbarger."

"I suppose it would be too much to hope that you'd let me know what you find out about the stake," Phyllis said.

"That's a matter for the police." Whitmire followed the Crime Scene officers out of the park.

Carolyn glared after him and said, "That man is one of the most infuriating people I've ever met."

"He's just trying to do his job the best way he knows how," Phyllis said.

"Then he ought to let you help him. You have a better track record at solving murders than he does!"

Phyllis shook her head. "I wouldn't go so far as to say that."

"Well, I would." Carolyn paused, then went on, "You were thinking maybe somebody stabbed Logan with that stake, weren't you?"

"The possibility occurred to me. If it pierced the heart, the wound might not have bled much."

"I didn't see any blood on the stake, though, did you?"

"No, it looked clean to me," Phyllis said.

"So we're back to not knowing how Logan was killed, or even if it was murder."

"I'm afraid so."

They left the park themselves then, each woman taking her own car back to the house.

Sam, Eve, and Bobby were waiting around the kitchen table when Phyllis and Carolyn came in. The containers of pumpkin muffins sat in the center of the table, and Bobby was eyeing them hungrily.

"We waited for you," Sam said, "but it was a little hard for some of us."

"Those are *good* punkin muffins," Bobby said.

"All right, you may have one," Phyllis told him with a smile. "But only one. I don't want you to ruin your appetite for supper."

"Does the same go for me?" Sam asked.

Phyllis laughed. "I don't see why not."

Each of them had a muffin; then Bobby went off to the living room to watch TV. Phyllis could tell from the sleepy look on the little boy's face that the long, busy day was catching up to him. She suspected that Bobby would be asleep on the sofa in just a few minutes.

"All right," Eve said as the four adults remained seated at the kitchen table. "What was that all about back there, Phyllis? What did you think of that made you and Carolyn stay at the park?"

"I'll bet it was somethin' to do with the murder," Sam said. "You just solved the case, didn't you, Phyllis?"

Phyllis shook her head. "Far from it. I have no idea what happened to Logan, or whether it was murder or not. But I did start thinking about something."

She explained about the hay bale and the stake that someone had put in the clump of yuccas.

"You could see part of it from the path," she concluded, "but I doubt if anyone would have really noticed it, or thought anything about it if they did."

"And now the police have it," Eve said.

"That's right. I'm sure if there's any real evidence there, they'll find it."

Carolyn said, "Well, you have more confidence in them than I do, then."

Phyllis didn't see where any good would come of continuing to discuss Carolyn's lack of confidence in the police, so she said, "From what I could tell, the festival is a big success, despite what happened. The volunteers must have taken in thousands of cans of food already, and it'll be going on until later tonight."

"I'm sure I'll find out the total number early next week," Carolyn said. "All the volunteers will be getting together to figure out the details of how we'll handle the deliveries on Thanksgiving morning. You're welcome to come to the meeting, Phyllis, since you said you wanted to help."

Phyllis nodded. "Just let me know when and where, and I'll be there."

"I could give you a hand with that, too," Sam said.

"And I'll stay here and keep an eye on Bobby," Eve added.

"That sounds fine to me," Phyllis said. "I'm glad we'll be able to help out some people—"

The phone interrupted her by ringing. She stood up and snagged the receiver from its base that sat on the counter, then frowned as she glanced at the caller ID readout.

It said W'FORD POLICE DEPT.

She couldn't think of any good reason the police would be calling her ... but she could come up with quite a few bad ones.

She thumbed the TALK button and said, "Hello?"

"Mrs. Newsom?"

Phyllis recognized Chief Ralph Whitmire's voice, and her apprehension grew stronger. "That's right," she told him.

"This is Chief Whitmire," he said unnecessarily. "Would you mind coming down to police headquarters for a few minutes? I'd like to talk to you."

"About Logan Powell?" she asked, and that caused eyebrows to go up all around the table.

"Yeah, we've got some preliminary results back from the medical examiner."

"He's already done the autopsy?" Phyllis asked, surprised that things were moving that quickly. Even in a relatively small city like Weatherford, the wheels of officialdom usually ground slowly.

"No, that's going on now," Whitmire said. "He was able to identify that unusual substance found in Powell's mouth, though."

Brown slime, the paramedic had called it, and the description fit as well as any, Phyllis thought. She didn't want to think about what Whitmire might tell her next, but she couldn't help herself. There was only one reason he would be calling *her* about this.

"What was it?" she forced herself to say.

"Well, this isn't a positive identification, you understand—that'll have to wait for further tests—but according to the ME, the substance appears to be what's left of some sort of ... baked good. A muffin, maybe. And the best guess is—"

"A pumpkin muffin," Phyllis said.

Chapter 17

$\mathscr{S}$am insisted on coming along with her to police headquarters. Carolyn wanted to come, too, but Phyllis talked her out of it. She didn't think her friend's hostile attitude toward the police would help matters right now.

Sam offered to drive and Phyllis accepted, glad that she wouldn't have to worry about the traffic. Her brain was spinning so much because of what Chief Whitmire had just told her that she wasn't sure it would be safe for her to get behind the wheel.

"I'm sure they don't think for a second it was one of your muffins that killed him, Phyllis," Sam told her as he headed his pickup toward police headquarters. "Shoot, I don't see how Powell would've even got hold of one of them. They've got to be wrong about what they found in Powell's mouth."

"I don't know," Phyllis said slowly. "When Dana stopped by the house looking for her keys yesterday evening, she ate one of the muffins and took another one with her."

Sam frowned. "Oh, yeah. I'd forgot about that." He glanced over at her. "So you're not worried about the cops blamin' you for what happened. You think this'll help 'em pin it on Mrs. Powell."

"I don't know. She's already admitted that she was at the park with her husband yesterday evening and that they argued. There were witnesses to that, including Carolyn."

"Maybe she poisoned the muffin and left it for him to eat, then came back later, after he was dead, and put him in that scarecrow outfit."

"I don't believe Dana would have killed him," Phyllis said, "but even if she did, why dress him like a scarecrow?"

Sam shook his head. "I got no clue. It's a crazy thing to do, all right."

When they walked into police headquarters, the officer on duty at the desk recognized Phyllis. "Chief Whitmire is waiting to see you, Mrs. Newsom," she said. "Do you know where his office is?"

"Yes, thank you," Phyllis said.

The officer picked up a phone. "You can go on back. I'll let him know you're here."

Whitmire was waiting in the open doorway of his office when Phyllis and Sam got there. He looked curiously at Sam, and Phyllis said, "You remember my friend Mr. Fletcher?"

"Yes, of course," Whitmire replied. "I thought you were a teacher, Mr. Fletcher, not a lawyer."

"Retired teacher," Sam said. "Not even close to a lawyer."

"Well, since you're not Mrs. Newsom's legal counsel, I'll have to ask you to wait for her back in the lobby."

"I don't know . . . ," Sam began with a frown.

Phyllis put a hand on his arm. "It's all right, Sam." She didn't want him getting on the chief's bad side. "If Carolyn were here, she might suggest they were going to bring out the bright lights and rubber hoses, but we know better, don't we?"

"I reckon so. But if you need me, you know where I'll be."

He stood there with his hands tucked into the hip pockets of his jeans while Whitmire ushered Phyllis into the comfortable, well-appointed office. Whitmire closed the door behind them.

"Please, have a seat," he said, holding out a hand to-

ward a red leather chair in front of his desk, which was a
little cluttered with papers but not too messy. "I'm sorry
to have to call you down here," he went on as both of
them settled down in their chairs. "I want this investigation to stay up to speed, though. Logan Powell was a
well-respected member of the business community here
in town. The sooner we know what killed him and why—
and who, if it comes to that—the better."

"I can't argue with that," Phyllis said. "We all just
want the truth to come out."

Whitmire clasped his hands together in front of him.
"You baked pumpkin muffins for the contest at the festival?"

"That's right," Phyllis said as she nodded. "But I brought
them with me to the park this morning. They were in
closed containers, and they were all accounted for."

"You can prove that?"

Phyllis realized suddenly that she and the others had
eaten some of those very muffins when they got back to
the house, so she no longer had the physical evidence that
she was telling the truth. But she said, "You saw them for
yourself, Chief, and so did a lot of other people. They
were still sitting right there on the table when Logan's
body was found. No one had gotten into them, or into
any of the contest entries."

Whitmire nodded. "Yeah, you're right about that. We
have pictures of the table, too, although they're not de-
tailed enough to tell us whether any of the muffins were
missing from those containers. But I think we can stipu-
late that there weren't."

"I think so, too," Phyllis said.

"Which leads to my next question: Have you ever
made muffins like that before, Mrs. Newsom?"

Phyllis wasn't surprised at the turn the conversation
was taking. "As a matter of fact, I have," she said. "I
wouldn't enter any recipe in a contest without trying it
out first, usually several times."

"I didn't think so. What happened to those other
muffins?"

"We ate them. Except . . . I believe there are still a

couple left from the last batch I made before the ones for the contest."

"And where are they?"

"At my house."

"No one's eaten any of them except you and the other folks who live there? Mrs. Wilbarger, Mrs. Turner, and Mr. Fletcher, if I remember right."

Phyllis nodded. "That's right. And my grandson, Bobby. He's staying with me right now."

"Mike's little boy." Whitmire's grim expression was relieved momentarily by a smile. "Cute kid. Where's Mike?"

"He and Sarah are visiting Sarah's family in California. Her father is in bad health."

"Sorry to hear that. How come Bobby didn't go with them?"

"He came down with an ear infection earlier this week and the doctor said he shouldn't fly."

"Well, that's a shame. Sorry to hear about that, too. How's he doing?"

"I believe he's just about over it." Phyllis didn't doubt that the chief's expressions of sympathy were sincere. She knew Ralph Whitmire was a decent man. He could be pretty dogged in his devotion to duty, but that was a good thing, after all.

"I'm glad to hear it. It looked like he was enjoying the festival today." Whitmire moved some papers around on his desk. Phyllis didn't think there was any reason for what he did, other than to signify that the interview was getting back to an official basis. "Now, you're sure nobody got any of the muffins from that earlier batch except the people in your house?"

Phyllis realized that she was at a crossroads. She could either lie and risk it coming out later on that Dana had taken one of the muffins with her, which would make things look even worse for both of them, or she could tell the truth, which is what all her instincts urged her to do anyway when she was talking to the police.

She made up her mind and said, "Actually, Dana

Powell had one yesterday evening when she stopped by the house."

Whitmire's bushy eyebrows rose. "Mrs. Powell was at your house yesterday evening?"

"That's right."

"Why?" Whitmire added quickly, "You realize you don't have to answer that, Mrs. Newsom. You haven't been charged with anything. You're within your rights not to talk to me at all."

"I know that. Mrs. Powell came by my house after school to see if I still had her keys."

"Her keys?"

"Earlier in the day, Mrs. Wilbarger and I stopped by the school to pick up the scarecrows that Mrs. Powell had in the back of her SUV. She gave us her keys so we could get the scarecrows; then I took them back to the school office. That's what Mrs. Powell asked me to do."

"Then why did she think you might still have them?"

"Because I left them with the school secretary, Katherine Felton, and then later Katherine couldn't find them and wasn't sure whether I'd given them to her or not."

"So Mrs. Powell's keys were missing." Whitmire picked up a pencil and made a note on a piece of paper. "Do you know if she ever found them?"

"No, I'm afraid I don't. The question didn't come up the next time I saw her, which was this morning."

Whitmire nodded. "So she ate one of the muffins at your house. I don't suppose she took any of them with her when she left?"

"As a matter of fact, I wrapped one up in a paper towel and gave it to her. I knew she was on her way to the park to help set everything up for the festival, and she hadn't had any supper yet."

Whitmire frowned across the desk. "She took one of your muffins with her, and then this morning what's left of a pumpkin muffin shows up in the mouth of her dead husband."

Phyllis said, "When you put it like that, Chief, you make it sound ... well ..."

"Suspicious?"

"Think about it," Phyllis said. "Logan was still alive when Dana left the park. You have eyewitness testimony to confirm that. Even if she gave him the muffin that I gave her, and he ate it, there wouldn't have been traces of it in his mouth this morning."

Whitmire leaned back in his chair. "You do have a knack for putting together evidence and testimony to build up a chain of events, don't you, Mrs. Newsom? I can see how you've been able to help out with those other cases." Before Phyllis could say anything, he went on, "But what if . . . what if Dana Powell came back to the park last night, while her husband was still there but everyone else was gone? They had argued earlier. Maybe she gave him the muffin and told him it was a peace offering. He started to eat it, but she'd poisoned it and he died before he could finish."

"She wouldn't do that," Phyllis insisted.

"But it could have happened that way." Whitmire was just as adamant.

"So you're suggesting that Dana Powell, who can't weigh much more than a hundred pounds soaking wet, undressed her dead husband, put that scarecrow's clothes on him, dragged a heavy bale of hay down to the cabin and into the dogtrot, and lifted his body onto it?" Phyllis shook her head in disbelief. "Even if she could do that, why would she?"

"Desperation gives people more strength than you might think they have," the chief said. "And killers sometimes do things that make sense to them but not to anybody else. Anyway . . . maybe she had help."

"Help?" Phyllis repeated with a confused frown. "What do you mean?"

Whitmire shrugged. "Logan Powell was supposedly cheating on his wife. Maybe she was fooling around on him, too. Maybe that's why she killed him, so she could be with a boyfriend."

"No," Phyllis said. "I don't believe it."

"You know her well enough to completely rule out the possibility that she could have been having an affair?"

"Well . . . no. I don't suppose I do. But I don't believe it."

Whitmire grunted. "I don't deal in opinion. I'm just concerned about facts."

"It sounds to me like you're dealing more in speculation. No one has said anything to you about Dana having an affair, have they?"

Whitmire frowned but didn't answer, which was an answer in itself, Phyllis thought. He toyed with the pencil on his desk and said, "I'll need a copy of your recipe for those muffins, so we can check the ingredients against the substance found in Powell's mouth. I'm pretty sure that's what it was, though."

"The recipe's not going to confirm anything," Phyllis pointed out. "There's nothing unusual in the muffins. Just common ingredients, including canned pumpkins and chopped pecans."

"Well, we'll check it anyway. You can drop the recipe off anytime, or just e-mail it to Detective Largo, if you want." Whitmire took one of his business cards from a holder on the desk, turned it over, and wrote on the back before sliding it across to Phyllis. "There's her e-mail address."

Phyllis picked up the card and put it away in her purse. "Where is Detective Largo? I halfway expected her to be here."

"She's still at the hospital, questioning Mrs. Powell."

"After all this time? Isn't that overdoing it?"

"We're just trying to get to the bottom of this," Whitmire said. "But no bright lights or rubber hoses; you have my word on that."

"Do you know what Dana's condition is?"

"From what I've heard, she's all right. She just fainted from the stress. I think they're gonna keep her overnight for observation, though."

"Fainting from stress," Phyllis said. "Doesn't that sound like something an innocent woman would do after seeing her husband's dead body?"

"I imagine trying to get away with murder is pretty stressful, too," Whitmire said.

Chapter 18

Sam was waiting for Phyllis when she got back to the lobby. As she came in, he stood up quickly from the metal chair where he'd been sitting.

"You all right?" he asked.

"Of course I am. You weren't really worried that I'd be interrogated, were you?"

"Not really, but I'm glad to see you anyway. What'd the chief want?"

Phyllis glanced at the officer on duty at the desk, then said, "We'll talk about it in the pickup."

Once they were back in the vehicle, she asked Sam whether he would mind driving back down by the park to see how the festival was going. He agreed readily and turned the pickup in that direction.

"I reckon we can even go back in if you want," he said as he held up his hand to indicate the duck figure stamped onto the back of it. "This is supposed to be so folks can go in and out after they drop off their canned goods. You'd think that with it bein' nearly Thanksgiving, though, they would've made it look like a turkey instead of a duck."

"I suppose they didn't think of it. Anyway, the lake is known for the ducks that live there. And it's not necessary for us to go back into the festival. I'm just curious to see how the attendance is holding up. I imagine that by now the news about Logan's death has gotten around town."

A few minutes later they reached the road that led to the park's north entrance. Phyllis was surprised to see that cars were parked along both sides of the road, even farther away from the park than they had been earlier.

"Doesn't look like what happened has hurt attendance," Sam said. "Fact is, I'd say it's more crowded now than it was this mornin'."

Phyllis nodded as they drove past. "Morbid curiosity, I suppose. People have heard about Logan and want to see where his body was found."

"They'll have to come up with a bag of canned goods to do it," Sam pointed out. "So that's something positive to come outta the whole mess, anyway."

"I suppose so," Phyllis said with a sigh.

"We headin' home now?"

"Yes, I don't think there's anything else I need to see here."

When Sam got back to the house, a blue SUV was parked at the curb where he usually left his pickup. He pulled into the driveway instead and said, "Looks like you got company. You know who that SUV belongs to?"

Phyllis shook her head. "No, I don't."

She didn't wait for Sam to come around and open her door for her. She opened it herself and got out of the pickup. The visitor didn't necessarily have to have something to do with Logan's death, but considering the way these things usually went, Phyllis would be surprised if that didn't turn out to be the case.

Sure enough, when she and Sam went inside, they found Carolyn and Eve sitting in the living room with Barbara Loomis, Jenna Grantham, Taryn Marshall, and Kendra Neville. The women had cups of coffee.

"Hello," Phyllis said.

Barbara Loomis put her cup back on its saucer on the coffee table in front of her and said, "I'm sorry we barged in on you like this, Phyllis. We just wanted to find out if you knew how Dana's doing. She's not home, and they wouldn't tell us at the hospital if she's still there."

Phyllis looked at the concerned expressions on the faces of the women. Of course they were worried about their friend. They had a right to be, considering everything that had happened.

"Carolyn told us you'd gone to the police station," Jenna added. "Did they tell you anything about Dana?"

"She's still at the hospital," Phyllis said. "According to Chief Whitmire, the doctor wants to keep her there overnight for observation. However, he didn't seem to think there was any real reason to worry. She just fainted from the stress."

Kendra said, "Yes, but he's a policeman, not a doctor."

"And he's the one who had poor Dana arrested," Taryn put in. "I don't trust him."

"It was the doctor's opinion that Dana's not in any danger from the fainting, not the chief's," Phyllis explained. "And she hasn't actually been arrested."

"They've questioned her, though," Jenna said. "How stupid is that? Dana wouldn't hurt Logan."

"Of course she wouldn't," Barbara agreed.

"Right now, the police don't even know how Logan died," Phyllis said. Chief Whitmire hadn't told her not to discuss the case, so she didn't see anything wrong with sharing what she knew with Dana's friends. Of course, what she knew didn't actually add up to very much, she reminded herself. Not even the proverbial hill of beans, in fact. She went on, "The autopsy was still going on when I talked to the chief."

"Did he call you down there to fill you in on what was going on?" Kendra asked. "You work for the police as a consultant of some sort, don't you, Phyllis?"

Carolyn scoffed. "She would if Chief Whitmire had any sense! The police wouldn't ever solve any murders around here if it wasn't for Phyllis's help."

"Do you really think Logan's death was murder?" Barbara asked. She caught her lower lip between her teeth, as if the question bothered her.

As well it might, Phyllis suddenly realized. Barbara's husband, Ben, was a business rival of Logan Powell's, she recalled. She had heard Logan threatening to kill

Ben Loomis the day before in the park, when Phyllis had accidentally eavesdropped on Logan's phone conversation. Maybe Ben had decided to strike first.

Of course, right after that, Logan had mentioned the golf game he and Ben were scheduled to play. The so-called threat had been nothing but a joke. Logan had said so himself.

But maybe it wasn't. Maybe the banter masked a real feud going on between the two men over that NorCen-Tex Development deal. That was something she could look into, Phyllis thought.

If she were investigating the case, and *if* there really was a case to investigate.

She knew she was grasping at straws. Logan's alleged affair was a much better motive for murder than some nebulous real estate deal.

Those thoughts flashed through Phyllis's mind. Barbara was looking at her, waiting for an answer to the question she had asked. Phyllis said, "I don't know. No one does, at this point. We'll have to wait until they find out the cause of death."

"Well, they ought to let us in to see Dana at the hospital," Jenna declared angrily. "We're her friends, and they don't have any right to keep us from visiting her."

"Maybe they'll let her go home tomorrow. I wouldn't be surprised if they gave her something to make her sleep after Detective Largo finished questioning her."

Taryn spoke up, asking, "Do we need to see about getting her a lawyer?"

Barbara nodded. "I was thinking the same thing. Her rights need to be protected." She looked around at the others. "I don't know any defense attorneys, though."

Phyllis did: Juliette Yorke. The woman was from back east somewhere, but she seemed like a highly competent lawyer. She had been involved in a couple of the cases that had ensnared Phyllis.

"I can recommend someone, if it comes to that," Phyllis told the four teachers. "Right now, though, I think we all need to just wait and see what happens over the next couple of days. It might not look good for Dana if she rushed right out and retained a defense attorney."

"No, I suppose not," Barbara said. "If there's anything we can do to help her, though, we're certainly willing." The other three women nodded.

"I'm sure she knows that," Phyllis said. "Once she's released from the hospital, one of you might even want to go and stay with her for a while."

"I could do that," Jenna said without hesitation.

"So could I," Taryn said, and Kendra nodded, too. Barbara was the only one of the four who was married, Phyllis recalled. The three single women would have an easier time of it if they wanted to drop everything and help out a friend.

"Do you know if she has any relatives around here?" Phyllis asked.

"Not any close ones," Barbara replied. "Some cousins, I think. But Dana's folks are dead, and she doesn't have any brothers or sisters."

"And she and Logan didn't have any children," Jenna added.

Phyllis remembered Dana mentioning that. She said, "It sounds like she's liable to need all of her friends, then."

"We'll be there for her," Carolyn said.

There wasn't much else to be said, at least not about Dana and Logan. The talk turned to the festival instead, and Phyllis told the visitors how she and Sam had driven by the park a short time earlier and found it more crowded than ever.

"Gawkers," Barbara said, tight-lipped with disapproval. "They just want to see the place where a man died."

Phyllis said, "I'm sure that's why some of them are there, but the afternoon usually has the biggest crowds at something like a harvest festival. Some people probably don't even know about Logan yet."

"I'll bet most of them do," Carolyn said.

Phyllis had to agree with that. "But as Sam pointed out to me," she said, "they still have to donate their canned goods to get in, no matter why they're there."

Barbara nodded. "There's that to consider, I suppose. A big crowd means there'll be plenty of food to deliver on Thanksgiving, I hope."

"And a bigger cleanup in the morning," Jenna added with a smile. "The trash collectors will be busy picking up everything that people leave behind."

Phyllis knew that to be true, as well. Anytime there was a large crowd anywhere, there was trash to be picked up.

"What about those other scarecrows we made?" Kendra asked. "Dana was going to get them in the morning and store them for next year's festival. Now, though . . ."

She didn't have to finish her sentence. They all knew what she meant. Dana wouldn't be able to pick up the scarecrows and probably wouldn't want to, even if she could. She probably wouldn't want to ever lay eyes on them again.

"I don't mind pickin' 'em up," Sam volunteered. "You think there's room in the toolshed for 'em, Phyllis?"

"I think we can make room if there's not," she said.

"And I'll be responsible for them," Carolyn offered. "If you're sure that's all right, Phyllis."

"I think it's a good idea," Phyllis said with a smile. "That way none of you ladies will have to bother with them, and they ought to be safe in the shed."

"That's very generous of you," Barbara said. "Thank you." She looked around at Carolyn and Sam. "All of you. I'm afraid Logan's death has really thrown things for a loop, and it's going to take some time to sort it all out. But if there's anything we can do to make it easier for Dana and help her get through it, I'd like to."

The others all nodded. Their concern for their friend was touching, Phyllis thought.

She just hoped that before all this was over, what Dana would really need to get through it wouldn't be the services of a good defense attorney like Juliette Yorke.

Chapter 19

The air the next morning was still cool and crisp, with enough of a north wind to carry away most of the pollution that drifted in from Dallas and Fort Worth and even from as far away as Houston. The deep blue color of the sky was broken here and there by small, puffy clouds as white as snow. It was beautiful fall weather in Texas.

Phyllis and Sam skipped church in the morning to go collect the scarecrows from the park. When they got there, a crew of inmates in orange and white coveralls from the county jail was already at work cleaning up the trash left over from the festival, under the watchful eyes of a couple of deputies. Mike had worked on cleanup details like that from time to time, Phyllis knew, but he didn't like it. He preferred being out on patrol where there were more opportunities to actually help people.

There were a handful of cars parked in the lot. Phyllis saw some children down around the playground equipment by the lake, and she spotted an elderly couple who appeared to be walking for exercise on the opposite shore.

She and Sam qualified as an elderly couple, she mused. There hadn't been any more talk about that whole boyfriend-girlfriend matter, but as far as she was concerned, it was settled and didn't need any more discussion. They would continue to take things slowly. That was just the opposite of someone like Eve, who had been known to comment more than once that she had only a certain amount of time left on this earth and she meant to make the most of it. Phyllis could see the logic in that approach, but it just didn't fit her personality. And she was too old to change now.

"We don't have to do anything with the hay bales, do we?" Sam asked as they got out of the pickup.

"No, I assume they're the responsibility of whoever provided them," Phyllis said. "I know there's not room for them and the scarecrows in our toolshed."

They came to the spot where the hay bale had been moved down to the dogtrot. Phyllis pointed it out to Sam, who paused and squinted as he looked back and forth from where he stood to the cabin.

"Seems like a long way for a little thing like Miz Powell to haul a bale of hay," he said after a moment.

"I pointed out that same thing to Chief Whitmire. He didn't seem to put much stock in it, though. He just said that desperate people are sometimes stronger than you think they would be."

"Well, I suppose he's right about that. If he wasn't, you wouldn't hear about mothers liftin' cars off their kids."

"True," Phyllis said. "I still can't see Dana doing it."

"Neither can I, to be honest. I guess this bale was as close to the cabin as any of 'em, come to think of it, if you wanted to dress a dead man up as a scarecrow and set him up down there."

"How do we know he was dead?" Phyllis asked.

"What do you mean?"

"Maybe Logan was still alive when he put on those old clothes. Maybe it was his idea."

"I can't see why he'd want to do that."

"Neither can I," she admitted. "But at this point we can't rule out any possibilities."

"You're right," Sam said. "Like ol' Sherlock Holmes, you just eliminate the *im*possible and see what you got left."

Phyllis didn't like being compared to Sherlock Holmes. For one thing, she thought she'd look ridiculous in a deerstalker hat, and for another, she had no interest in using cocaine.

She couldn't help but wonder, though, what Holmes would have made of a dead man dressed up like a scarecrow stuffed with one of her muffins. If in fact it was one of her muffins. She had e-mailed her pumpkin muffin recipe to Detective Largo the day before but hadn't heard anything back. Not that she really expected to hear back from Detective Largo.

It took them about half an hour to pile all eleven scarecrows into the back of Sam's pickup. When Phyllis looked at them, she couldn't help but be reminded of what she had said a couple of days earlier when they saw the scarecrows in the back of Dana's SUV at the elementary school. Like a pile of bodies, she had described them, and the remark had proven to be grimly prophetic, though only one of the scarecrows had turned out to be a body.

So far, Phyllis reminded herself. If this were a movie or a TV show or a best-selling thriller with a hundred chapters, none of them more than four pages long, Logan would turn out to be just the first victim of a madman known as the Scarecrow Killer who taunted the authorities through the media while frustrating the efforts of a beautiful, dauntless female FBI agent and a rumpled but ruggedly handsome journalist to catch him. . . .

This was none of those things, though, and Phyllis hoped and prayed that there wouldn't be any more bodies dressed like scarecrows.

A car door closed nearby, breaking into Phyllis's thoughts, and a familiar voice said, "Hi, Mrs. Newsom."

She looked over to see Jenna Grantham coming toward them. "Good morning," Phyllis said. "What are you doing here?"

"I just thought I'd stop by and see if you needed any help with those scarecrows," Jenna said. She nodded toward the stack of overall-clad figures in the back of Sam's pickup. "I see you've already got them, though."

"That's right. But thank you."

"I'm supposed to meet Barbara, Kendra, and Taryn at the hospital, too. We're going to try to see Dana again. Now that we know she's there, I don't think Barbara will take no for an answer." Jenna smiled. "She's really stubborn about getting what she wants."

"I wouldn't get your hopes up," Phyllis cautioned. "If Dana's still in the hospital, she's probably under a police guard."

"Really?" Jenna shook her head. "She's really a . . . a suspect? That just seems so crazy to me."

"To me, too," Phyllis said. "The police should have the results of the autopsy by now, though. Maybe it found something that will clear Dana's name."

"Gee, I hope so." Jenna opened her car door and lifted a hand. "Well, I'll see you. Two more days of school this week, then the Thanksgiving break. I'm ready for it, too."

"Oh? You have big plans?"

"No." A wistful tone came into Jenna's voice as she went on. "No, not really. I don't have any family around here—I'm from Wisconsin—and I can't afford to fly back up there just for a few days."

Sam said, "Well, you can spend Thanksgiving with your boyfriend, I guess."

Jenna shook her head. "No boyfriend. Not right now. There are places over in Fort Worth that are open for Thanksgiving dinner. I guess I'll try one of them, or just have something in my apartment."

"That's a shame," Phyllis said. "You'll be able to go back home for Christmas, won't you?"

Jenna brightened. "Sure. I can justify the airfare for a longer trip like that." She waved again. "So long."

As Jenna drove away, Sam looked over at Phyllis and said, "You're thinkin' about somethin', aren't you? Somethin' about the case?"

"Not at all," Phyllis said. "I was thinking about how that girl's going to be spending Thanksgiving all alone."

"I'd figure any time a girl that good-lookin' spends alone is by her own choice," Sam pointed out.

"You'd think so because you're a man. Being attractive doesn't guarantee that men are going to be flocking around all the time. From what I've heard, really attractive single women are alone more than you'd believe."

"So what are you gonna do? Invite her to the house for Thanksgivin' dinner?"

"Oh, I doubt that she'd want to come spend her holiday with a bunch of old folks like us," Phyllis said. "But I might call Dolly and see if she knows of any other teachers who are going to have the same problem."

A grin split Sam's face. "Have a real houseful, eh?"

"Would that bother you?"

"Shoot, no. Back when I was married and the whole family would visit durin' the holidays, sometimes there'd be forty or fifty people in the house for Thanksgiving or Christmas or New Year's Eve. Everybody's all scattered now, though, or too busy with their own lives to get together, so I sort of miss those days."

"Well, I'll think about it," Phyllis said. "It would mean making more food, but I'm sure Carolyn wouldn't mind pitching in to help."

"I reckon you can count on that," Sam said drily. They both knew how much Carolyn liked to get in the kitchen and roll up her sleeves to get to work, especially if everybody else was willing to let her think that she was the boss.

They got in the pickup and headed back to the house. Sam drove up the alley behind the property, which would give them easier access to the toolshed. Earlier, he had pushed the riding lawn mower a little to make room for the scarecrows against the rear wall. Phyllis took them out of the pickup and handed them into the shed to Sam, who stacked them in place.

"There," he said as he brushed his hands together when they were finished. "They'll be ready for next year's Harvest Festival. Wonder if anybody will dress up a twelfth one, or if they'll make do with eleven. Odd numbers like that drive some folks nuts."

"It doesn't really matter to me," Phyllis said. "I can make one, if anybody wants me to."

Sam took the pickup around front while Phyllis walked into the house through the back door. She found Carolyn waiting for her with a tense look on her face.

"What's wrong?" Phyllis asked, knowing that her old friend was upset about something.

"Detective Largo is here," Carolyn said in a low voice.

For a second Phyllis thought she must not have heard correctly. "Detective Largo?" she repeated.

"That's right. She just got here a few minutes ago. I told her that you'd be back anytime now, and she asked if she could wait and talk to you. Of course I said yes. She's the police, after all. I offered to call you on your cell phone, but she said to wait a little while first." Carolyn's voice took on a scornful tone. "She said she didn't want to interrupt what you were doing."

"Well . . . all right. I suppose I'll talk to her. Where is she?"

"In the living room."

Something else occurred to Phyllis. "Where's Bobby?"

"Upstairs." Carolyn frowned. "I think."

As Phyllis went along the hall toward the living room, though, she heard Bobby's voice. "My daddy is a deputy sheriff," he was saying.

"I know," Isabel Largo replied in her throaty voice. "I've worked with him before, coordinating things between the sheriff's office and the police department."

"You're a detective?"

"That's right." Largo sounded a little amused. Bobby's precocious intelligence had that effect on some adults. He was so bright that they enjoyed talking to him.

"My gran'mama catches bad guys, like my daddy."

"I know that, too."

"Do you have any kids?"

"A little boy who's not quite three years old. How old are you?"

"I'm four! What's your little boy's name?"

"Victor," Detective Largo said. "The two of you will probably be in school together someday."

"I'll be a grade ahead of him."

"Maybe you'll know each other anyway."

"Yeah, I hope so."

Phyllis had paused to listen to the conversation, but

she didn't want to wait too long. She was curious about what brought Detective Largo here. She stepped around the corner into the living room and said, "Good morning, Detective. Mrs. Wilbarger told me you were here."

"Gran'mama!" Bobby greeted her with his usual enthusiasm. "Did you get the scarecrows?"

"We did," she told him, smiling. "Maybe Sam will take you out to the shed later to look at them."

"Are they scary?" he asked with a sudden frown.

"Well, they're scarecrows. They're supposed to scare off birds."

"Yeah, but one of 'em turned out to be a dead guy."

"You don't have to worry about *that*," Phyllis said firmly. "The ones in the shed are just scarecrows. They can't hurt you."

"Okay."

"Why don't you run on out to the kitchen and see what Carolyn is doing?"

He was an agreeable child most of the time, thank goodness. He nodded and said again, "Okay."

When Bobby was gone, Detective Largo said, "What a smart little boy. And adorable."

"He's definitely both of those things," Phyllis said as she sat down on the sofa opposite the armchair where Largo sat. "What brings you here on a Sunday morning, Detective?"

"Chief Whitmire asked me to stop by and talk to you."

"More questions?"

Largo shook her head. "No, he wanted me to tell you the results of the autopsy on Logan Powell, as long as you promise to be discreet and not tell anyone else."

Phyllis leaned back, taken by surprise. "He did? Why in the world would he do that?"

With a faint smile, Detective Largo said, "You may not believe it, Mrs. Newsom, but the chief really does appreciate the things you've done to help the department in the past. And he has a great deal of respect for your son. I think he'd like to hire Mike away from Ross Haney."

Phyllis knew that was true. Mike had been the object of a tug-of-war between Whitmire and Sheriff Haney for a while now.

"I appreciate the chief feeling that way," Phyllis said. "And he's right—I'd be very interested to know what the medical examiner found out."

"Again, this is confidential," Largo said.

Phyllis nodded.

"Logan Powell died of a heart attack."

Phyllis drew in a deep breath. "A heart attack," she repeated. That left the question of why Logan had been dressed like a scarecrow and propped up in the dogtrot, but at least it settled one thing. "Then it wasn't murder after all."

"Oh, yes," Detective Largo said. "It was murder, all right."

Chapter 20

𝒫hyllis stared at Detective Largo for a moment, unable to comprehend what the woman had just told her. Finally, she said, "I don't understand. How could Logan's death be murder when you said he died of a heart attack?"

"Mr. Powell had a number of different medical conditions, Mrs. Newsom. Were you aware of that?"

Phyllis shook her head. "Not at all. Every time I saw him, he looked so . . . so healthy." She paused, then added, "Well, except for the last time, of course."

"Evidently he drank heavily when he was younger and damaged his liver. That caused him to be hypoglycemic. Do you know what that means?"

Phyllis thought that Largo's question was a little condescending, but she was too interested in what the detective was telling her to be offended. "Of course I do," she said. "It means he suffered from low blood sugar."

Largo nodded. "That's right. It was aggravated by the fact that he was slightly diabetic and was on medication for that. He had to maintain exactly the right dosage, taken at exactly the same time every day, and stay on a very strict diet, or else his blood sugar would either spike to dangerous levels or plunge so low that he risked going into a coma and dying."

"I didn't know any of that," Phyllis said. "Of course, I only met the man a few times."

"According to what Mrs. Powell told us, her husband tended to disregard his doctor's orders. He was always busy with his work, and he would sometimes forget to eat a meal when he should, which could cause problems for him."

Something clicked together in Phyllis's head. "That's why he was always eating those peppermints he carried. He used them to keep his blood sugar from dropping when he wasn't eating properly."

Detective Largo nodded and said, "That's right. He was self-medicating, in a way, and in the end it backfired on him. He came to rely on those peppermints to keep his blood sugar up."

"How did that backfire on him?" Phyllis asked.

"Because someone switched the peppermints he normally carried for sugar-free ones. They were in the same wrappers as the ones with sugar in them, and I guess they tasted similar enough that Powell didn't notice the difference until it was too late."

"You said he died of a heart attack," Phyllis reminded the detective.

Largo nodded again. "Brought on by the stress caused by his plummeting blood sugar. Powell must have been incoherent and only semiconscious there at the end, and if his heart hadn't given out on him, he would have slipped into a coma and died from that if he didn't receive immediate medical attention. Either way, it would have been murder."

"Because someone switched the peppermints."

"That's right. The fact that whoever it was changed the wrappers and made the sugar-free candies look just like the ones with sugar in them means it was deliberate."

Phyllis sat back on the sofa, trying to process everything that Detective Largo had just told her. She had suspected all along that Logan's death might be murder, but she never would have dreamed that anyone could come up with such an arcane method. In order to do so, whoever had killed him would have had to know him very well indeed. . . .

"You said that Dana Powell told you about her husband's medical problems?" Phyllis asked suddenly.

Largo smiled faintly. "That's right. She didn't know at the time that we had already determined what killed her husband. I'm sure she thought she had gotten away with it."

"I knew it!" Phyllis said. "You think she killed him."

"Of course she did. She had argued with him about his affairs. That gave her a strong motive, and she had plenty of opportunity. She could have been switching his peppermints without him knowing for days or even weeks or months, a few at a time to bring his blood sugar down slowly, and then all of them to make it drop suddenly and dangerously."

"Then why would she even tell you about it?" Phyllis wanted to know. "She could have kept her mouth shut about his medical problems."

"She knew they would show up in the autopsy and in his medical history. I'm sure she thought it would look better for her if she told us, rather than letting us find out on our own. She was confident enough—or arrogant enough—that she thought we'd never discover the business about the peppermints being switched. Powell didn't have any of them on his body, after all, either sugar-free or the regular kind."

"That's right; his regular clothes and everything else he had on him were gone, weren't they?" Phyllis asked, still struggling with the idea that Dana Powell had killed her husband. "Have they been found yet?"

"No, I'm sure the killer took them away and disposed of them somehow, and it's our theory that the peppermints were the reason why. By dressing him in that scarecrow costume and leaving him there at the festival, she thought the circumstances of him being found like that would be so bizarre, we wouldn't even think about what he might have had in his pockets."

Phyllis supposed that a killer could have thought that way. It was a bit of a stretch, but someone's reasoning powers would have to be a little flawed to start with if they were going to seriously consider murder.

"So how *did* you find out about them?" she asked.

"When we searched Powell's car, which was still

parked in the lot, we found some of them. A chemical analysis told us that they contained an artificial sweetener, not sugar. The autopsy had already confirmed that Powell died of a heart attack, as well as the dangerously low amount of sugar in his blood. I discussed everything with the medical examiner early this morning, and he agreed that the heart attack could have been brought on by a severe attack of hypoglycemia. That makes it murder."

"You got the results of the chemical analysis that fast?" Phyllis asked with a surprised frown.

Detective Largo smiled. "I called in some favors over in Tarrant County and got their forensics lab to run the tests right away. Chief Whitmire regards this case as high priority."

Phyllis wasn't surprised by that, considering both the victim and the circumstances. Logan's status in the community and the bizarre nature of the case made it prime fodder for the media. It had been featured on the newcasts of the Fort Worth and Dallas television stations the night before, and there was a big story on the front page of the Fort Worth newspaper that morning.

"Were they able to get any fingerprints off that stake?"

Detective Largo shook her head. "Not off that rough wood."

"What about the other forensics tests?"

"We recovered a number of hairs, but that doesn't really mean anything. Several different women worked on those scarecrows and handled the costumes. It's possible some of the hairs we found belong to you, Mrs. Newsom."

A shiver went through Phyllis at that thought.

The detective went on. "None of the evidence clears Mrs. Powell, and since she's the only one who had both the knowledge and the opportunity to kill her husband in this particular manner . . ." Her shrug was eloquent.

"Have you arrested Dana yet?"

"Mrs. Powell was taken into custody a short time ago. Just before I came over here, in fact. The chief wanted me to let you know about that, too."

Phyllis looked intently at Detective Largo and said, "You're wrong, you know. Dana didn't kill him."

"Means, motive, and opportunity, Mrs. Newsom. I know it's a cliché, but Mrs. Powell had all three of them."

"You've tied her to the sugar-free peppermints?"

Largo shrugged. "Not yet. I'll admit, we may not be able to. But you can buy them in any grocery store. It's not like she didn't have access to them."

"So did everyone else in town."

"Everyone else in town didn't have a reason to kill Logan Powell, nor the opportunity to switch the peppermints without him knowing about it."

Unfortunately, that was true, Phyllis thought. She still didn't believe that Dana was guilty.

"What about the affairs? All you know for sure is that Dana suspected Logan was cheating on her. You don't have any proof that he really was."

"We don't need it," Largo said. "Mrs. Powell's suspicions alone are enough to constitute motive. It doesn't matter whether Powell was actually having an affair as long as she *believed* that he was." The detective paused. "But you can be sure that we'll be investigating Mr. Powell's background thoroughly. If he was involved with anyone else, chances are that we'll find out about it."

Phyllis sat there, unsure what to say next. The way Detective Largo summed up the case, it certainly sounded damning to Dana.

Phyllis didn't have to say anything, because at that moment, Carolyn stepped into the living room and snapped at Detective Largo, "You're insane. Dana Powell never killed anyone."

Anger flashed in the detective's eyes. "You've been eavesdropping, Mrs. Wilbarger?"

"I have a right to be in this house," Carolyn declared. "More of a right than you do. I overheard what you were saying about Dana. It's not true. Not any of it."

"That'll be up to the legal system to determine, starting with the district attorney. He'll have to decide whether to prosecute Mrs. Powell."

"Don't you mean persecute?"

Detective Largo stood up. "We're done here," she said. "Mrs. Wilbarger, I'll tell you what I told Mrs. Newsom. You're not to discuss this case with anyone. The only reason I came here today was because Chief Whitmire asked me to. I think it was a mistake to let a civilian in on police department business, no matter how much help she may have been in the past."

"I won't say anything," Phyllis told the detective, "and neither will Carolyn."

"Speak for yourself," Carolyn said.

"I'm warning you, you'll be facing obstruction of justice charges if you disregard what I just told you," Largo said. "Do you understand that, Mrs. Wilbarger?"

"I understand that you're going to try to railroad poor Dana Powell. That's what I understand."

Largo sighed and shook her head. She turned toward the door and said over her shoulder, "Good-bye, Mrs. Newsom. Be smart. Stay out of this from now on."

When the door had closed behind the detective, Carolyn said, "That . . . that . . ." She obviously couldn't find the words to describe Detective Largo, not any that she was willing to use, anyway. She turned to Phyllis and went on, "You don't think she's right about Dana, do you?"

"No, I don't," Phyllis said. "But from the sound of it, they have a pretty strong case against her. How much of it did you hear?"

"Enough to know that she thinks Dana killed Logan."

"It's worse than that," Phyllis told her friend. "They've already arrested her."

"My God," Carolyn murmured. "We have to go down there and make sure she has a lawyer."

"That's exactly what I was thinking. Where's Bobby?"

"He went out into the garage with Sam. I think he was going to watch Sam work on those bookshelves he's making."

Phyllis started toward the kitchen. "I'll make sure it's all right with Sam if he keeps an eye on Bobby for a while. Then we'll go see what we can do to help Dana."

Chapter 21

Phyllis had Juliette Yorke's cell phone number, so she called the attorney from the car as she and Carolyn headed toward police headquarters. She didn't know whether Dana was being held there or had already been transferred to the county jail, although it seemed unlikely that she would have been moved this soon.

Juliette Yorke didn't answer, so Phyllis left a message on her voice mail, asking that the lawyer call her right away. Juliette returned the call just as Phyllis was pulling into the parking lot in front of the police building.

As Phyllis parked, she quickly explained the situation. Juliette listened, then said, "I know you're worried about your friend, Mrs. Newsom, but I can't just come down there and offer to represent Mrs. Powell. It wouldn't be ethical. She's going to have to call me, or at least ask you to retain me on her behalf. But there's really nothing I can do to help her today."

"Why not?" Phyllis asked. "Because it's Sunday?"

"That's right. There won't be any bail hearings until tomorrow morning."

"Will they even let Dana out on bail, since she's being charged with murder?"

"That's hard to say, but it's possible. Of course, just because she's been arrested doesn't necessarily mean that she'll be formally charged. The district attorney

could decide not to go forward with the case. That would
be the best outcome, because then Mrs. Powell would be
freed without her having to raise bail, and there
wouldn't be any charges hanging over her head. Of
course, that wouldn't stop the police from arresting her
again later on and charging her then, if they thought
they had new evidence to make their case stronger."

Phyllis sighed. Carolyn was watching her intently
from the passenger seat, clearly frustrated by being able
to hear only Phyllis's side of the conversation.

"Right now, try to talk to Mrs. Powell," Juliette went
on, "although they may not let you see her. If they do,
find out if she wants me to represent her. If she does, let
me know and I'll do what I can to make sure she gets a
bail hearing tomorrow. They may want to postpone that
until the arraignment, though, if they've decided to
move quickly on that."

It was all a labyrinth of rules and procedures to Phyllis, and she hoped that Dana would be able to hire Juliette Yorke or someone equally competent to help
guide her through it. She said, "I'll be in touch," and
closed the cell phone.

"Is she going to be able to help us?" Carolyn asked.

"I don't know yet. The first thing we have to do is see
if they'll let us talk to Dana."

"They have to, don't they? They can't just hold her
prisoner and not allow anyone to see her or talk to her."

"Actually, they can hold her for a while without
charging her," Phyllis said. "I don't really know how
much time they're allowed to do that."

"What about her one phone call?" Carolyn demanded indignantly.

"Maybe she's already called a lawyer. We don't know.
But we'll try to find out."

The two women went into the building, and as they
did so, Phyllis thought that even though the weather
was every bit as beautiful as it had been earlier, the day
seemed to have a pall hanging over it now.

When they told the tall, burly officer at the desk what

they wanted, he said, "You'll have to talk to Detective Largo. That's her case."

"We just spoke with Detective Largo a short time ago," Phyllis explained.

"And what did she tell you?"

To stay out of the case, Phyllis thought, but she didn't say that to the officer because she knew he would take it to mean that they couldn't talk to Dana Powell.

"She said that Chief Whitmire specifically told her to bring us up to date on what's happening in the Powell case," Phyllis said instead. That was true enough, and it made her and Carolyn sound like insiders who might be allowed a few special privileges.

"Well, I'm sorry," the officer said with a shake of his head, "but I can't help you without specific authorization. You'll have to talk to Detective Largo." He reached for the phone. "I can see if she's in her office and has time to see you."

Phyllis shook her head, knowing that it wouldn't do any good to talk to Largo again. She had started to turn away, hoping that she wouldn't have to drag Carolyn out of there, when the officer went on, "Say, Mike Newsom's your son, isn't he?"

Phyllis nodded. "That's right. Do you know him?"

"We were in some of the same criminal justice classes. He's a really good guy. How's he doing over there in the sheriff's department?"

"He's doing fine," Phyllis said.

"Next time you see him, tell him that Warren Schofield says hello."

Phyllis smiled and said, "I'll do that, Officer Schofield."

"You know . . ." Schofield leaned back in his chair. "Detective Largo didn't actually order me not to let anybody see the prisoner. And it's not like you ladies are reporters or anything like that. You're more like friends of the family, right?"

"That's exactly what we are," Carolyn said. "Old friends."

"Hang on a minute. Let me call back there and see what I can do."

Still smiling, Phyllis said, "We'd really appreciate that."

A few minutes later, after Officer Warren Schofield had navigated through a small sea of red tape for them, Phyllis found herself in a tiny room, sitting in an uncomfortable wooden chair on one side of a table divided by a screen and glass barrier. An officer brought Dana Powell in through a door on the other side of the room and motioned for her to sit in the chair on the other side of the table. There was no telephone like on the TV shows. Phyllis and Dana could talk through the square of wire mesh in the center of the glass wall.

Dana wore the same clothes she'd been wearing at the park the day before. That was probably all she had with her when she was arrested at the hospital. She wouldn't be issued coveralls until she was transferred to the county jail.

Her hair was tangled and her face was haggard. She looked twenty years older than she had a couple of days earlier when Phyllis and Carolyn had gone to the school to pick up those scarecrows. Mostly, though, she just looked scared and confused.

She leaned toward the mesh and said, "Phyllis, what are you doing here?" Her voice sounded dull and stunned.

"Carolyn and I came to see if we can help you," Phyllis said. "She's here, too, just outside. They'd only let one of us come in, and she said I should do it."

You're the one who's going to figure out who really killed Logan and clear Dana's name, Carolyn had said when they'd reached the door of this room, accompanied by Officer Schofield. *You should talk to her.*

"You can't help me," Dana said. "Nobody can help me. My husband is dead, and . . . and they . . . they think I killed him."

Phyllis could tell that Dana's grip on her emotions was fragile at best. She might collapse into sobs at any moment. So Phyllis said quickly, "Listen to me, Dana. Have you called a lawyer?"

"What? A lawyer? No, I . . . I don't really know any lawyers. . . ."

"Well, I do. I know a good one named Juliette Yorke. Is it all right if I call her and ask her to defend you?"

"I suppose so. I'll need a lawyer, won't I? They think I killed Logan. They really do. It's the craziest thing. It's just . . . crazy. . . ."

With that, tears began to roll down Dana's cheeks, and she put her head on her arms where they lay on the table in front of her. Her shoulders shook from her sobs. Phyllis looked up, unsure what to do, but the door on the other side of the room was already opening. The officer who had brought Dana here came in. He must have been watching through the small window in the door and seen Dana break down, Phyllis thought.

"You'll have to go now, ma'am," he told her through the glass and wire as he took hold of Dana's arms and lifted her to her feet. As little as she weighed, it wasn't much trouble for him.

Phyllis nodded and said, "Thank you." She stood up and watched the officer lead Dana out of the room, then went out through the other door into the hall.

Carolyn and Warren Schofield were waiting there for her. "She asked me to call Juliette for her," she said.

"Good," Carolyn said. "That's all we needed to hear."

Schofield said, "I'd appreciate it if you ladies wouldn't mention my part in this to Detective Largo. I don't know if she'd object or not, but I'd just as soon not take that chance."

"Of course," Phyllis promised.

Schofield led them back through a maze of hallways to the front of the building. As they stepped into the lobby, he muttered, "Oh, shoot," and Phyllis immediately saw what had caused him to react that way.

Detective Isabel Largo stood in the lobby, arms crossed over her chest and a glare on her face.

"Officer Schofield, you *are* familiar with proper procedure around here, aren't you?" she snapped at him.

"Yes, ma'am, Detective," Schofield replied, obviously trying not to gulp.

"Did you think I wouldn't find out what you were doing? I'm sure you just wanted to help out a couple of nice little old ladies—"

"Don't blame Officer Schofield," Phyllis cut in, not bothering to rein in the anger she felt at being described as a nice little old lady. "You may have told him to direct any inquiries about Mrs. Powell to you, but you didn't tell him that she couldn't have visitors."

"He knows the policies."

"Anyway, Mrs. Powell has the right to call an attorney," Phyllis said.

"The last time I checked, neither of you ladies has a law degree."

"No, but we were arranging for her to have legal counsel. She was too upset, and too shocked at being accused of her husband's murder, to think of it. Why don't you let the chief and Juliette Yorke hash this out, and leave Officer Schofield out of it?"

Detective Largo frowned. "You're getting Yorke to represent Mrs. Powell?"

"That's right."

After a couple of seconds, Largo shrugged. "She has a right to legal counsel. She was advised of that right. I suppose there's no harm done here." She pointed a finger at Schofield. "But you're on my list now."

"Sorry, Detective," he muttered.

Phyllis patted him on the arm. "We're sorry, too, Officer. If you'd like me to speak to the chief on your behalf . . ."

"No, ma'am. It's fine."

"All right. I'll say hello to Mike for you."

Schofield grinned. "Thanks." He leaned closer to Phyllis and lowered his voice. "I may need him to put in a good word for me over at the sheriff's office."

Detective Largo got in their way as Phyllis and Carolyn headed for the door. "I'd like to know what Mrs. Powell said to you."

"I'm not sure I have to tell you that," Phyllis said.

"They probably have those visiting rooms bugged anyway," Carolyn put in.

"But really, I just asked her if she had already called a lawyer," Phyllis went on. "She said she hadn't and that she didn't know any. I told her I did and asked her if she wanted me to call Juliette Yorke for her. She agreed." Phyllis spread her hands. "That was all of it, Detective. Dana started to cry again. The very idea that she's in jail and being blamed for her husband's death is just too much for her to handle. That ought to tell you right there that she's innocent."

"Or putting on a good act," Largo said.

Phyllis shook her head. "That was no act." She had looked into Dana's eyes and seen nothing except grief and pain and shock. Dana had been too overwhelmed to even feel any anger at being arrested.

"All right, you ignored what I told you about staying out of this," Detective Largo said, "and you didn't waste any time about it, either. What are you going to do now?"

"Ms. Yorke is waiting for me to call her," Phyllis said. "After I've done that, I suppose I'm through. I don't know what else I can do to help Dana."

"Good. I hope you continue to feel that way."

With a curt nod, Detective Largo stalked out of the lobby and disappeared down one of the corridors.

"I'm sorry again, Officer," Phyllis called to Schofield as she and Carolyn went to the front door of the building.

"Don't worry about it," he said with a grin. "But don't forget to say something to Mike. By the time Detective Largo gets through with me, I really might be looking for a job!"

Chapter 22

Once they were back in the car, Phyllis called Juliette Yorke right away and told her what had happened.

"All right, I'll be down there later today to talk to Mrs. Powell and let her know that I'll be representing her," Juliette said when Phyllis was finished. "She'll have to sign some paperwork. Then I'll call the district attorney and find out what his plans are. If there was any way to get her out today, I would, but as I told you earlier, that's impossible. First thing in the morning, though, I'll be doing everything I can to secure bail for her, assuming that she's still going to be charged with murder."

"I think you can assume that," Phyllis said. "Detective Largo is sure that Dana's guilty."

"It's Isabel Largo's case, is it?" Phyllis thought she heard the same sort of guarded hostility in Juliette's voice that she had heard in Detective Largo's when she mentioned the lawyer. Maybe there was some sort of bad blood between the two women. "Well, luckily, from this point on, what happens isn't really Largo's call. Her part of the process is pretty much over. It'll be up to the district attorney whether to proceed or not."

"Thank you again for taking this case. I didn't expect you to drop everything to handle it."

"My schedule isn't that full right now," Juliette said. "Besides, what lawyer doesn't like a good murder case?"

Phyllis wasn't sure there was such a thing as a good murder case, but she didn't say that. Instead, she told Juliette, "If there's anything I can do to help, please let me know."

"All right. I'll try to keep you informed as to what's going on, but you realize that my first responsibility is to my client now."

"I wouldn't have it any other way," Phyllis said.

She hung up and related Juliette Yorke's plans to Carolyn, who nodded in satisfaction. "From what I've seen of Ms. Yorke, she's a good lawyer," Carolyn said. "I just hope she can help Dana."

Phyllis started the car. "I'm sure she can."

"What about you?"

"What about me?" Phyllis asked with a frown.

"You're going to investigate, too, aren't you?"

"I don't want to interfere with whatever Ms. Yorke has planned."

"If anyone can come up with the evidence to clear Dana's name, it's you, Phyllis, and you know it," Carolyn said. "That lawyer can handle all the legal technicalities, but you're the one who can uncover the truth. You know the police won't do it. They're satisfied that they already have Logan's killer, and they're not going to be looking for anything that might contradict that."

Carolyn had a point. As far as Detective Largo and the rest of the police force were concerned, the investigation had been concluded successfully. All that was left for them was the prosecution of the case against Dana Powell.

"I'll think about it," Phyllis said. "I might be able to come up with a few questions. If I do, I suppose it wouldn't hurt anything to ask around...."

"That's what I thought. I'd be glad to help you."

"I'll let you know." When she had found herself investigating murders in the past, Sam had usually been at her side. As he put it, she was the brains and he was the brawn. Mostly, though, his intelligence and common sense made him the perfect person to bounce things off of as she was trying to figure out what had really happened. Given Carolyn's argumentative nature, Phyllis wasn't sure she could fill that role as well, but she didn't want to say that to her old friend.

She drove back to the house, mulling over everything Detective Largo had said. Largo seemed to have an answer for everything, but there was one question they hadn't covered, Phyllis realized.

What was the significance of the pumpkin muffin in Logan's mouth, and how had it gotten there? If, indeed, Phyllis reminded herself, it really was a pumpkin muffin....

When they got back to the house, they found Sam and Bobby in the garage, standing by the workbench. Bobby was wearing the outsized goggles, and he grinned as he said, "Look at me, Gran'mama. I'm a Martian again!"

"You certainly are," Phyllis told him. "Thank you for looking after Bobby, Sam."

"My pleasure," Sam said. "Heck, I put him to work. He does a good job handin' boards to me."

Phyllis saw the curiosity in his eyes and knew he wanted to ask how it had gone with Dana, but he didn't want to bring up the case in front of the little boy. She said, "Bobby, why don't you go inside with Carolyn now? I'll be in in a few minutes."

Bobby pulled the goggles off. "Okay. I'll help you paint those boards later, Sam."

"Sounds like a deal," Sam told him.

When Carolyn and Bobby had gone in the house, Phyllis said, "We got Juliette Yorke to handle Dana's case. She's going to try to get her out on bail tomorrow."

"That lady lawyer seems pretty smart, from what I've seen of her," Sam said. "How's Miz Powell holdin' up?"

"Not well," Phyllis replied with a shake of her head. "I don't know how she's going to get through this."

"With help from all her friends—that's how she's gonna get through it. Same as anybody else."

Phyllis patted his shoulder. "That's a nice thought, but there's only so much that friends can do." She smiled and shook her head again. "Carolyn thinks that I should investigate the case and try to find out who really killed Logan."

"So do I," Sam declared. "Let's face it: You're good at pokin' around in things like that."

"The last time, my poking around almost got both of us killed."

"Yeah, but we're still here and a killer's behind bars."

Phyllis couldn't dispute that point. "I told Carolyn I'd think about it," she admitted. "I'd really like to know whether or not that was part of a pumpkin muffin in Logan's mouth, and if it was, how it got there."

"There you go," Sam said. "Start with that."

"Someone needs to look deeper into Logan's background, too," Phyllis went on, becoming enthused with the idea despite herself. "The reason he was murdered has to be there. This wasn't a random killing. It was too well planned for that. Someone must have really hated him to go to so much trouble."

Sam nodded. "Sounds to me like you're on the right track. If I can give you a hand, just let me know."

"I will," Phyllis promised. She went in the house and got out the phone book. She had some calls to make.

Not all the numbers Phyllis was looking for were in the book. These days, some people didn't even have regular telephones, only cell phones, especially younger folks. But Carolyn had the numbers Phyllis couldn't find, since she had worked with everyone involved in getting ready for the Harvest Festival.

Phyllis made the calls to Kendra Neville, Taryn Marshall, and Jenna Grantham first. She had to leave messages for Taryn and Jenna, but Kendra answered her phone and agreed to meet at Phyllis's house that afternoon around three o'clock. Then Phyllis called Barbara Loomis, the only one of the three teachers who had a regular phone number listed in the directory.

A man answered. Phyllis said, "Mr. Loomis?"

"Yeah, this is Ben Loomis, if that's who you're looking for."

"Actually, I was hoping to speak to your wife. This is Phyllis Newsom calling."

"Barbara? Yeah, she's here somewhere. Wait just a— Hey, I know your name! You're the lady who's solved all those murders."

"Well, there haven't really been *that* many. . . ."

Loomis laughed. "Hey, solving even one murder is more than I could do. I can't even tell what's gonna happen on the TV shows I watch." The man's tone grew solemn as he went on. "Is this about what happened to Logan Powell?"

"That's right," Phyllis said. She decided that since she was already talking to Ben Loomis, she might as well take advantage of the opportunity to ask him a few questions.

"That was a terrible thing, just terrible," Loomis went on before Phyllis could say anything. "Logan and I were, I guess you'd say, friendly rivals for several years."

"That's right; you were in the same business, weren't you?"

"Yeah, real estate. Commercial development, mostly. Logan was working on a really big deal. I don't know what's gonna happen with it, now that he's gone."

"You mean NorCenTex Development?" Phyllis asked.

"That's right! Say, you must really keep up with the real estate market if you know about that, Mrs. Newsom."

"Well, I'm always on the lookout for good investments, you know," she said. She thought dangling the prospect of potential investment money in front of Loomis, so to speak, would keep him talking.

"You couldn't do better than that mall. When it goes in on the west side of town, once all the zoning issues are taken care of, it'll be quite a boon now that the economy's recovered. The slump around here was never as bad as it was in other places, you know."

"I know," Phyllis said, trying to sound like she knew what she was talking about. As a matter of fact, even during the economy's bad times, it had seemed to her that Weatherford and the surrounding area just kept growing by leaps and bounds.

With a rueful chuckle, Loomis said, "I tried to talk Logan into letting me in on the main deal, but he had that pretty well sewed up. I've managed to get some of the leavings, though, in locations around the mall property. I should do okay."

"I certainly hope so."

Loomis laughed again. "Here I am, yammering on about business, when you called to talk to my wife. You should never ask a salesman about his job, I guess. I'll go find Barbara."

"Thank you."

"Hang on."

Phyllis heard him put the phone down. The few minutes while Ben Loomis went to look for his wife gave Phyllis time to think about what she had just learned. A full-fledged mall being built here in town was a big deal indeed. Weatherford had a lot of shopping developments, especially along the interstate, but the closest actual mall was twenty miles away, in Fort Worth. With the population growing like it was, Phyllis thought, such an enterprise would probably be a big success . . . and it would mean a lot of money for whoever handled the sale of the property.

Earlier she had toyed with the notion that Ben Loomis might have had something to do with Logan's death. Now it appeared that the stakes were high enough to provide a possible motive. Someone would have to take over the NorCenTex Development deal. Phyllis needed to talk to Dana and find out whether Logan had any associates who could do so, or if the whole thing would be up for grabs again.

Of course, talking to Dana was dependent on her actually getting out of jail.

"Mrs. Newsom? Phyllis?"

That was Barbara Loomis's voice. "Yes, Barbara," Phyllis said. "How are you?"

"Not good," Barbara said. "Have you heard that

Dana's been arrested? We found out when we went to the hospital to try to see her. I can barely believe it, but it's true!"

"I know," Phyllis said. "That's why I'm calling. I'd like to talk to you and Dana's other friends, so I thought maybe you could come by my house this afternoon? About three o'clock?"

"You want to talk about what we can do to help her?"

"Exactly."

"Then I'll be there," Barbara said with grim determination. "I can call Jenna and Kendra and Taryn, too, if you'd like."

"I've spoken to Kendra already and left messages for the other two."

"I'll make sure they're there," Barbara promised. "You can call it a council of war if you want, because if going to war is what it takes to clear Dana's name, then that's what we'll do!"

Chapter 23

A Sunday afternoon in the fall usually meant that the Dallas Cowboys were playing, and in this part of the world, even for someone who wasn't a football fan, it was almost impossible not to hear and read about the games. Phyllis, for example, knew that the Cowboys were playing one of their main rivals, the Philadelphia Eagles, that afternoon. She offered to meet with the ladies somewhere else in the house so that Sam could watch the game on the big TV, but he wouldn't hear of it.

"The set in my room's just fine," he told her. "Me and Bobby can watch the game there, can't we, Bobby?"

"Yep," the little boy said. He had been tagging along with Sam for most of the day.

"Anyway, it doesn't really matter," Sam went on. "The Cowboys are probably gonna lose. I've never really forgiven 'em for gettin' rid of Tom Landry the way they did."

"Who's Tom Landry?" Bobby asked.

Sam peered down at him for a long moment, then said, "Boy, your daddy's been neglectin' your education. You come along with me, and I'll tell you all about Roger the Dodger and Dandy Don and Bullet Bob and, most of all, the Man in the Hat."

Phyllis smiled as Sam led Bobby out of the living room.

"I'm sitting in on this meeting," Carolyn announced.

"I'm not," Eve said. "I have some errands to run, and Sunday afternoon is a good time to do them. There aren't very many people out during the game."

Phyllis nodded and said an all-inclusive, "That's fine," to both of them. She knew that Carolyn would want to be part of any effort to help Dana. The challenge would be to keep her from losing her temper and making things more difficult when they were dealing with the authorities.

The four teachers showed up only minutes apart. Phyllis had coffee and tea ready, along with some of the pumpkin muffins from the canceled contest. She hoped that none of the visitors would regard her serving them as being in bad taste.

When the six of them were settled in around the living room with cups of whichever hot beverage they preferred, Phyllis began by saying, "I suppose I should bring you up to date on what's happened since Dana was arrested this morning."

She told them about her conversations with Juliette Yorke and her visit to police headquarters to see Dana. When she described Dana's tortured emotional state, expressions of anger and pity appeared on the women's faces.

"They can't get away with this," Barbara said. "Is this lawyer you've arranged for any good, Phyllis?"

"I think so," Phyllis replied. "She's the only defense attorney I actually know, but she seems quite competent. And Detective Largo didn't seem happy that Ms. Yorke was going to be representing Dana, so that bodes well, I think."

"I agree," Carolyn said. "That detective wouldn't be worried if she didn't think Ms. Yorke was a good lawyer."

Phyllis went on. "I don't know of any delicate way to put this, but how well is Dana fixed, financially? Can she afford to pay Ms. Yorke, or do we need to start thinking about raising funds for that?"

"Oh, goodness, I think she can pay," Jenna said.

"Logan was doing really well in his business, and Dana's been teaching long enough that she makes a pretty good salary, too." She looked around at the others. "Don't you think?"

They all nodded, and Barbara said, "Money shouldn't be a problem, as long as the district attorney doesn't try to freeze their assets or something like that." She frowned. "Can he do that if she's charged with murder?"

"I don't know," Phyllis said. "That's something I can ask Ms. Yorke the next time I talk to her, though." She paused, then said, "There's something else I need to be blunt about. Detective Largo believes that Dana killed Logan because he was having an affair. Do any of you know anything about that?"

Kendra stared wide-eyed at Phyllis and asked in a voice that had a little surprised squeak in it, "Are you saying that the police think Logan was cheating with one of *us*?"

"What?" Phyllis stared back at her for a second, then exclaimed, "Oh, no! That's not what I meant at all! I just wondered if Dana had ever said anything to you about being suspicious of Logan."

"She never said anything to me," Barbara said, "and anyway, I don't believe it. Logan had his faults—to be honest, he sort of neglected Dana in favor of his work most of the time—but I don't think he was cheating on her."

"I never heard anything about that," Taryn said, and Kendra chimed in, "Neither did I."

Phyllis said, "Detective Largo claims that it doesn't matter whether Logan was really cheating. She says that if Dana believed he was, that's enough to constitute a motive." She glanced over at Carolyn. "And we know that she *did* believe it, because she fought with Logan about it at the park on Friday night and then said something about it to Carolyn and me yesterday morning before his body was discovered."

"That's terrible," Barbara murmured as she looked down at the floor and shook her head. "I'm surprised she kept it from us like that. We were all so close. But honestly, she never said anything to me about suspecting Logan of such a thing."

"So none of you would have any idea whether or not it was true?"

Jenna said, "Even if it was, I don't see how it's going to help matters to dig up a bunch of dirty laundry now. Say that you proved Logan was fooling around. Wouldn't you just be making the police's theory stronger?"

"Not necessarily," Phyllis said. "You see, if we're assuming that Dana didn't kill him—"

"She didn't," Carolyn said.

"Then the unavoidable conclusion is that someone else killed him," Phyllis continued. "It seems to me that the most likely suspect would be the woman he was having an affair with. Maybe she wanted Logan to leave Dana, and he refused."

The four teachers exchanged long looks; then Barbara shook her head. "I'm sorry, Phyllis," she said. "We'd help you if we could, but we just don't know anything about that."

Phyllis was disappointed, but she had no choice but to believe them. She knew it was entirely possible that Dana had held in all her worries about Logan and never shared them with her friends. Phyllis hoped she could ask Dana about that directly, once Dana was out of jail. Until she heard differently, she was going to hope for the best and assume that Juliette Yorke would be able to arrange bail.

"All right," she said. "None of you know whether Logan was having an affair or not. What *can* you tell me about him? What do you know about his business, his background, anything that might give someone a reason to want him dead?"

"Well, he was in business, right?" Taryn said. "He's bound to have had some enemies." She glanced at Barbara. "No offense. I don't mean to say that Ben has enemies."

Barbara laughed and shook her head. "None taken, because of course he does. Anytime someone's successful, there's going to be somebody out there who's jealous of that success, at the very least. Or someone who thinks that they've been done wrong. And I know from experience that real estate can be pretty cutthroat. I'm not saying there's anybody out there who'd like to murder Ben, but I'm sure there are people who wouldn't mind seeing him fail or even go broke. They'd get a big kick out of it, in fact."

"But not Logan Powell, right?" Phyllis said.

"No, not Logan. They were friends, even if they were competitors. Oh, Logan might have felt a little resentment if Ben snapped up some juicy deal he had his eye on, and vice versa, but—" Barbara stopped short, her eyes widening. A look of anger appeared on her face. "Wait just a minute! You're not saying that *Ben* could have had something to do with Logan's death!"

"Not at all," Phyllis said quickly, although in truth she hadn't ruled out that possibility. She needed Barbara as an ally, though, so she tried to smooth the waters by saying, "I was thinking about some of the other people involved in Logan's business. Do you happen to know, was he a one-man operation, or did he have some associates?"

Barbara seemed slightly mollified by Phyllis's explanation. "It was Logan's business, all the way. He had a secretary and a bookkeeper, but he was the only agent at his firm. He always said that he liked being a lone wolf. That way all the responsibility was his, but so were all the rewards."

Phyllis nodded as she filed away that information. The fact that Logan didn't have a partner who could take over for him or anything like that removed one possible motive and suspect.

Unfortunately, that brought them right back to Logan and Dana's marital troubles as the most likely motive for his death.

"What about Logan's family? Where was he from? Did you know about all his medical problems and his drinking?"

"His drinking?" Kendra repeated. "I don't think I ever saw Logan take a drink."

"He always seemed very fit to me," Jenna said. "What sort of medical problems?"

Phyllis looked around at them and realized that they didn't know how Logan had been killed. No one had told them the details of the case, so all they really knew was that Dana had been arrested. Detective Largo had given Phyllis the results of the autopsy and the forensics tests in confidence, and against her better judgment, as she had made clear. Phyllis wasn't sure she felt comfortable about betraying that confidence, even though she had already done so to a certain extent by bringing up Logan's medical history.

"I can't really say any more . . . ," she began.

That brought a chorus of angry objections from the four teachers. "We're Dana's best friends," Jenna declared. "If you know something about how Logan died, you can tell us, Mrs. Newsom."

"I'm sorry. I shouldn't have said what I did. I don't want to jeopardize her defense."

"Or maybe you just want to make sure that if anybody gets the credit for solving his murder, it's you," Barbara said. She clasped her purse tightly and stood up. "I think we should go."

"Please don't," Phyllis said. "I understand how you feel. It's not like I'm trying to keep secrets from you. I was told some things in confidence, that's all. And it might really help if you told me everything you know about Logan."

Barbara looked at her friends. Jenna shrugged. Barbara sighed and sat down again. "I probably knew him better than anyone," she said, "since Ben and I were friends with him and Dana for quite a while."

"We just saw Dana, mostly at school," Taryn put in. "So I never knew that much about Logan."

"He talked a lot whenever he was around," Kendra added, "but he never really seemed to say all that much, if you know what I mean."

Phyllis knew, all right. Logan had had a natural salesman's ability to keep up a conversation. He could run quite a line of bull, as Sam would put it.

"Logan never revealed that much about himself, even to their friends like Ben and me," Barbara said. "He would brag about his business, or talk about sports, or almost anything else. I know he grew up somewhere around here. Granbury, I think. He and Dana met while they were both in college at North Texas."

Phyllis knew that Barbara was talking about the University of North Texas in Denton, which had been North Texas State University when she went there, and when Dana and Logan did, too.

"So they were college sweethearts."

"Not really," Barbara said. "They knew each other, but they didn't start dating until they were in their thirties." A smile touched her lips. "It seemed to be a good match, though. They were suited for each other. Logan could be a little ... brash ... and Dana was just always so sweet, but they got along well."

"Dana said she couldn't have children."

"That's right. She worried that Logan would be disappointed, but I never got the sense that he was."

That jibed with what Dana had told Phyllis. She asked a few more questions, standard things like whether or not Logan had any enemies they knew of, or whether there had ever been any serious trouble between Logan and Dana until a couple of nights earlier. None of the four knew anything that looked promising.

"We're just spinning our wheels here, aren't we?" Jenna said suddenly. "There's not any evidence against anyone else. The police are going to put Dana on trial and convict her."

"No!" Barbara said. "There has to be something." She cast an appealing look toward Phyllis. "Doesn't there?"

Phyllis sighed. "Right now, I don't see anything to cast suspicion on anyone else. But I'm sure Ms. Yorke will dig into Logan's background, and if there's anything there, she'll find it."

"What about you?" Carolyn asked. "Does this mean you're giving up?"

Phyllis shook her head. "No. I'll keep digging, too. Maybe it'll help when I can talk to Dana again."

They all looked so downcast that Phyllis wanted to raise their spirits. "I have some pumpkin muffins in the kitchen," she went on. "I'll get them."

"We really ought to be going . . . ," Jenna said.

"Please. Stay and have a muffin." Phyllis managed to laugh. "If you don't, my grandson will just try to eat all of them."

"All right," Barbara said with a smile. "I've heard that you're a great baker, Mrs. Newsom."

Carolyn cleared her throat, prompting Barbara to add, "And I know you are, Carolyn."

Phyllis brought out the muffins and passed them around on small paper plates. Jenna was the only one who turned down a muffin, citing a diet she was on. Phyllis didn't think Jenna weighed enough to be worrying about a diet, but that was none of her business.

It reminded her of something, though, and she said, "Were all four of you at the park on Friday night, helping to get ready for the festival?"

"That's right," Barbara said, nodding.

"Did you happen to see Dana eating a muffin like this?"

That brought puzzled frowns from all four of them. "I didn't see her eating anything," Kendra said.

"Me, neither," Taryn agreed.

"Why do you ask?" Jenna wanted to know.

"She stopped by here before she went to the park. She had one of the muffins, and I gave her another to take with her. I was just wondering if she got to enjoy it before that argument with Logan broke out."

Barbara shook her head. "I have no idea. You'll have to ask Dana."

"Why did she come by here?" Jenna asked.

Phyllis explained about the missing keys. "I don't guess she ever found them. She hadn't when we talked to her yesterday morning, and she hasn't had a chance to since then."

Kendra said, "That's scary, to think that your house keys are out floating around somewhere."

Phyllis nodded. "I'll say something to Juliette Yorke.

The locks ought to be changed on Dana's house, just to make sure that no one can get in there."

Everyone talked about how good the muffins were, and then Phyllis couldn't think of any other reason to keep them there. They said their good-byes and trooped out, still filled with worry for their friend in jail.

"That didn't go well," Carolyn said when the four teachers were gone. "They didn't know anything that would help you figure out who really killed Logan. From the sound of it, Dana's still the only one with any reason to want Logan dead."

Phyllis wasn't sure about that. She wanted to find out more about the NorCenTex Development deal and any possible involvement that Ben Loomis might have in it. It made her uncomfortable to think that she might wind up ferreting out evidence against Barbara's husband, because she liked Barbara. But she liked Dana, too. And right now, Phyllis's main interest was in finding out the truth. As Sam had said, she had to proceed like Sherlock Holmes and eliminate the impossible.

And hope that the only remaining possibility didn't point straight at Dana.

Chapter 24

Despite Sam's prediction, the Cowboys won their game after all, prompting him to declare that evening that he supposed he wasn't such a great football prognosticator after all. Bobby seemed to have enjoyed watching the game with him, which was all Phyllis really cared about.

She was at the computer in the living room at about eight o'clock that night when the phone rang. The caller ID screen told her that Mike was at the other end of the call, two hours earlier in California.

She hadn't talked to him since he'd called Friday evening to check on Bobby, so there was a certain amount of eagerness in her voice as she said, "Hello, Mike."

"Hi, Mom. How are you?"

"I'm all right, I suppose."

"You suppose?" Mike was quick to pick up on such things. "What does that mean?"

She laughed. "Oh, don't worry about me. I'm fine. There have just been some things going on around here. . . . Not about Bobby, though," she added quickly, so he wouldn't worry. "He's fine. His fever is gone, he's not complaining about his ear hurting him anymore, and he seems to be having a wonderful time helping me around the house and spending time with Sam."

"That sounds great. I know I've told you this before,

but Sarah and I really appreciate you taking care of him."

"How's Bud doing?" Phyllis hoped that Mike wasn't calling with bad news.

"He's hanging in there. Says he's looking forward to Thanksgiving dinner."

"I'm glad to hear that." Phyllis knew that Sarah's father wanted to be around for one more Thanksgiving, and if he accomplished that, then maybe he could make it his goal to see another Christmas. Such mental ploys didn't have any medical reason for being effective, but sometimes the human spirit responded to things that had no medical basis.

"Now, what's this about something going on there?" Mike persisted.

Phyllis sighed. He would have found out what had happened at the Harvest Festival sooner or later, but she would have preferred that it waited until he and Sarah got home. She knew better than to think that she could dodge Mike's questions, though. He was too good at finding out things, which helped make him such a well-respected law enforcement officer.

"There was some trouble at the Harvest Festival yesterday," she said.

"I'm sure it wasn't too bad, as long as you didn't stumble over another dead body."

Phyllis didn't say anything.

Mike was silent for a moment, too, and when he spoke, his voice had a sharper edge to it. "Mom? You didn't actually find a body, did you?"

"Well, I certainly didn't set out to," Phyllis replied with a note of exasperation in her own voice. "But then Carolyn and I started to move one of the scarecrows that were set up at the park as decorations, and we discovered that the scarecrow was actually, well, a man who'd been murdered."

"A murder victim inside a scarecrow," Mike said, sounding now as if he were torn between disbelief and resignation. "Of course there was. Are you really all right?"

"I'm fine," Phyllis insisted. "It's not like this is the first time such a thing has happened."

"No, unfortunately it's not. What about Carolyn?"

"She's all right. We're both just worried about the case."

"The case?"

"Of the murdered man. You might have known him, by the way. His name was Logan Powell."

"The real estate guy?" Mike sounded surprised now. "Why would anybody want to kill him?"

"The police have arrested his wife," Phyllis said. "She's a teacher."

"Which means you and Carolyn probably know her."

Mike's comment wasn't actually a question, but Phyllis said, "That's right. Carolyn knows her better than I do, but I've been acquainted with her for quite some time. And neither one of us believes that she's capable of murder."

There was a note of genuine alarm in Mike's voice now as he said, "We're coming home."

"Oh, no!" Phyllis exclaimed. "There's no need for you to do that. Let Sarah stay there and enjoy Thanksgiving with her dad."

"Then she can stay and I'll come home," Mike insisted. "I know you, Mom. If you think this lady is innocent but the cops have arrested her for the murder anyway, you're going to try to prove that she's not guilty. The only way to do that is to find out who the real killer is."

"Juliette Yorke has taken Dana's case. I'm sure Ms. Yorke will be able to handle things."

"She's good, all right, but I've got a hunch that won't stop you from nosing around yourself."

Phyllis looked at the computer monitor in front of her. There on the screen were the results of the search she'd just done for NorCenTex Development.

"I'm really convinced that Dana Powell is innocent, Mike," she said. "If there's anything I can do to help her, I intend to do it. But that's no reason for you to cut your trip short. I'll be fine."

"I'm sure that's what you thought when you were down at the coast last year, too, and you know what happened there."

Phyllis couldn't dispute that, so she asked, "When were you and Sarah planning to fly back? Next Saturday, right?"

"Yeah, we thought we'd miss the worst of the holiday travel congestion on Sunday. Of course, that depends to a certain extent on what happens with her dad."

"According to Ms. Yorke, nothing is going to happen in the case between now and then except maybe a bail hearing for Dana," Phyllis said. "So there's no reason for you to come back early."

"Are you sure about that?"

"Positive."

"Well . . . no promises, but tell me about what happened. The full story."

For the next half hour, Phyllis did just that, giving Mike every detail she could remember since first becoming involved with Logan and Dana Powell and the preparations for the Harvest Festival. Putting it into words like that gave her a chance to go over all of it again in her mind, but she was disappointed when nothing new sprang out at her. She had hoped she would see some connections she had missed before. When she finished, she had to admit to herself that the evidence was just as damning toward Dana as it had seemed to be starting out.

Mike must have come to that same conclusion, because he said, "You know that anytime someone is murdered, the spouse is always the first person we look at. There's a good reason for that."

"Yes, of course. And I suppose in most cases the police are right to think that way."

"The statistics are pretty overwhelming, actually. Nothing leads to murder as much as love and money, and you have both of those elements in a marriage." Mike paused. "Although I'll admit that I'm a little intrigued by this NorCenTex Development connection. I hadn't heard anything about a mall being built in town."

"Neither had I, until this came up," Phyllis said. "I've done some searching on the Internet, and from the looks of it, the company has bought some existing malls in other towns, but they haven't actually built one before."

"So this would be a big deal for them," Mike mused. "Lots of money involved, more than likely."

"I would think so, yes."

"That might be worth looking into . . . for Juliette Yorke, though, not you, Mom. And I really shouldn't say anything else, because the sheriff's office and the police department are supposed to be on the same side, and I shouldn't be trying to undermine their case."

"Well, I think we should all be on the side of justice," Phyllis said, "and it'll be an injustice if Dana Powell is convicted of her husband's murder."

"Not if she did it."

Phyllis didn't say anything. She knew that Mike was right about what he'd just said, but she was stubborn enough to believe that she was right about Dana, too.

"Tell you what," he went on after a moment, "I'll call some of my friends back there on the police force and see what I can find out. Maybe they have some evidence that you don't know about. If they do, I can't pass along the details to you, but I can at least tell you for sure that your friend is guilty."

"In the opinion of the police. Of course they're not going to look for anything that contradicts that theory."

She felt a surge of anger as she heard him sigh. When you got to be a certain age, your children thought they knew everything again and you knew nothing, just like they did when they were teenagers. She kept herself from making the sharp comment that she wanted to, though.

"I'll stay in touch," Mike said. "You're right, with Thanksgiving coming up in just a few days, not much is going to get done this week. The bail hearing, maybe the arraignment, that's about it. I'll be back by the time the case really starts to get going."

"So you'll stay in California and let Sarah enjoy the time she has left with her dad?"

"I guess so. If you'll promise to stay out of trouble."

This time she couldn't hold it in. "Bobby's your child, Michael, not me."

She heard him take a deep breath. "You're right. Sorry. I didn't mean that the way it sounded."

Yes, he had, she thought, but in the interest of keeping the peace, she didn't say it.

They said their good-byes instead, and then, feeling vaguely unsettled after she'd hung up the phone, Phyllis went back to the page of hits she'd gotten in response to her NorCenTex Development search. She went to the company's Web site and got a list of the commercial properties it owned, but the site was lacking in any real information about the company itself beyond a post office box address in Fort Worth, a telephone number, and an e-mail link.

Clicking back to the search page, Phyllis scrolled down the links to newspaper stories that mentioned NorCenTex Development. There were quite a few of them. She had read some of them before Mike called and now checked out several more of them, confirming her impression that NorCenTex Development was primarily an investment holdings company that bought up failing or borderline commercial properties and made successes out of them. The company seemed to have a good track record at that.

There was nothing, though, about a pending mall-construction deal in Weatherford. If it was true, though, and she had no reason to doubt what she had heard from both Logan Powell and Ben Loomis, it would be a big step for the company, as Mike had pointed out.

She couldn't imagine what Logan could have done to jeopardize that deal—he had been hoping to cash in on it himself, in fact—but if circumstances had changed abruptly and Logan suddenly represented an obstacle to the mall, how far would the other people in the deal go to make sure it wasn't ruined?

Phyllis knew that was pure speculation on her part, but she thought it was a question worth asking . . . and answering. She wasn't sure how to go about doing that, but she was going to give it some thought.

Sam came into the room behind her and rested a familiar hand on her shoulder. "Thinkin' about the case?" he asked as he looked at the list of links on the monitor.

"That's right. That was Mike on the phone a little while ago. I told him all about it."

"Let me guess. He told you to keep your nose out of the case and stay out of trouble."

Phyllis laughed and reached up to pat his hand where it rested on her shoulder. "How did you know?"

"Hey, I got grown kids, too, who think I'm a dodderin' old fool."

"Mike doesn't think I'm doddering."

"Well, we're in agreement on that. You're about as far from dodderin' as anybody I know."

"Can we stop using the word *doddering*?"

"Fine by me. What did you tell him?"

"That there probably won't be anything going on in the case this week except Dana's bail hearing. He agreed."

"So you didn't actually promise not to nose around in the case?"

Phyllis shook her head and said, "Not in so many words, no."

Both of them knew what she meant by that. Sam chuckled and tightened his grip on her shoulder for a second. "Here we go again," he said.

Chapter 25

Phyllis had some vague plans for Monday morning, but before she could get started on them, the phone rang. Phyllis, Sam, Carolyn, Eve, and Bobby were in the kitchen at the time eating breakfast, and Carolyn was the closest to the phone, since she was up pouring herself another cup of coffee.

She picked up the phone, checked the caller ID screen, and said, "It's Dolly."

Phyllis stood up and held out her hand. "I called and left a message for her yesterday, asking her to call me back." Carolyn handed her the phone, and Phyllis pressed the TALK button and said, "Hello."

"Phyllis? This is Dolly Williamson. I got your message. Sorry I wasn't able to get back to you yesterday. I was tied up at church nearly all day."

"That's all right," Phyllis assured the former superintendent. "I was calling about Thanksgiving. I got to thinking about people who are going to be alone on that day, without families to gather around them."

"Oh, Phyllis! How lovely that you thought of me. I'd love to come and spend Thanksgiving with you and Carolyn and Eve. And Sam, too, of course."

Phyllis's eyes widened in surprise. She hadn't really meant to invite Dolly. She had just planned to ask her for suggestions of teachers who might be alone on the holiday. Dolly had grown children with families of their own, and they usually all got together on Thanksgiving.

"You're not going to be with your own family this year?" Phyllis asked.

"No, they're all flying off to Disney World or some such. Why anybody would want to spend Thanksgiving in some hotel, I don't know, but what can you do? This younger generation certainly has a mind of its own."

The members of that "younger generation" Dolly referred to were middle-aged adults, since she was in her late seventies. Phyllis didn't point that out, though. She did the only thing she could and made the best of the situation by saying, "Of course we'd love to have you spend the day with us, Dolly. In fact, I was thinking about inviting several teachers who might be alone otherwise."

"What a wonderful idea! Who did you have in mind?"

"Well, Jenna Grantham mentioned that she couldn't afford to fly back home to Wisconsin. . . ."

"I know Jenna. Lovely girl."

Phyllis wasn't surprised that Dolly was acquainted with Jenna. Dolly might be retired, but she kept a finger on the pulse of the school district. Phyllis sometimes thought that Dolly knew every teacher who had ever taught in Weatherford, going all the way back forty years or more and continuing right up to the present day. She was familiar with a lot of teachers from surrounding districts, too, such as Sam, who had taught at Poolville for most of his career.

"What about her friends Taryn Marshall and Kendra Neville? I know they're both single, but I don't know what their plans are for Thanksgiving."

"Let me find out about that," Dolly volunteered. She loved to organize things, so the offer came as no surprise to Phyllis. "I'm sure I can come up with some other teachers who'd be glad to have a place to go for Thanksgiving, too. How many people can you handle? A dozen?"

Phyllis had been thinking more along the lines of three or four guests, but she had to admit that a dozen would help fill the house up and make it feel more like an old-fashioned Thanksgiving. She said, "Around a dozen would be good."

"But of course we can't expect you to prepare a dinner for that many people all by yourself."

"I won't be," Phyllis said. "Carolyn will be helping me."

"That's still not enough. I can bring my baked mashed potatoes with sour cream and cream cheese. They're wonderful. I'll tell everyone who's coming to bring a side dish or dessert. How will that be?"

It would certainly be easier if everyone pitched in by bringing food, Phyllis thought. And that was something of a tradition at family get-togethers, too. This was shaping up to be a bigger affair than she had expected, but she found herself looking forward to it.

"All right, that's fine," she told Dolly.

"This will be fun. It's a wonderful, generous idea on your part, Phyllis. Now, you just relax and let me handle all the details."

"Okay," Phyllis said with a smile. Despite her age, Dolly was a force of nature, like a blizzard or a typhoon. There was no stopping her, and it was a waste of time and energy to try.

"All right, I'll stay in touch, and I'll let you know exactly who's coming and what they're going to bring."

"That's fine, Dolly, thank you."

They said their good-byes and hung up. As Phyllis replaced the cordless phone on its base, Carolyn said, "You just got steamrollered by Dolly, didn't you?"

Sam grinned and put in, "I always thought of her as more like a velvet sledgehammer."

Phyllis thought both of those descriptions were pretty accurate. She said, "Dolly sort of invited herself for Thanksgiving, and she's going to line up some other teachers who'd be alone for the holiday otherwise. We may have a dozen people here." She looked around the table. "I hope that's all right with the rest of you. I mean, this is your home, too."

Sam shrugged. "The more the merrier, as far as I'm concerned."

"I think it's a fine idea," Eve said.

"We don't have to cook for that many people, do we?" Carolyn asked. "I don't really mind, but I've spent a lot of Thanksgivings where I hardly got out of the kitchen all day."

Phyllis shook her head. "No, we'll just prepare like we would have anyway, although I might go ahead and cook an extra turkey. But everyone who comes is supposed to bring a covered dish, so we should have plenty of food."

Bobby asked, "Who's Dolly? What's a covered dish?"

"Dolly is the lady that all of us used to work for," Phyllis explained. "Except for Sam, because he taught in a different school district."

"But I know her," Sam added. "Dolly knows all the teachers for miles around."

"And a covered dish is food," Phyllis went on. "People make green-bean casserole, Jell-O salad or desserts, things like that, then cover the dish with aluminum foil and bring it with them so that everybody can have some of it."

"That sounds good," Bobby said. "Well, maybe not the green-bean part."

Phyllis smiled. She was about to tell him that she could prepare green beans so that he would like them, but the phone rang again first. This time she was the closest, so she picked it up and saw that Juliette Yorke was calling.

"Hello? Ms. Yorke?"

"That's right," the lawyer said, "but you might as well call me Juliette. I just wanted to let you know that Ms. Powell will be arraigned at nine o'clock, and I plan to ask for bail at that time. I think it would be a good idea for you to be there, in case I need to show that she has the support of some solid citizens in the community."

"Of course," Phyllis said. She could pick up with her other plans later. "I can do that. Should I bring Carolyn with me? What about her friends who are still teaching? It's kind of short notice for them to get substitutes. . . ."

"I think you and Ms. Wilbarger will be sufficient. I

don't see any need to take those other ladies away from their jobs. And I know this is short notice for you, too, so I appreciate it."

Phyllis glanced at the clock and saw that it was a few minutes past eight o'clock. "That's all right. We'll be there."

Juliette gave her the number of the courtroom, which was in the district court building a block off the square in downtown. Phyllis still thought of it as the old post office building, which it had been for years before the post office moved to a larger facility on the south side of town.

"Who'll be where?" Carolyn asked as Phyllis hung up the phone.

"You and I are going to Dana's arraignment and bail hearing." Phyllis looked at Sam and Eve. "I hate to ask the two of you to be responsible for looking after Bobby again...."

"Shoot, it's no problem," Sam said. "I got boards that need sandin'. I reckon he can handle a piece of sandpaper without hurtin' himself, can't he?"

Bobby looked at Phyllis and nodded eagerly. She smiled and said, "I'm sure that will be all right." She drank the last of the coffee from her cup, then told Carolyn, "Now I guess we'd better go and get ready."

They made it to the courthouse with a little time to spare and found Juliette talking to a slender, dark-haired man in a gray suit just outside the courtroom. Phyllis and Carolyn kept their distance until the conversation was over. The man didn't seem too happy as he walked away, and Juliette didn't look pleased, either. She was in her thirties, with chestnut hair pulled back in a conservative style. She wore glasses and carried a briefcase, and her dark green suit over a white blouse, along with her low heels and lack of jewelry except for a watch, marked her as all business. The few times Phyllis had met the woman, Juliette had struck her as being perhaps a little too tightly wound. But when people's lives and well-being were in her hands, maybe that was a good thing.

Juliette smiled thinly as she nodded to Phyllis and Carolyn. "Ms. Newsom. Ms. Wilbarger. Thank you for coming."

"We're on time, aren't we?" Phyllis asked.

"Yes, court won't be in session for another ten minutes or so. That was the district attorney I was just talking to."

"I thought I recognized him. Is it too much to hope that you were able to make a deal regarding bail for Dana?"

"I'm afraid so." Juliette shook her head. "He's going to ask that she be denied bail."

"On what grounds?" Carolyn asked. "Dana's certainly no danger to the community."

"He's going to argue that the method used to kill Logan Powell was so ingenious that it demonstrates Dana's ability to slip out of this jurisdiction if she wants to. In other words, he's going to say that she's a flight risk."

Carolyn snorted. "That's absurd. Her job and all her friends are here. She's not going anywhere."

"The school district isn't going to allow anyone who's charged with a felony to teach elementary children, certainly not when that felony is murder," Juliette said. "So she won't have a job until her name is cleared. And friends won't count for as much as family would have with the judge, I'm afraid. Still, we'll play the cards we're dealt. I think there's a good chance that the judge will see things our way. It'll be up to his discretion, though."

"If you need to call on us as character witnesses, feel free," Phyllis said. "That's why we're here, to help Dana in any way we can."

Juliette suddenly cocked her head slightly to the side, as if an idea had just come to her. "If you mean that, I may know of a way," she said.

"Whatever it takes," Phyllis said. "What did you have in mind?"

Before Juliette could explain, though, the district attorney walked back past them, opened the door of the courtroom, and went in. "You'll see," Juliette said to Phyllis. "Right now, it's time to get started."

Chapter 26

$\mathcal{P}$hyllis had never liked being in a courtroom. They were intimidating by their very nature. Things happened there that could determine the course of a person's life from that point on. The atmosphere was often solemn and a little scary, sort of like a hospital.

Yet the people who worked there every day, the judges and bailiffs and clerks, often joked around with each other, trading quips and stories about their personal lives. Phyllis understood that—the surroundings were commonplace to them—but it still struck her as odd and somewhat unsettling.

There was no levity going on in this courtroom today. The district attorney sat at one of the tables in front of the judge's bench and talked with a severe-looking woman who was probably an assistant DA. Juliette Yorke waited alone at the other table. Quite a few people sat on the benches behind the railing that separated the rest of the courtroom from the tables and the judge's bench. As Phyllis and Carolyn found a place to sit, Phyllis thought that court was sort of like church, too, with those pewlike benches. Nobody was going to pass the plate, though.

Phyllis knew that several dozen cases might be arraigned this morning, most of them minor offenses ranging from petty theft to possession of drugs. Normally a case might have to wait several weeks or even longer after the arrest before arraignment took place, which was why bail hearings usually preceded arraignments. Because of the seriousness of the charge against Dana, Juliette Yorke must have been able to get the case added to the docket on short notice, Phyllis thought.

She wouldn't have known so much about court procedures if she hadn't heard Mike talking about various cases. Also, she had been called as a prosecution witness on several occasions when her efforts had helped uncover the identity of a murderer.

Looking around at the other people on the benches, Phyllis saw that many of them looked worried, and her heart went out to them. Some of them were there with relatives while others were defendants themselves. Some might well deserve whatever course the legal system took, but others had simply made mistakes, maybe never even been in trouble with the law until they did something without thinking. Phyllis could feel sorry for them and hope that their lives worked out better from now on.

After a few more minutes, the bailiff called out, "All rise." Everyone stood as the judge came in through a door to the left of his bench. He was a short, fair-haired man in late middle age. Phyllis didn't know him. He took his place behind the bench and leaned forward to say into the microphone in front of him, "Please be seated." With a rustle of clothes and feet, the spectators followed that instruction.

The lawyers remained on their feet, though, and the district attorney half turned to motion toward the bailiff, who nodded and opened a door behind the court clerk's desk. Phyllis's breath hissed between her teeth as a couple of uniformed female officers brought Dana into the courtroom and escorted her over to the table where Juliette Yorke waited for her.

Dana was still dressed in her own clothes. They were starting to look pretty wrinkled and shapeless by now. Phyllis couldn't tell if she was wearing any makeup, but she had brushed her hair. That didn't really make her look much better, though. Her face was still stunned and haggard. She wore handcuffs, and a chain attached them to a ring on a broad leather belt strapped around her waist, so she couldn't raise her arms very high. At least she didn't have shackles on her ankles, Phyllis noted.

The court clerk read the case number and the charge. This was the most high-profile case, so they were getting it out of the way first. The judge looked over the paperwork the bailiff had given him and then asked, "How does the defendant plead?"

"Not guilty, Your Honor," Juliette Yorke said.

The judge looked directly at Dana, who stood next to Juliette, and said, "Is that a true plea, Ms. Powell?"

"It is, Your Honor," Dana said. Phyllis could tell from the rote sound of her voice that Juliette had coached her on what to expect and how to respond.

The judge picked up a pen and marked off something on a document. The mundane nature of the proceedings when it was Dana's life at stake bothered Phyllis. She knew that was the nature of the system, though. The courts had to have their routines and paperwork in order to function.

"All right, you're being bound over for a grand jury hearing," the judge went on. "The grand jury will decide whether there's enough evidence against you to warrant an indictment on the charge of murder in the first degree. Do you understand that, Ms. Powell?"

"Yes, Your Honor," Dana said, again sounding like she was reciting a poem learned in school.

"In the matter of bail, Your Honor—," Juliette began.

The district attorney said, "The state requests that bail be denied, Your Honor."

The judge looked at him and said, "You're aware that bail is usually granted these days even in murder cases, Mr. Sullivan?"

"With all due respect, not in high-profile murder cases where the defendant poses a flight risk, Your Honor."

"Ms. Powell poses absolutely *no* flight risk, Your Honor," Juliette said. "She pled not guilty because she is innocent of this charge and is eager to clear her name so that the police can go about discovering who actually killed her husband."

"Your Honor, the state believes that Ms. Powell committed this crime; otherwise, the charge would not have been brought against her."

"Presumption of innocence," Juliette snapped as she glanced over at the district attorney.

"You've read the charge, Your Honor," Sullivan insisted. "Logan Powell was killed in a particularly devious and cruel fashion, indicating that his murderer possesses a high degree of intelligence and no moral compunctions whatsoever. We believe that if Ms. Powell is freed from custody, no matter what precautions are taken, she will find a way to circumvent them and will flee from justice."

"Your Honor, Ms. Powell is a highly respected educator and member of the community," Juliette argued. "She has one of the most important jobs to be found anywhere, that of teaching our children. And I might add, the community has trusted Ms. Powell with those children for many years. Not only that, but she has many, many friends, including Mrs. Phyllis Newsom and Mrs. Carolyn Wilbarger, who are here in court today to testify on her behalf if needed."

The district attorney said, "I'm sure Ms. Powell can find many people who will tell you what a fine person she is, Your Honor. That doesn't change the facts of the case."

"Mrs. Newsom is prepared to do more than testify on my client's behalf," Juliette said. She glanced back at Phyllis, who had an idea of what was coming next. It had occurred to her while Juliette and District Attorney Sullivan were arguing back and forth. She gave Juliette a tiny nod now to indicate that it was all right. Juliette faced the judge again and went on, "Mrs. Newsom is willing to open her own home to Ms. Powell and allow her to stay there until the case comes to trial."

Next to Phyllis, Carolyn made a little noise of surprise. She leaned over and whispered, "Really?"

Phyllis nodded.

"That's a good idea—," Carolyn started to say.

The judge silenced her by saying, "Order, please." He looked past the attorneys' tables and gazed directly at Phyllis. "Mrs. Newsom, would you stand up, please?"

Phyllis got to her feet and stood there clutching her purse.

"Mrs. Newsom, is this true? If Ms. Powell is released on bail, you'd like for her to come stay with you?"

"That's right, Your Honor," Phyllis said. "I have a spare bedroom in my house."

That was true. The extra room had sat there empty ever since Mattie Harris had passed away. Phyllis hadn't been able to bring herself to rent it out again. Besides, she and Carolyn and Eve and Sam all got along so well, she hesitated to bring in someone else who might upset the dynamics of the house.

This would only be temporary, though, so Phyllis thought it would be all right. She glanced at Carolyn, who nodded to show that she thought it was all right, too.

The district attorney looked annoyed. Obviously, he hadn't anticipated this ploy from Juliette. He said, "Your Honor, the state has the highest admiration and respect for Mrs. Newsom. No one has forgotten how helpful she's been to the authorities in the past. But that doesn't mean she's qualified to take responsibility for a dangerous prisoner."

"Ms. Powell is not dangerous, Your Honor," Juliette insisted. "In fact, she's as much a victim here as her husband. Whoever killed him has struck at her, too. I respectfully ask that this tragedy not be compounded by forcing her to remain in custody until her case comes before the grand jury."

The judge steepled his fingers together in front of him. "If I grant bail now, and then the grand jury indicts your client, Ms. Yorke, I may have to consider revoking it."

Juliette nodded. "I understand that, Your Honor."

"All right, then." The judge reached for his gavel. "I hereby grant bail to the defendant in the amount of two hundred and fifty thousand dollars."

Sullivan's expression was bleak and angry, but he responded quickly to the ruling. "Your Honor, the state requests that a higher amount be set, not less than one million dollars."

"I've made my decision, Mr. Sullivan," the judge said. "We'll move along to the next case."

Juliette glanced down at the papers spread out on the table in front of her. From where Phyllis was sitting, she couldn't be sure, but she thought she saw a smile play briefly across Juliette's face. Then Juliette turned to Dana and spoke to her for a moment in a low voice. The officers who had brought Dana into the courtroom came over and took charge of her again, escorting her back out the way she had come in. Juliette gathered up her papers, placed them in her briefcase, snapped the case closed, and came through the gate in the railing to join Phyllis and Carolyn. She inclined her head toward the lobby outside the courtroom, indicating that they would talk there.

"That went even better than I'd hoped," Juliette said once they were out of the courtroom.

"Two hundred and fifty thousand dollars is a lot of money," Carolyn pointed out. "I don't know if Dana can raise that much."

"She won't have to. I know several bail bondsmen who'll put up ninety percent of it, and Dana's given me power of attorney to get a certified check for the balance from her account at the bank. It'll take an hour or so to do all the paperwork, but I'll have her out and at your house before the morning is over, Mrs. Newsom."

Phyllis nodded. "That's fine. I'll go get the spare room ready for her and let the others in the house know that we'll be having company."

"They won't object, will they?"

"Sam and Eve?" Phyllis shook her head. "I'm sure they won't."

"What happens after that?" Carolyn wanted to know.

Juliette smiled. "The grand jury won't meet again until the first of next month. We can all sit back and take a deep breath right now. Thanksgiving is in three days, and I suggest we all try to enjoy it as much as we can. After the holiday will be soon enough to start digging deeper into the case."

Phyllis knew the lawyer was probably right, but it still struck her as a waste of time. They ought to be trying to prove that Dana was innocent *now*.

Maybe she would have an opportunity to do so, she told herself. After all, Dana was going to be right there in her house, where Phyllis could ask all the questions she wanted. There were still questions for which she definitely wanted answers.

Beginning with a certain pumpkin muffin.

Chapter 27

As she and Carolyn drove away from the court building, something nagged at Phyllis's brain. She had a feeling that she had seen or heard something back there in the courtroom that would go a long way toward explaining Logan Powell's death and maybe even lead to his killer.

But no matter how hard she tried, the thought eluded her. Finally, she stopped worrying about it, knowing from experience that sometimes that would make the idea pop into her mental grasp.

Not today, though. By the time they reached the house, Phyllis still had no idea what it was that had tantalized her like that.

"Dana looked like she's been through a terrible ordeal," Carolyn commented as Phyllis pulled into the garage. "It was a good idea to let her stay here. I'm not sure she needs to be by herself right now."

"That's what I thought," Phyllis said. "I'm glad Juliette came up with it. It might have helped influence the judge to grant bail, too."

"You looked like you were a million miles away while we were driving back over here. What were you thinking about?"

"I'm not sure." Phyllis smiled slightly. "That's the problem."

She didn't explain any further, because they were out of the car now and Bobby came running to greet her. He held up a smooth piece of board.

"Sam let me practice on this, and then he let me sand one of the boards for the bookshelves! Look what a good job I did!"

Phyllis ran her fingers over the surface of the board. "Yes, you did," she told the little boy. "That's very good work."

Sam propped a hip against the bench and grinned. "Bobby's a natural-born woodworker," he said.

Eve opened the door between the garage and the kitchen and asked, "What happened? Did the judge set bail for Dana?"

Phyllis nodded, glad that they were all here so she could go ahead and tell them the news. "Yes, Ms. Yorke is arranging for her to be released right now. And when that's done, Dana is going to come here and stay with us for a while."

Sam's bushy eyebrows lifted slightly in surprise, while Eve frowned. "Are you sure that's a good idea, dear?" she asked.

Phyllis didn't answer right away. Instead she patted Bobby on the shoulder and said, "Why don't you run along inside for a few minutes, Bobby? The grown-ups need to talk."

"I want to sand some more boards!"

"I got plenty of boards for you to sand, pardner," Sam said as he steered Bobby toward the door. "We'll work on 'em again in a little while, okay?"

"Yeah, okay," Bobby agreed a little grudgingly.

Once he was gone, Carolyn said, "I'm surprised at you, Eve. I didn't think you'd object to the idea."

"It's just that Dana's been accused of murder—," Eve began.

"You didn't move out when the police thought *I'd* killed someone!"

"That was different," Eve said. "I knew you couldn't have killed anyone, Carolyn."

"Well, I know Dana didn't kill anyone, either."

"Anyway, it's not because of me that I'm worried," Eve went on. "I just wondered how Mike and Sarah are going to feel about having an accused murderer staying in the same house as Bobby."

"Falsely accused murderer," Carolyn insisted. "But ... I hadn't thought about that."

"Neither did I," Phyllis admitted. "But Mike knows I would never do anything that I thought would put Bobby in the least bit of jeopardy. I'm sure he and Sarah will understand."

She hoped that would be the case, anyway.

And if nothing else, it was one more good reason to get to the bottom of this business as soon as possible, so the spectre of being accused of killing her own husband wouldn't be hanging over Dana any longer than necessary.

"I'm sure you know what you're doing," Eve said. "Where is Dana going to stay? In Mattie's old room?"

"That's right. And I guess she'll be here for Thanksgiving, too, along with Dolly and whoever else she rounds up."

Phyllis went upstairs to dust the room and make sure everything was in order, even though she was confident that it was. She cleaned this room every week, just like she did all the others. Just about the time she was finished, she got a cell phone call from Juliette Yorke saying that she and Dana were on their way.

Phyllis told the others, and they were all waiting in the living room, even Bobby, when Juliette parked her car at the curb in front of the house. Juliette and Dana got out and started up the walk.

"She doesn't have any bags," Carolyn commented. "Someone will need to go over to her house and pick up some clothes and other things for her."

"That's a good idea," Phyllis said as she went to the front door. "Dana may not feel like doing it herself right now."

"Who is this lady again?" Bobby asked.

"A friend of ours," Phyllis said. "Some bad things have happened, and she can't stay at her house right now. So we're letting her stay here for a while."

"Oh." Bobby nodded as if that explanation satisfied him.

Phyllis opened the door and put a smile on her face. "Come in," she said with the same sort of welcome cheeriness in her voice that would have been there if she'd been welcoming any other friend or relative for a visit. Somehow it rang hollow in her own ears, though, and she wondered if it sounded the same way to Dana.

Summoning up a smile of her own with obvious effort, Dana stepped into the house, followed by Juliette. Dana was able to nod and say, "Hello."

"I think you know everyone except my grandson," Phyllis said. "This is Bobby."

Dana's smile was a little more genuine as she looked down and said, "Hello, Bobby."

"Hi," he said. "I'm stayin' here 'cause I had a ear 'fection."

"Oh, that's too bad. Are you feeling better now?"

"Yes, ma'am."

Dana glanced up at Phyllis. "He's very polite. Of course, I wouldn't have expected anything else."

Phyllis said, "It's been wonderful having him here. He's really livened things up."

"He's been a big help to me in my woodworkin', too," Sam put in. "We don't know each other very well, Miz Powell, but it's good to have you here with us."

"That's right," Eve added, and Phyllis was grateful to her friends for trying to make Dana feel comfortable about being here.

"Why don't we all sit down?" Phyllis suggested.

Sam put a hand on Bobby's shoulder and said, "Bobby and I can't. We've got boards waitin' for us out in the garage. They won't sand and stain themselves, you know."

"That's all right," Phyllis told him. "We'll let you know when lunch is ready."

Sam and Bobby left the living room, and the five women sat down on the sofa and chairs arranged around the room. Dana's control slipped for a second, and the strain she was under showed on her face as she sank down on the sofa next to Juliette Yorke.

"Thank you so much, Phyllis," she murmured. "I . . . I couldn't have faced going back home right now. There's too much there that would remind me of . . . Anyway, I'm not sure the judge would have agreed to bail if you hadn't said you'd take me in." She smiled, but it was one of the saddest smiles Phyllis had ever seen. "I'm just a homeless waif right now."

"That's not true at all," Carolyn insisted. "For the time being, this is your home, and I'm sure that when you've put all this behind you, you'll go back to your own house."

Dana shook her head. "If that district attorney has his way, my next home will be in Gatesville."

That was the central Texas town where most of the state's female prison inmates were housed, Phyllis knew. Obviously, Dana knew that, too.

"It's not going to come to that," Carolyn insisted. "Phyllis and Juliette will find out who . . . I mean, they'll find out what really happened."

Juliette looked at Phyllis and said, "I wasn't aware that you were working as my investigator now, Mrs. Newsom."

"I'm not," Phyllis said, wishing that Carolyn hadn't said that. "I don't want to interfere with anything that you're planning to do to build Dana's defense. But if there's anything I can do to help, I hope you'll feel free to let me know."

"Right now, what you're doing is important. Dana needs a place to stay that's safe and secure. You're providing that."

Phyllis wanted to provide a lot more, such as the identity of whoever had killed Logan, but that would have to wait. She said, "I had better go get started on lunch."

"Eve and I can do that," Carolyn offered before Phyllis could get up. "Why don't you stay and talk to Dana and Ms. Yorke?"

Why didn't she stay and ask questions—that was what Carolyn meant, Phyllis thought. That wasn't a bad idea, although she wasn't sure how much Juliette would allow her client to say. She might not want Dana talking about the case at all.

"All right, that'll be fine," Phyllis said. When Carolyn and Eve had stood up and gone to the kitchen, she went on, "If you'd like, Dana, Carolyn and I can go over to your house this afternoon and bring you back some clothes and anything else you might need."

She wanted to take Carolyn along because she wasn't sure she would feel comfortable going into Dana's house by herself. She didn't really know Dana *that* well.

Dana didn't really seem to think anything of it, though. She just nodded and said, "I'd appreciate that very much. Like I said, I don't really want to go there right now."

"Do you have any pets that need to be cared for? Maybe we could make arrangements with your neighbors. . . ."

Phyllis stopped because Dana was shaking her head. "No, we don't have any pets," she said. "We were both so busy it didn't seem like there was really time for them. It would have been unfair to the animals."

"I understand."

Juliette stood up. "You seem to have things well under control here, Mrs. Newsom," she said. "I should be going."

"I hoped you'd stay for lunch," Phyllis said.

Juliette smiled and shook her head. "Thank you, though. I have some other things I need to do."

Dana got to her feet as well, held out her hand as if she were going to shake with Juliette, and then suddenly put her arms around the lawyer instead. "Thank you so much," Dana said in a husky half whisper. "I don't know what I would have done without you helping me, Ms. Yorke."

Looking a little uncomfortable with the hug, Juliette slipped out of Dana's arms and gave her hand an encouraging squeeze. "It's going to be all right," she said. "For now, just take it easy and try to recover from what's happened. I know it'll be difficult, but try not to worry. That's what I'll be doing for you."

Dana managed another tiny smile. "All right," she said. "I'll try."

She didn't sound like she thought she had a chance of succeeding, though, Phyllis thought.

With Juliette leaving, that meant she could ask Dana whatever she wanted to. Phyllis hated the idea of forcing Dana to revisit any of the terrible things that had happened, but the sooner the truth came out, the sooner Dana could begin to really put the tragedy behind her and get on with her life.

As they sat back down once Juliette had left, Phyllis said, "There was something I was wondering about, Dana, if you don't mind."

"About . . . what happened to Logan?"

"Well, yes. We don't have to talk about it now. . . ."

Dana shook her head. "Nothing we say here can make things any worse than they already are. I'll tell you whatever I know, Phyllis."

"All right. Here's my first question." Phyllis leaned forward. "What happened to that pumpkin muffin I gave you Friday night?"

Chapter 28

*J*udging by the expression on Dana's face, the question took her completely by surprise.

"The pumpkin muffin?" she repeated. "What pumpkin muffin?"

"Remember you ate one here, and then I gave you another to take with you because you hadn't had any supper and you were going to the park to help with the festival preparations?"

The frown on Dana's forehead deepened. "Wait a minute. Let me think. I recall eating the muffin here. It was good. And, yes, now I remember you gave me another one to take with me. It was wrapped up in a paper towel, wasn't it?"

"That's right," Phyllis said with a nod. "Did you eat it on your way to the park, or at the park?"

Dana shook her head. "No, I'm sure I didn't. I had calmed down a little after being so upset about my keys being missing, but I wasn't actually very hungry. I set it on the passenger seat...." She looked intently at Phyllis. "That's the last I remember seeing of it."

"Could it still be there in your SUV?"

"Why does it matter?" Dana asked. She was starting to sound a little annoyed now. "Do you want it back or something?"

"No, no, not at all," Phyllis said quickly. It seemed

that Dana didn't know about the muffinlike substance that had been found in Logan's mouth after he was dead. Phyllis didn't really want to tell her about it, either, because the whole thing might turn out to be meaningless. Dana didn't need any false hopes at this point. "I just wondered what happened to it."

"Well, I don't see how it's important," Dana said, "but I don't know. It's not in my car, though; I'm sure of that. It would be pretty stale by now, though, if it was."

Phyllis didn't doubt that. She said, "When you drove home from the park that night, was the muffin still there then?"

"I don't know. Let me think. . . ." Dana concentrated for a moment, then went on. "I can't say for sure, but I don't think it was. I would have seen it either then or the next morning when I got in to drive to the park, wouldn't I?"

"I would think so," Phyllis agreed.

"And since I don't have any memory of it at all, I don't see how it could have been there. But that means . . . What *does* that mean? I'm having so much trouble thinking straight. . . ."

"It means someone took it, probably while you were parked there on Friday evening."

"My missing keys!" Dana suddenly exclaimed. "Somebody used them to get into my car. But why go to that much trouble just to steal a muffin? I mean, yes, the one I ate here was really good, but it just doesn't make sense to me."

"Not to me, either," Phyllis said. "Not yet, anyway. But we know now that someone got into your car. Was anything else missing?"

"Not that I know of. I . . . I didn't notice anything being gone on Friday night or Saturday morning. And I think I would have if it was something that was usually there. I just didn't think about the muffin because I had so much else on my mind."

"The argument with Logan about his affairs." Phyllis knew her words would be blunt and painful to Dana, but it couldn't be helped.

Dana grimaced and nodded. "That's right. When you're scared that your marriage is falling apart, you don't worry about something like a . . . a muffin."

"Of course not. I'm sorry to have to be asking you about all this, Dana, but are you sure Logan was cheating on you?"

"Shouldn't I be talking with my lawyer about these things?" Dana asked. Then understanding abruptly dawned on her face. "You're going to try to find out who killed Logan! Carolyn's told me about how . . . how you've solved all those murders."

"I've gotten lucky a few times." Phyllis smiled encouragingly. "But who's to say I won't get lucky again?"

A hollow laugh came from Dana. "That's what Logan and I argued about . . . his habit of getting lucky, although in a totally different way from what you mean, Phyllis. Was I sure he was cheating on me? I never actually caught him in bed with another woman, if that's what you mean. I don't have motel receipts or anything like that. But I know. A wife knows. He . . . he spent so much time away from home, so many late nights when he didn't come in until after midnight. Some nights he never came home at all. He blamed it on his business and said that sometimes he slept at the office, and I wanted to believe him, but after so long a time . . . I just couldn't anymore."

Phyllis could understand why eventually Dana would get suspicious about her husband's behavior. She wasn't sure she agreed, though, about a wife being able to just tell if her husband was cheating. She had learned that the depths of human deception were sometimes limitless . . . and that people generally believed what was easiest and most convenient—and least painful—for them to believe.

"I wish there was some way not to hurt you like this," Phyllis went on, "but do you have any idea who Logan was seeing, if he was?"

Dana shook her head. "No, I don't. There are a lot of women who work in real estate, though. Or I suppose it could have been someone in some other business who came in contact with him. There may have been more than one of them, for all I know."

"Don't get caught up in wild imaginings," Phyllis advised.

"There's nothing wild about it," Dana insisted. "Logan spent enough time away from home that he could have had three or four women on the string!"

Phyllis considered that unlikely, but she really didn't know. Maybe Dana was right about Logan. Maybe he was a compulsive womanizer who had cut a broad swath through Weatherford. In that case, there might be several potential suspects out there, including the women he'd slept with and any jealous husbands or boyfriends who found out about it.

The police should be looking into this, she thought. It was their job to get to the truth. But they weren't going to do that as long as they thought they could convict Dana, which left it up to other people, like Dana's lawyer . . . and her friends.

Dana's face was pale and drawn, and she was starting to get a wild, hunted look in her eyes. Maybe it would be better to back off for the moment, Phyllis decided. After all, as Juliette Yorke had pointed out, they had time. Nothing else was going to happen until after Thanksgiving.

Anyway, it was almost lunchtime, so any more questions could be postponed until later. In fact, Eve came into the living room just a few moments later and announced that the food was ready.

"I don't think I can eat," Dana said with a shake of her head.

"Of course you can, dear," Eve insisted. "Why, you don't have enough meat on your bones to be able to afford to miss too many meals."

That was the sort of blunt comment Carolyn usually made, but instead of taking offense at it, Dana actually smiled. "No, I guess I don't," she said. "You wouldn't know it to look at me, but I've always been able to eat everything I wanted and never gain a pound."

"I'd hate you for that, dear, but I'm too busy admir-

ing you." Eve smiled. "Come on. Carolyn has made
some excellent sandwiches."

To Carolyn, making a sandwich had never meant just
slapping together meat, cheese, and bread with some
mayonnaise or mustard. Each sandwich was a minor
production for her and included an assortment of lettuce, tomatoes, avocado slices, cream cheese, and exotic
dressings. A sandwich made by Carolyn was a full-
course meal in itself, occasionally worthy of Dagwood
Bumstead, Phyllis thought.

The Caesar sandwiches they had for lunch this day
were no exception, made with leftover pork roast and
served on croissants. Phyllis was glad to see that Dana's
appetite returned when she sampled Carolyn's effort.
Nothing would help Dana get over her loss quicker and
better than good food and plenty of rest. Phyllis intended to see to it that Dana got plenty of both of those
things.

The talk over lunch was about Thanksgiving. Dana
had helped in the planning of the food drive that culmi-
nated in the Harvest Festival, so naturally she was still
interested in it despite what had happened.

"Do you think it would be all right if I helped distribute the food on Thanksgiving morning, the way I was
supposed to?" she asked.

"I don't know," Phyllis said. "We can ask Ms. Yorke
what she thinks, though."

"I'd like to, if she says it's all right."

"We're going to have a houseful of guests for Thanksgiving, you know," Carolyn said. "Dolly Williamson is
coming, and she'll be bringing some of the other teachers who don't have anyplace else to go."

Dana smiled and said, "That'll be wonderful," but
Phyllis thought she looked a little intimidated by the
idea of having so many people around.

After lunch, when they went back into the living
room, Dana tugged at the wrinkled blouse she wore.
"I'd really love to get out of these clothes and take a
shower, then maybe lie down for a while, but I don't
have anything else to wear."

"Carolyn and I will go get what you need," Phyllis said, "but there's no reason for you to wait for us to get back. I have a nice comfortable robe I think you can wear. It'll be a little big on you, but not too bad, maybe."

"That's really kind of you. I appreciate it."

"Come on. I'll show you your room."

She took Dana upstairs, pointed out the other bedrooms and the bathroom, and took her to the room she'd be using. Leaving her there, Phyllis fetched the bathrobe and returned with it.

"We won't disturb your nap when we get back. Just let us know when you're awake again, and we'll bring everything upstairs."

"I doubt if I'll be able to doze off," Dana said. She muffled a yawn. "I haven't slept much at all the past two nights."

She left unsaid the fact that she had spent those nights in jail, which Phyllis imagined would make it difficult for anyone to sleep. She just said, "Well, try to rest some, anyway. You may find out that a nice, long, hot shower will make you feel relaxed enough to doze off."

"I hope so."

Phyllis went back downstairs and collected Carolyn, who'd been more than willing to come along and help her gather some of Dana's clothes and other belongings. Phyllis thought that between the two of them, they could pick out enough so that Dana would be comfortable for a while.

"I don't actually know where Dana lives," Phyllis said as they left the house in her car. "You'll have to tell me how to get there."

"I've been there several times. It won't be a problem," Carolyn said.

She directed Phyllis to one of the relatively new, upscale housing developments in the southeastern part of town, on the other side of the interstate. As Phyllis drove across an overpass spanning the highway, she glanced along the divided lanes to the west and said, "I may want to make one other stop before we go back home."

"That's fine with me," Carolyn said. "I'm in no hurry, and if Dana lies down like she said she was going to, she won't be, either. The poor thing looked exhausted. If she ever goes to sleep, she may not wake up for a while."

Phyllis thought the same thing. The rest would do Dana good.

It took them about fifteen minutes to reach the street where Dana lived, and where Logan had lived until he was murdered. Phyllis didn't need any reminders of that, but she got one anyway as she turned onto the street Carolyn pointed out and immediately spotted flashing lights a couple of blocks ahead of them. As they drew closer, she saw two police cars parked in front of a house, with an unmarked car that was probably a police vehicle parked between them.

"Is that . . . ?" she began.

"Dana's house," Carolyn said in a grim voice. "Yes. It most certainly is."

Chapter 29

For a second, Phyllis thought about turning around and driving back to her house. But she had promised Dana that they would fetch her things, and Phyllis didn't like to go back on her word.

Besides, she wanted to find out what was happening. Now that she thought about it, she had a pretty good idea, but she wanted to be sure.

"What are we doing?" Carolyn asked as Phyllis pulled up behind the rear police car with its flashing lights. At other houses up and down the street, people stood on their lawns watching. If it hadn't been the middle of the day on a workday, the curious crowd would have been even bigger.

"What we told Dana we'd do," Phyllis said. "We're going to get her some clean clothes and anything else she might need while she's staying with us."

"Assuming that the police will let us in."

"They'll let us in, or I'll call Ms. Yorke. Dana is out on bail, and they shouldn't interfere with her leading a normal life until the grand jury convenes."

Phyllis had already noticed a uniformed officer standing on the front porch of the impressive brick home. As she and Carolyn got out of the car and started up the walk, the cop moved to meet them.

"I'm sorry, ladies," he said. "I don't know who you're looking for, but there's no one here."

"You're here," Phyllis said in a challenging tone, "and I'd be willing to bet that Detective Isabel Largo is, too."

The look of surprise in the officer's eyes told Phyllis that her guess was a good one.

"I assume that Detective Largo has a search warrant," Phyllis went on.

"You'd have to talk to her about that, ma'am. My job is just to keep civilians out of that house."

"Can you tell her that Phyllis Newsom is here?"

The officer looked surprised again. "You're her? The lady who catches killers?"

That wasn't a reputation that Phyllis had ever wanted, and most of the time it made her decidedly uncomfortable. There were times, though, she supposed, when it came in handy.

"That's right."

The officer reached for the walkie-talkie on his belt. "I'll call Detective Largo—"

"That won't be necessary, Officer," Isabel Largo said from the porch, where she had emerged from the house. She came down the walk, wearing a long coat against the coolness in the air, and gave Phyllis and Carolyn a curt nod. "Ladies. What are you doing here?"

"I imagine you heard that Dana Powell is staying at my house while she's out on bail," Phyllis said.

Largo nodded again. "I heard. Generous of you, opening your home to a killer."

Phyllis didn't rise to that bait. She said, "Mrs. Wilbarger and I came to get some clean clothes and personal items for Mrs. Powell."

"That's certainly reasonable, I suppose," Largo said with a shrug. "Come on inside. You realize, though, that I can't allow you to walk around unsupervised. The house is still being searched for evidence. I'll have to make an inventory of everything that you take with you, too."

"I'm surprised that you haven't searched the house before now," Phyllis commented as the three of them started inside.

"We have. We made a general search Saturday afternoon, after Mr. Powell's body was discovered, as well as impounding both of their vehicles that were left at the park and searching them. But at that time we didn't know the cause of death. It took until today to get another warrant signed for a more specific search." Largo paused on the porch and frowned at Phyllis. "None of which is any of your business. How do you get people to talk to you without them even realizing what they're doing? Is it because you look like everyone's kindly aunt or grandmother?"

"I just ask questions," Phyllis said. "I'm not big enough or strong enough to make anyone answer them unless they want to."

Largo grunted and shook her head. "Come on. I don't have a lot of time. Don't touch anything except the specific items you're after, and you'd better ask me about them first."

Phyllis thought that Detective Largo was being a little heavy-handed, but she didn't say anything. She followed the detective's order not to touch anything as they went into Dana's living room.

But Largo hadn't said anything about not looking around.

Phyllis's gaze roved quickly over the room. It was comfortably, even expensively, furnished, with thick carpet on the floor, heavy furniture, and some beautiful antiques to go along with an ultramodern plasma TV and media center. Phyllis's eyes paused briefly on a crystal bowl that sat on a coffee table. The bowl had individually wrapped peppermints in it, but it was less than half full, as if someone had scooped some of its contents out. Phyllis suspected that was exactly what had happened. Detective Largo had probably taken some of the peppermints to have them tested.

Another bowl of the candies rested on an antique breakfront, and as Phyllis looked through a door into the dining room, she spotted yet another bowl of peppermints on an antique china cabinet. Largo had probably taken samples from each of them.

Logan had believed in keeping the peppermints

within easy reach at all times, Phyllis mused. Of course, with his blood sugar the way it was, he had no way of knowing when he might need several of them in a hurry, to keep from slipping into the sort of distress that had caused his heart to fail. When Detective Largo led them upstairs to Dana's bedroom, Phyllis wasn't surprised to see bowls of peppermints on the nightstands on both sides of the bed. More of the individually wrapped candies were scattered on the vanity in the bathroom, she noted as she began gathering up personal items Dana might need, while Carolyn took clothes from the closet and the drawers in a lovely antique dresser and chest.

Detective Largo stood in the open doorway between the master bedroom and bath, keeping an eye on Phyllis and Carolyn at the same time and jotting down in a notebook a list of everything they picked up. Phyllis gestured toward the peppermints on the vanity and asked, "Is it all right if I take some of these for Mrs. Powell? She must like them, too, the way they're all over the house."

Largo shook her head. "All the peppermints stay where they are, except the ones we've already collected as evidence. If they're sugar free, they might be considered potential murder weapons."

"You're joking," Phyllis said.

"I never joke about evidence."

Or probably about much of anything else, Phyllis thought. Surely Detective Largo wasn't dour and humorless *all* the time, but she took her job seriously; that was for sure.

She checked all the things Phyllis and Carolyn gathered for Dana, then nodded her head in approval as they were packed away in a couple of suitcases Carolyn found in a closet. "You shouldn't need to come back over here," Largo said, "but if you do, be sure to check with me first."

"Mrs. Powell was released on bail," Phyllis reminded the detective again. "She could have come back here to stay. Would you have tried to keep her out of her own house?"

"That would be different. Since she's *not* here, I'd like to preserve the scene in its current condition as much as possible."

"It's not a 'scene,'" Carolyn said. "It's someone's home."

"It was home to two people," Largo shot back, "until one of them was murdered."

She left unsaid the part about the other one being the killer, but Phyllis could hear it in Largo's voice anyway.

The detective escorted them back downstairs and through the living room. As they went out, Phyllis looked once more at the mantel over the fireplace. Several large, framed photographs of Dana and Logan sat there, all of the two of them together, including a wedding picture. It made a pang go through Phyllis's chest. Their marriage, like so many others, had started out full of hope and love, and over the years it had turned into something else. Phyllis thanked God every day that she and Kenny hadn't ended up like that. They had loved each other just as much at the end as they had at the beginning, which in this world made them very, very lucky.

"Good-bye, ladies," Detective Largo said as Phyllis and Carolyn started down the walk. She didn't sound sad to see them go.

They put the suitcases in the trunk of Phyllis's car and drove away. "That woman is positively infuriating," Carolyn said, and Phyllis had no doubt that she was referring to Isabel Largo.

"She probably feels the same way about us. The way she sees it, she's just doing her job."

"You're so fair-minded, I figured you'd defend her," Carolyn said. "I can't, though. I think she and all the rest of the authorities are trying to railroad Dana. They don't care if she's guilty or not. All that matters to them is whether they think they can get a conviction."

"I'd hate to think that was true," Phyllis said, but as a matter of fact, the same thought had crossed her mind earlier as they were driving over here.

"You think that just because Mike is honest and de-

voted to his job, all of the authorities are. But it's not
true, Phyllis. I hate to think about how many innocent
people have been convicted because of the sheer, blind
stubbornness of the police and prosecutors."

Phyllis had heard people argue the exact opposite,
that no one would be arrested in the first place if there
wasn't a good reason to think they were guilty. As in
most things, the truth probably lay somewhere in between, she thought.

In this case, though, she believed that Carolyn was
right. Dana was innocent, but the police weren't going
to try to prove that. With that thought in her mind, Phyllis turned left when they reached the interstate. As she
accelerated out onto the highway, Carolyn asked,
"Where are we going?"

"Remember I said I needed to make another stop on
the way home?"

"Oh, yes, of course. Where?"

"That's just it. I don't know exactly where I'm going."

Carolyn frowned. "What does that mean?" They
were speeding past the area where shopping centers
had sprouted on both sides of the highway in recent
years. "There's not much else out in this direction."

"I know. But that doesn't mean there couldn't be."

That statement appeared to puzzle Carolyn even
more. But she just sat back and muttered, "All right, I
suppose you'll explain when you're good and ready."

They passed what Phyllis still thought of as the new
high school, even though it had been there for a number
of years. As they continued west, open fields began to
line the highway on both sides.

She asked Carolyn, "Can you watch on your side for
official signs posted out in the fields?"

"Official signs?" Carolyn repeated. "What's going on
here, Phyllis?"

"One of Logan's real estate deals had to do with the
building of a big mall somewhere out here," Phyllis explained. "I'd like to find the spot."

"Why?"

"I just want to have a look at it, that's all." Phyllis

couldn't explain why she felt that way, but she thought some instinct was telling her that it might be important.

She spotted what she thought looked like official signs on a long stretch of undeveloped property on the south side of the highway. Taking the next exit, she turned left under the highway and started back up the frontage road the other way.

"This could be it," she said.

There was no traffic on the frontage road at the moment, so she was able to stop when she drew even with the first of the signs. In big letters, it announced ZONING CHANGE APPLIED FOR. Under that in smaller print was a phone number that could be called for more information.

Phyllis drove slowly and saw several more of the signs. The property stretched for at least a mile. That was too big even for a mall, but Phyllis recalled Ben Loomis saying that some of the property around the actual mall site was going to be developed, too. In fact, they came to a sign that read PAD SITES AVAILABLE. WILL BUILD TO SUIT. LOOMIS REALTY. There was a phone number on that sign, too.

Carolyn stared at it for a moment, then said, "You think Logan was killed because of this mall development business."

"I think there's a lot of money tied up in this," Phyllis said. "People sometimes do things they might not otherwise do when there are fortunes to be made or lost."

"I suppose you're right about that. What are you going to do?"

Phyllis took a little notebook out of her purse and wrote down the number of Loomis Realty, as well as the phone number that was on the signs announcing the potential zoning change and several other numbers that might be important.

"I'll do the only thing I can," she said. "Keep asking questions."

Chapter 30

The questions would have to wait, though, until after they got back to the house with the things they had picked up for Dana. When they reached the house and carried the bags in, Eve reported that Dana hadn't come down from her shower and nap.

"The poor dear must have been exhausted," she said.

Phyllis nodded. She was glad that Dana was getting some rest, but at the same time, a worry nagged at her. The strain of everything that had happened had taken a terrible toll on Dana. She had been depressed, stressed out, driven to distraction, and stricken by grief over Logan's death, despite her suspicions of him. She probably felt some guilt, as well, because her last conversation with him had been an angry one, the argument on the bridge at the park. People under that much pressure had been known to take desperate measures and end their own lives, just to make the pain stop. Phyllis didn't want that happening.

"If she doesn't come down in a little while, I think I'll go up and check on her," she said.

"You're worried about her mental state, too?" Carolyn asked.

"That's right."

"Let me do it. I don't mind disturbing her to make sure she's all right."

"Let's give it a little while longer," Phyllis suggested. "I don't want Dana to think that we don't trust her."

"Well . . . all right. But I'm going to worry about her."

"So am I," Phyllis said.

As it turned out, though, they didn't have to worry for very long, because Dana came downstairs about twenty minutes later, barefoot but wrapped up in the thick robe Phyllis had loaned her. Her hair was a little tousled from being damp when she lay down for her nap, but her color was better and she looked more rested. Phyllis was glad to see that.

"The shower helped, didn't it?" she asked.

"Yes, it did," Dana said. She ran her hand over the fleece robe. "So did this. It's so warm and comfortable, I couldn't help but go to sleep. Thank you, Phyllis."

"We're just trying to help." Phyllis paused. "Unfortunately, that means I need to ask you some more questions."

Dana's smile slipped a little. "Of course. Just give me those suitcases. I'll go upstairs and get dressed and be back down in a few minutes."

Sam had come out of the kitchen, trailed by Bobby. He reached for the suitcases and said, "Let me get those for you. Men are beasts of burden by nature, I reckon."

He carried the suitcases upstairs with Dana following him. Phyllis turned to Bobby and asked, "Are you and Sam still working on the bookshelves?"

"Yeah. He says we'll have 'em ready in a few more days."

"I'm sure you will."

"Can I stay here when Mama and Daddy come back from Cal'fornia?"

The question took Phyllis by surprise. "Don't you want to go home and sleep in your own bed and be with your parents again?"

"No, I like it better here."

Eve laughed. "You're doing your job, Phyllis. You've thoroughly spoiled him."

Phyllis didn't think she had been *that* lax with Bobby. But maybe she had. She said to him, "You know you don't really want to stay here. You'd miss your parents too much. And you'll enjoy being back in your own room and having all your own things around you again."

Bobby thought it over and then shrugged. "Yeah, I guess so. But it sure has been fun stayin' here."

Phyllis smiled at him. "It's been fun having you here, too."

"Can I have a snack?"

"Maybe a little one."

Bobby hustled off to the kitchen. Phyllis would have followed him, but Sam came back down the stairs just then.

"Miz Powell was glad to have some of her stuff back," he reported. "She said to thank the two of you again."

"She may not be so grateful when she hears what we found going on at her house," Carolyn said.

Sam frowned, but Carolyn didn't offer any explanations and neither did Phyllis. They would go over the whole thing when Dana came back downstairs.

She did so about ten minutes later, dressed in a pair of brown slacks and a cream-colored blouse. Her hair was brushed and she had put on a little makeup. She looked better than Phyllis had seen her since before all this began.

Dana went into the living room with Phyllis and Carolyn, and as they all sat down, she said, "All right. Ask me anything you want to. I'll tell you the truth, Phyllis. Clearing my name is the only way to put all this behind me."

Phyllis began, "Well, before I ask you anything, I should tell you that someone was at your house when Carolyn and I got there. Detective Largo and some other officers were carrying out another search."

"What?" Dana's eyes widened and then began to blaze with anger. "She had no right to do that!"

"She said she had a search warrant. I'm sure Ms. Yorke could get a copy of it if you'd like."

"What were they after?"

"Well, I don't know, specifically, but I have a feeling they took some of the candy from the bowls scattered around the house."

"Because they think that's how I killed Logan," Dana said. "By switching his regular peppermints for sugar-free ones. It's crazy! Who would even think about murdering a person like that?"

"Someone did," Phyllis pointed out. "The medical examiner was certain that Logan's low blood sugar brought on his heart attack. Did you know about all his medical problems, Dana?"

"Of course I did," she replied with a shrug. "I'm his wife." She drew in a deep breath. "I *was* his wife."

"Did anyone else know? Every time I saw Logan, he looked and acted like he was as healthy as a horse."

"That's what he wanted everyone to think. It was all part of his image. You couldn't really call it macho. But he liked for people to think he was a hard-driving businessman. He said that gave clients more confidence in him. And he tried to live the life, too, working long hours, skipping meals. . . . That was why he had to have the peppermints to keep him going."

"So if you knew all that, you would have known that switching them out for sugar-free ones might hurt his health," Phyllis pointed out.

"I suppose so. I never really thought about it, though, because I didn't want to hurt him." Dana swallowed hard. "Even when I began to suspect he was cheating on me, I didn't want to hurt him. I just wanted him to stop. I . . . I would have forgiven him. I would have gone on."

Phyllis didn't doubt that. In nearly every relationship, there were moments when a person had to just forgive something and go on, in order to save what they had.

Seeing the shine of tears in Dana's eyes, Phyllis waited a moment for her to compose herself. Then she said gently, "So you're sure no one else knew about Logan's medical condition?"

"You mean other than his doctor, and a few people who work in the doctor's office?" Dana shook her head. "I wouldn't think so. Logan wouldn't have told anyone. I'm certain of that."

"He must have," Carolyn blurted out. "Otherwise how did the real killer know what to do?"

Phyllis had already thought of the same thing. Dana's answers were just pointing even more suspicion right at her.

"I don't know what to tell you," Dana said miserably. "It's the truth."

There was another answer somewhere, Phyllis thought, another way of looking at things so that they made sense. It was just that she couldn't see it yet.

She switched tacks by saying, "What about Logan's business? Did he confide in you about it?"

"Oh, to a certain extent. I didn't know all the details about every deal he was working on, of course. I mean, I have my own job, and that takes up a lot of time." Dana wiped at a tear that had trickled out of her right eye. "I hope I can get back to my class soon. I . . . I miss the kids. I want to know how they're doing. We have benchmark tests coming up, and I need to be there to help them."

Phyllis and Carolyn both nodded in understanding. As stressful as the job of teaching could be, as maddening as the students sometimes were, the good teachers always felt a bond with them. If not, what was the point of getting into that line of work to start with?

"Maybe you will be," Phyllis said. "Maybe some new information will come to light."

Dana shook her head. "I don't know what it would be."

"What about something connected with that new mall on the west side of town?"

"You know about that?"

"Why wouldn't we?" Phyllis countered.

"Well, Logan was trying to keep it as quiet as he could until everything was set. He swore me to secrecy every time he mentioned it. He was afraid that someone would—I don't know—horn in on it."

Like Ben Loomis, Phyllis thought.

"And he was afraid it would all fall through because of the zoning problem," Dana continued.

"What zoning problem?"

"The property isn't zoned for a mall. The zoning will have to be changed, and not all the members of the Planning and Zoning Commission are in favor of it." Dana gave a hollow laugh. "Logan said it was going to be an expensive proposition to change their minds, but that it would be worth it in the long run."

Phyllis leaned back in the chair where she was sitting. "You mean that he hinted he was going to *bribe* them?"

"I shouldn't have said that," Dana replied quickly. "I don't know that's what he meant. But I'd heard him say things before . . . about other projects . . . about greasing the wheels of the process, and I just assumed that was what he meant."

Phyllis thought that was very likely, and if it was true, then it opened up the proverbial new can of worms. If Logan had been involved in crooked land deals in the past, and was mixed up in a gigantic one now, then surely a motive for murder could be buried in that morass of corruption.

"You have to tell Juliette Yorke all about this," Phyllis said. "This could establish reasonable doubt by itself."

"And ruin Logan's reputation as an honest businessman," Dana said. She shook her head. "No. I shouldn't have even said anything to you. It's bad enough that he's dead, and, yes, I was angry with him before he died, but I love him, and I won't see his name dragged through the mud."

Carolyn said, "It's too late for that, Dana. It's your life at stake, and that's worth more than Logan's reputation."

"That's my choice to make; no one else's." Phyllis heard the rock-hard stubbornness in Dana's voice.

"There's no point in arguing about this now," she said. "Anyway, it's just a starting point. We still don't know how anyone involved in the mall deal could have known about Logan's illness, if he was as secretive about it as you say."

"He was," Dana insisted.

"We'll mull it all over until after Thanksgiving. Then we'll sit down with Juliette and have a long talk about strategy."

"You mean I will," Dana said. "I don't want to seem ungrateful after everything you and Carolyn have done for me, Phyllis, but these are my decisions to make, not yours."

Phyllis opened her mouth to argue, then realized that Dana was right. Helping out was one thing; meddling was something else entirely.

"All right," she said. "To change the subject, do you have any special traditional dishes you like to make for Thanksgiving? We'd be perfectly happy to let you have some time in the kitchen as we're getting ready for Thursday, wouldn't we, Carolyn?"

"Of course," Carolyn said.

Dana smiled and shook her head. "I'm afraid that I'm not much of a cook. Most years when Logan and I weren't going out of town to relatives for the holiday, I'd buy one of those prepared Thanksgiving dinners from one of the grocery stores and pick it up the day before. That was better than what either of us could make."

Phyllis thought that was a shame, but she reminded herself that not everyone enjoyed cooking as much as she did. She said, "That's fine. We'll be fixing plenty of food, and Dolly and the guests who come with her will be bringing covered dishes, too. One thing I can promise you: No one around here will go hungry on Thanksgiving!"

Chapter 31

🧁

*N*othing else was said about Logan's death or the case against Dana that day. In the evening, Phyllis and Carolyn drove out to the elementary school, where the meeting was being held to discuss the delivery of the canned goods and Thanksgiving dinners on Thursday morning.

Jenna Grantham walked up to them right after they came into the school cafeteria and greeted them with a smile. "Thanks so much for inviting me to spend Thanksgiving at your house, Mrs. Newsom," she said. "It'll be almost like going home for the holiday."

This was the first that Phyllis had heard of her coming for Thanksgiving, but she quickly made the assumption that Jenna was one of the guests Dolly Williamson had rounded up. She smiled and said, "I take it Dolly talked to you?"

"That's right. It's really a generous gesture on your part to have us over for dinner."

Taryn Marshall and Kendra Neville saw them talking and came over as well, and Phyllis wasn't surprised when both of them expressed their gratitude as well.

"We would have been alone on Thanksgiving if not for you," Taryn said.

"And that would have been really depressing," Kendra added.

"We'll be glad to have you," Phyllis assured them. "Do you know who else is coming besides Dolly?"

"No, but there she is," Jenna replied, nodding across the room. "You can ask her."

Phyllis nodded and started to turn away, but Kendra stopped her by asking, "Is it true that Dana is staying with you? We heard some talk about that after school today."

"Yes, it's true," Phyllis confirmed.

"How's she doing?" Jenna wanted to know. "I'm really looking forward to seeing her again on Thursday."

"So am I," Taryn said.

Phyllis said, "She's doing as well as can be expected, I suppose." She didn't want to go into detail about the discussions she'd had with Dana. "I'm sure she'll be glad to see the three of you, too."

Phyllis started across the room toward Dolly Williamson, but before she could reach the former school superintendent, Barbara Loomis intercepted her. A stocky, red-haired man with a broad, friendly face was with her.

"Mrs. Newsom, it's good to see you again," Barbara said. "This is my husband, Ben."

Phyllis shook hands with Ben Loomis, who grinned and said, "Yeah, sure, I remember you. We talked on the phone the other day. Nice to meet you, Mrs. Newsom. Still thinking about investing in some real estate?"

Barbara slapped him lightly on the shoulder. "This is a volunteer meeting, Ben!" she scolded him with a smile. "No talking business."

"Okay, okay," he said as he held up his hands in surrender. "But you gimme a call if you're interested, Mrs. Newsom, okay?"

"Of course," Phyllis said, then added, "I'm pretty cautious by nature, though. I might want to wait until all the zoning problems have been ironed out."

She caught the glint of surprise in Ben Loomis's eyes. He had to be wondering where she had heard about those potential problems. But he controlled the reaction almost instantly and said, "Oh, that's nothing to worry about. It'll all get straightened out."

So he knew about the problems, too. Had he known that Logan planned to make them go away with bribes? Had he maybe even been involved in the whole situation, which was rife with the potential for double-crosses, blackmail, and all sorts of other graft and corruption? It was a web of chicanery built for murder, as far as Phyllis was concerned.

She didn't get to talk to Dolly before the meeting was called to order. Dolly, in fact, was chairing it, which came as no surprise to Phyllis. With the efficiency and take-charge attitude she had learned over decades of running a school district, Dolly had the volunteers assigned to their respective tasks and clear on what they were supposed to do in less than an hour. The canned goods collected at the festival were being stored in the fellowship hall of one of the local churches. Everyone would show up there bright and early on Thanksgiving Day, pick up the boxes they were supposed to deliver, and set out with the list of addresses they were given at the meeting tonight.

Afterward, Phyllis finally managed to talk to Dolly, who, with her tightly curled iron gray hair and weathered face, looked her age but didn't act it.

"I have eight people lined up for Thursday, Phyllis," Dolly said, "not counting myself. Everyone else I talked to already had plans."

"That's fine," Phyllis assured her. "With everyone bringing something, we should have plenty of food."

"Well, a couple of the ones I invited are men, so I'm sure they'll have to *buy* something to bring," Dolly said with a note of scorn in her voice. She came from a generation where men did little if any of the cooking, so she didn't have a very high opinion of their culinary skills, even the younger ones.

"That's fine," Phyllis said.

Dolly lowered her voice from its usual booming tone. "How's poor Dana doing?"

"As well as can be expected, I suppose. She wants to help out on Thursday, but she didn't think it would be a good idea to come to this meeting tonight. Not so soon after . . . well, she was just released from custody this morning, after all."

Dolly nodded. "She can help you and Carolyn, if she'd like."

Something else occurred to Phyllis. "Dolly, I know this hadn't even come up when we started making plans for Thanksgiving, but do the people who are coming know that Dana will be there?"

"Why should that matter?" Dolly asked with a frown.

"Well, she *has* been accused of murder. I don't want anyone to be uncomfortable. I'm not worried about Jenna and Kendra and Taryn—they're all Dana's friends and think she's innocent—but I don't know about some of the others."

"I'll speak to them," Dolly said, and her tone made it clear that anyone who didn't want to come to Phyllis's house simply because Dana was going to be there would face her wrath.

"I don't want to cause a problem for anyone. . . ."

Dolly patted her on the arm. "You let me worry about that. Solving problems is my business."

Phyllis didn't doubt for a second that Dolly would take care of it.

With the meeting over, the gathering had begun to break up. Some people had left already, and others were walking past the office and out the front door of the school. Carolyn was still talking to several of her old friends, though, so Phyllis stepped around a corner and down a hall to the faculty restrooms.

As she approached them, she saw Ben Loomis standing in the hall, probably waiting for Barbara. He hadn't noticed her yet, and Phyllis was struck by how angry he looked. But then he saw her coming and that ready grin reappeared on his face.

"I meant what I said about giving me a call," he said as she went past him.

"I'll do that," Phyllis said, even though she knew she probably never would. She wondered what Loomis was upset about. He hadn't gotten that grin in place in time to keep her from seeing how furious he was.

When she stepped into the restroom, she found Barbara standing in front of the sinks, dabbing at her eyes with a tissue. Barbara said, "Oh," and stuffed the tissue back in her purse. She summoned up a smile.

"I saw Ben waiting for you outside," Phyllis said.

"Did he . . . say anything?"

"Not really."

Relief appeared in Barbara's eyes. She forced a laugh. "I thought he might have told you that we were fighting and that I'd run off in here to cry."

"He didn't say a word about it," Phyllis assured her, "and it's none of my business."

"But there's no use denying it. I mean, you came in and found me crying, right?"

"All married couples argue. Kenny and I had some doozies." That was true. It didn't mean they loved each other any less, but they had still disagreed passionately on some subjects.

"I suppose."

"Would you like to talk about it?"

"No, but thank you. I need to get going." Barbara paused as she started to leave the restroom, though. "Is Dana eating well? It's very important that she take care of her health, you know."

"She ate a good lunch and supper both," Phyllis said. "In fact, she surprised me a little with her appetite."

"Well, she knows what she has to do. But I'm glad she's not alone. Someone in her condition doesn't need to be alone."

Phyllis wondered what Barbara meant by that, and she would have asked if Ben hadn't chosen that moment to call from outside, "Barbara? You all right in there?"

"Oh, good grief," Barbara muttered. She raised her voice. "I'm fine. Hang on." Then she said to Phyllis, "I've got to go," and hurried out before Phyllis could ask her anything else.

"Well," Phyllis said into the silence that filled the restroom, "that was odd."

When she came out into the hall a few minutes later,

206 • LIVIA J. WASHBURN

Barbara and Ben Loomis were gone. Carolyn was there, though. "I thought you might have stepped into the restroom," she said. "Are you ready to go?"

"Yes, I suppose." As they left the building and started through the parking lot, Phyllis went on, "How well do you know the Loomises?"

"Barbara and Ben? I know her fairly well. She started teaching here two or three years before I retired. I'm not sure I've ever seen Ben except on social occasions with Barbara. Why do you ask?"

"I was just wondering if there was any trouble between them." Quickly, Phyllis told her friend about what she had seen outside and inside the restroom, and what Barbara had said.

For a moment, Carolyn didn't say anything, but when they were both in the car, she said, "This is veering dangously close to gossip—and you know how I feel about gossip."

Phyllis nodded.

"But there was a rumor that Barbara wasn't necessarily a hundred percent faithful to Ben," Carolyn went on. "I don't know the truth of it myself, and I hate to repeat such things, but that's what I heard."

"I wonder . . . ," Phyllis said.

"Wonder what?" Carolyn asked. Then she suddenly looked shocked. "Barbara and Logan? No! Not possible. Barbara and Dana are friends."

"People have had affairs with the spouses of their friends before now," Phyllis pointed out.

"Yes, I suppose so, but I just . . . Well, that would be a terrible thing to do!"

"You'll get no argument from me about that," Phyllis said, "but think about it. Since they both taught at the same school, Barbara would know Dana's schedule. She would know when Dana was going to be busy, so that she and Logan could grab a few minutes together."

"That's true," Carolyn admitted grudgingly. "But an affair with Logan is an awful lot to infer from the fact that Ben looked angry and Barbara was crying."

"You're right," Phyllis said. "Whatever was going on

between them tonight, it probably has nothing to do with what happened to Logan."

"I should hope not. If you're going to suspect Barbara of cheating with Logan because she knew Dana's schedule, you might as well suspect every teacher in the school!"

"That's right," Phyllis said. "I might as well."

"And remember, he was in bad health. Good grief, just how much stamina do you think he had?"

"Not enough, obviously." Carolyn's comment about Logan's bad health had dashed the thoughts that were starting to play around in Phyllis's mind. Dana had insisted that Logan kept his medical condition a secret, and it didn't make sense that he would have told a mistress about it. That would have ruined his image as a dashing, rakish businessman, something that clearly he had carefully cultivated. As far as Phyllis could see, Dana was still the only suspect who had the right combination of motive, opportunity, and the knowledge required to make this particular murder method work.

But that didn't mean she was going to give up trying to get to the bottom of this mystery. In fact, she already had an idea about where to start the next morning.

__ __ ____ __ __ __ __ _ ___ __ _ __ __ ___ exchange.

Chapter 32

After cleaning up the breakfast dishes, Phyllis fetched the little notebook from her purse and opened it to the page where she had written down the phone number from the sign on the property where the new mall was to be located. It rang a couple of times; then a woman's voice answered and said, "Planning and Zoning Commission."

"Yes, I have some questions about a proposed zoning change on some property."

"What parcel and lot numbers?"

Phyllis consulted the notes she had made the day before and read off what she hoped were the right numbers. She heard the faint sound of computer keys clicking, followed by a moment of silence. Then the woman who'd answered the phone said, "The vote on that change is scheduled for next week."

"What else can you tell me about it?" Phyllis asked.

"Nothing, really. It's a fairly standard request for a zoning change upgrading the property from standard commercial to a higher level."

"Who filed the request?"

"That would be—let me see—NorCenTex Development."

Phyllis was about to ask something else when a man's voice suddenly said, "Who is this? Can I help you?" Obviously he had taken the phone away from the woman Phyllis had been talking to, and she didn't think it was coincidental that it had happened right after the woman mentioned NorCenTex Development.

"I was just asking about a proposed zoning change."

"Those are matters of public record."

"Yes, I know. That's why I was asking."

"We can't really help you unless you file an open-records request with the state."

"Why would I want to do that?" Phyllis asked.

"You're not a journalist?"

"No, I'm just a concerned citizen."

"You'll still have to file an open-records request. Sorry."

The man didn't sound sorry at all, though. And the sharp click the phone made in Phyllis's ear as he hung up didn't sound too apologetic, either. She frowned at the phone in consternation and said, "Well."

It certainly seemed that something shady might be going on with that zoning change. Why else would the man have been so defensive?

Juliette Yorke was certainly going to have some ammunition to work with once she started putting together Dana's defense after the holiday, Phyllis thought as she replaced the phone on its base.

With that call out of the way, Phyllis turned her attention to the preparations for Thanksgiving Day. She and Carolyn had most of the ingredients on hand for the dishes they were going to prepare, but Phyllis still needed to pick up a few things, and there was one major item still missing: a second turkey. With this being Tuesday, the pickings at the store might already be getting slim, she thought. She couldn't afford to wait any longer. It was already too late to defrost one, so she would have to get a turkey that was just refrigerated, not frozen.

As usual, Sam was happy to watch Bobby, and Bobby was happy to hang around with his new best friend, Sam. Eve had gone somewhere—lately Eve had been gone more than usual, Phyllis thought—but Carolyn was willing to venture out to Wal-Mart with Phyllis.

Dana didn't want to join them, but she told Phyllis and Carolyn to go on and not worry about her. "I don't think I could face a lot of people right now," she said.

"I don't blame you," Carolyn told her. "Shopping at this time of year can be a little overwhelming."

When they got there, the parking lot was even more crowded than usual. "You can tell that it's a holiday in a couple of days," Carolyn commented. "People are getting ready for it."

"We'll just have to brave the mob," Phyllis said.

They went inside the store, and sure enough, there was something of a mob waiting for them. The aisles were crowded. Phyllis maneuvered her buggy carefully around the other shoppers. She paused as she passed the aisle where the candy was located and was about to go down it when Carolyn said, "I think we should get some more pumpkin pie filling."

"You're right," Phyllis said as she turned the buggy around. She wasn't sure if she would make any more pumpkin muffins, but she would probably bake at least one pumpkin pie. It wouldn't be Thanksgiving without one.

By the time they reached the turkeys, Phyllis had bought more than she'd really intended to. There was still room in the buggy for the bird, though. She had to wait while several other women made their selections; then she leaned over the refrigerated case and looked for a good one. She hefted a couple of turkeys before deciding on one that was a little over ten pounds. With the twelve-pounder she already had defrosting in the refrigerator, that ought to be plenty of meat for the meal and a little left over, she decided.

They checked out and left the store, and as Phyllis pushed the buggy through the parking lot toward her car, she thought that there was something she'd forgotten to get. She nearly always felt that way when she went shopping, though, and as far as she could tell, she hadn't actually forgotten anything. She told herself not to worry about it.

Phyllis spent the rest of the day happily baking several pies. Carolyn worked alongside her, and Dana came into the kitchen as well and joined in their conversation, which was heavily oriented toward past holiday celebrations. As Dana laughed and reminisced about things that had happened while she was growing up, Phyllis thought about how good this little slice of normalcy was for her. Phyllis hoped it would last through the holiday and on past it for a while. Dana needed to recover and get as much of her strength back as she could before the ordeal of defending herself from murder charges began again.

It didn't help matters when Chief Whitmire called and asked for Dana. With a feeling of apprehension, Phyllis handed over the phone, then watched and listened as Dana replied in clipped tones to the chief's questions, finally naming one of the town's funeral homes.

Phyllis and Carolyn exchanged a glance. Logan's funeral . . . of course, Phyllis thought. The police were finished with the body, and it was being released so that Dana could make funeral arrangements.

When Dana hung up the phone, the color was gone from her face again. "You know what that was about," she said.

Phyllis nodded. "Logan's funeral."

"Yes. I . . . I need to call the funeral home. I'm sure I'll have to go down there and talk to them. . . ."

Carolyn said, "I'll come with you. You don't have to handle all this by yourself, Dana. If there's anything any of us can do, we want to."

"That's right," Phyllis added. "Just let us know how we can help."

"Thank you," Dana murmured. "I'm not sure how I would have ever made it through this without the two of you."

"You would have figured out a way," Carolyn told her. "People are stronger than they think they are."

Dana called the funeral home, and then she and Carolyn left to go there and make the arrangements. What a terrible juxtaposition, Phyllis thought, to have to have a funeral right around the same time as a holiday of giving thanks.

She tried to concentrate on her baking while Dana and Carolyn were gone, but it was difficult to do so. Bobby provided some distraction, though, when he came in from the garage with Sam and had to tell Phyllis all about what they'd been doing.

Finally, the two women returned. Dana, looking pale and drawn, went right upstairs. Carolyn paused in the kitchen and told Phyllis, "The funeral is tomorrow afternoon at three o'clock."

"The day before Thanksgiving?"

"It was that or wait until Saturday, and Dana didn't want to wait that long. She said she'd rather not have it looming over her for any longer than she had to."

"Well, I can understand that, I suppose," Phyllis said.

"School will be out tomorrow, so her friends can be there. The ones who are willing to stick by her, anyway. I'm not sure all of them will."

"We will," Phyllis said. "Someone will have to stay here with Bobby. I wouldn't want to take him to a funeral without talking to Mike and Sarah about it first, and I don't think he needs to attend this one, anyway."

"Yes, it would probably bring up even more awkward questions than having Dana staying here with us," Carolyn agreed.

"Do we need to have lunch for the family before the service?"

Carolyn shook her head. "Dana said she didn't want to do that. She said she didn't think she could face Logan's family in a setting like that."

"Don't you think that makes her look even more guilty?" Phyllis asked with a frown.

"I don't care. If that's what she wants, then that's the way things will be. Anyway, we know she's not guilty, and eventually, everyone else will, too."

Phyllis wanted to believe that, and she knew that Carolyn did, too, but for the first time, she thought that she detected just the faintest trace of doubt in her friend's voice.

What if Dana was lying? Phyllis wanted to believe that she was a good enough judge of character not to be fooled easily . . . but what if that wasn't true this time? Maybe Dana had played them all for fools.

What it all boiled down to, Phyllis thought, was a need to know the truth. Once that was out in the open, then either Dana would be as much a victim as her husband had been, or else she would be revealed as a cold-blooded murderer. Either way, it would be over.

With that thought whirling around in her head, it wasn't easy for Phyllis to go to back to concentrating on pumpkin pies. But she managed.

Chapter 33

The next morning dawned gray and overcast. Appropriate weather for a funeral, Phyllis thought. Another front had blown through, bringing with it clouds, occasional drizzle, and colder temperatures, a reminder that winter was not that far off.

Phyllis explained to Bobby that there was something she and Carolyn and Eve had to do that afternoon, but that he could stay there with Sam. She didn't go into any detail, and he didn't seem to want any. He just said, "Okay, Gran'mama," and she was grateful once again that he had been easy to take care of during this difficult time.

The service was being held at the funeral home. Phyllis offered to drive all of them, since hers was the largest and most comfortable car. Dana rode in the front passenger seat, and on the way there that afternoon, she said, "I'm dreading this."

Carolyn leaned forward from the backseat to rest a hand on her shoulder. "I know you are. Just be strong and remember that we'll all be right there for you."

Dana wore an elegant black suit and looked every inch the grieving widow. The contrast with her dark clothes made her face seem even more washed out. Despite the overcast day, she slipped a pair of sunglasses out of her purse and put them on. Maybe she wanted to hide eyes that were red rimmed from crying, Phyllis thought.

Or maybe she just didn't trust anyone to see the expression in her eyes.

That nagging thought was disturbing. Ever since the day before, Phyllis hadn't been able to shake the idea that maybe she was wrong this time, that her instincts had failed her and she was harboring a killer in her home. Goodness knew, the evidence pointed to Dana. There were some unexplained questions, mostly about Logan's business and that NorCenTex Development deal, but was there enough in that to create any real doubt?

Phyllis wasn't thinking about the sort of reasonable doubt that was enough to keep a person from being convicted in court. Someone could be guilty of a crime and still be acquitted, simply because the state had failed to provide enough evidence against them. So far, despite her digging into the case, Phyllis still hadn't found anything to indicate that someone besides Dana had had a good reason to kill Logan and the knowledge needed to do so in the manner that had been employed by the murderer.

Was a hunch enough? Phyllis asked herself. Because that was really all she had, a hunch that Dana wasn't guilty, other than the feeling that she wasn't looking at something from the proper angle.

There weren't many cars at the funeral home when they got there. Of course, it was early yet. The funeral director met them at the door with his usual comforting smile and took charge of Dana, expecting to lead her to a small room where the family would wait for the service to begin.

Dana balked at that. "I don't want to wait with Logan's family," she said, her voice shaking a little. "I hope you understand."

"Of course," the man murmured. It was his job to act like he understood, whether he really did or not. "We have another small waiting room, Mrs. Powell. Come with me."

Dana turned her head and said, "Carolyn, can you ... ?"

"Of course," Carolyn replied without hesitation. She looked at the funeral director. "If that's all right?"

"Yes, please, Mrs. Wilbarger, come with us," the man said. He led both of them down a hallway and through a door.

"I hate funerals," Eve said to Phyllis as they stood in front of the double doors of the chapel. "Weddings are so much more fun."

"If Carolyn were here, she'd say that you ought to know, you've had so many of them," Phyllis said.

Eve laughed softly. "Thank you, dear, for taking up the slack. That's exactly what she would have said, and it makes me feel better to hear it. I'm going to get married again one of these days, you know."

"I don't doubt it," Phyllis said, although as far as she knew, Eve wasn't even dating anyone at the moment, which would make getting married a little harder.

They went into the chapel, where a few people were already sitting. Solemn music played very quietly from hidden speakers, just loud enough to hear without really intruding itself onto a person's consciousness. Phyllis and Eve took seats near the front and waited. They hadn't been there long when Ben and Barbara Loomis came in.

"Do you mind if we sit with you?" Barbara asked.

"No, of course not," Phyllis said. Barbara sat down next to her, with Ben on the other side of his wife.

"How are you?"

"Getting ready for Thanksgiving," Phyllis said in reply to Barbara's question. "We just have to get through this first."

"Yes. It's a terrible thing to have the day before, isn't it?"

Phyllis nodded. She looked over at Ben and saw that he wasn't his usual jovial self today. Well, who would be in a funeral home?

Ben didn't look sad, though. He looked angry, as if he didn't want to be here and Barbara had forced him to come. Maybe that was because he would rather be working, Phyllis thought.

Or maybe it was because there was something to the theory that had popped into her mind a couple of nights earlier, the possibility that something had been going on between Logan and Barbara. Phyllis could understand why a man might not be too happy about being forced to attend the funeral of his wife's lover.

She was getting *way* ahead of herself, she thought. Dana had suspected Logan of cheating, and Barbara and her husband were having some sort of trouble between them, but those two facts weren't necessarily connected.

Something occurred to Phyllis, something that Barbara had said in the restroom there at the school that she'd meant to ask her about. This wasn't a very good place to do it, but she didn't know when she'd get another chance. Keeping her voice low, she leaned closer to Barbara and said, "A couple of days ago, you mentioned something about Dana's condition. What did you mean by that? She can't be pregnant. She told me she can't have children."

"Pregnant? Oh, no, it's nothing like that. But she's not in good health at all. To tell you the truth, I never expected her to outlive Logan. He was so vital, so full of life, and she was so fragile."

Fragile? Other than being a little too slender, Dana seemed to be in perfect health, Phyllis thought. But then she remembered back to how Logan had seemed to her, and she never would have dreamed that he had so many medical problems.

"You mean they were both in bad health?"

"What?" Barbara frowned. "No. Logan was fine. He was the one who had to take care of Dana all the time."

Phyllis drew in a deep breath. She thought back quickly over everything she had read in the newspapers and seen on television about Logan's death. Nothing had ever been said about the cause of death, although in the absence of an official statement, the stories had hinted that Logan might have been poisoned. The authorities were keeping the exact cause of death to themselves for the moment, although Phyllis knew it. Barbara Loomis, clearly, did not.

Barbara didn't know that she had it backward about which of the Powells was in poor health, either. That had to mean something, Phyllis told herself.

Before she could puzzle out what it was, more mourners began to arrive. Not surprisingly, Jenna, Taryn, and Kendra were together. They filed into the same row where Phyllis, Eve, and the Loomises were sitting, and with a solemn smile, Jenna asked, "Can we join you?"

Ben stood up. "Why don't you ladies sit together?" he suggested. "I'll just move farther back."

"Oh, no, Ben," Barbara said quickly. "That's not necessary."

"I think it is," he said, clearly struggling to keep a curt note out of his voice. He waved a big hand toward the bench. "Ladies."

The other three teachers moved past him and sat down. If Phyllis had had any doubts about there being problems between the Loomises, they were gone now.

As soon as Kendra sat down, she took a handkerchief from her purse and began dabbing at her eyes. Phyllis saw how she kept looking at the closed casket sitting in front of the altar at the front of the chapel.

She wasn't the only one, though. Taryn and Jenna were staring at Logan's casket as well. It was difficult *not* to look at the casket when you were at a funeral, Phyllis thought, but the three teachers—four if you counted Barbara, who was also starting to look teary eyed—seemed to be regarding it with more than the usual intensity. It was almost like they had come not to support Dana in her grief . . .

But to say good-bye to Logan Powell.

Phyllis closed her eyes. The thoughts that began to whirl through her head were insane, and she knew it. Carolyn had said a couple of days earlier that if Phyllis was going to suspect Barbara of having an affair with Logan, she might as well suspect every teacher in the school.

Not *every* teacher, Phyllis thought now. But maybe four in particular.

On the other hand, suppose that wild theory was right. Phyllis had just come up with even more reason for Dana to hate her husband enough to kill him. It would have been bad enough if Logan was playing around with one of her close friends. But all four of them . . . ?

That would be enough to drive some women to murder, all right.

And if Dana really had killed Logan on Friday night, what better way to try to throw suspicion off herself than to show up at the park on Saturday morning looking for him and acting scared that something had happened to him? It hadn't worked, of course, but it was the sort of thing that someone might think, especially someone desperate with guilt. The more Phyllis turned everything over in her mind, the more it all fit.

But if it was true, then wasn't it possible that sooner or later Dana might try to strike back against the women who had befriended her and then betrayed her? Phyllis caught her breath as she looked along the line of grieving teachers. All four of them might be in danger.

She couldn't very well warn them in the middle of a funeral, though, and the service was about to get under way. The music had just gotten louder. Sad-faced men and women filed in from a side door and took their places on one of the front benches reserved for family. Those would be Logan's relatives, Phyllis thought.

A moment later, the funeral director brought Dana and Carolyn in. Phyllis saw the angry, suspicious glances that Logan's relatives directed toward Dana. They probably didn't know many of the details of the case, only that Logan was dead and Dana had been arrested for his murder. Yet here she was, out of jail and at his funeral. No wonder they felt considerable resentment.

The chapel was only about half full as the service started with a prayer. Phyllis recognized some of the mourners as teachers, while others were probably business associates of Logan's. Dana and Logan weren't regular churchgoers, but like Carolyn, they were members of one of the local Methodist churches, so the pastor from there conducted the service. There was no such thing as a "good" funeral, Phyllis supposed, but this one was more awkward and uncomfortable than most because of the circumstances.

It was made even more so for her by the speculation that filled her mind. Maybe Logan really had been a womanizing, philandering snake. That just gave his wife more of a reason to want him dead. And there was no getting around the fact that Dana was the only one who knew that switching his regular peppermints for sugar-free ones would probably kill him.

Even though she felt terrible about it, Phyllis resolved to keep a very close eye on Dana while the woman was staying at her house. She almost wished now that she hadn't agreed to it.

The funeral service really wasn't very long, but it seemed interminable. Finally it was over, though. Dana must have requested that the casket not be opened for a last look, because it remained closed. Everyone filed out to get in their cars and drive to the cemetery for the graveside service. Dana and Carolyn rode in the funeral director's car, directly behind the hearse, and Phyllis's car was the third one in the procession.

The clouds had continued their gray march across the heavens while the funeral was going on. Phyllis had to turn the windshield wipers on once to clear mist off the glass, but nothing was coming down when they got to the cemetery. The sky continued to threaten, however, so the minister didn't waste any time once everyone was gathered under the canopy that had been set up next to the open grave. He said a few words thanking everyone who had come, read a scripture, and said a prayer. The pallbearers added their boutonnieres to the flowers arranged on top of the casket, the mourners filed by and shook hands with Dana and with Logan's relatives— they had kept an empty folding chair between her and them, and her eyes were turned straight ahead and never wavered—and then it was finished. People scattered, heading for their cars.

Carolyn had sat with Phyllis, Eve, and the teachers from Loving Elementary during the graveside service. She stood up and went over to Dana, taking her arm. "We'll take you back to the house now," she said quietly.

"Yes. Thank you." Dana paused, though, and looked over her shoulder toward the casket as it sat on the apparatus that would lower it into the ground when everyone was gone except the cemetery workers. Phyllis tried not to look at the bulldozer that sat unobtrusively about fifty yards away and tried even harder not to think about how it would soon be used.

A long sigh escaped from Dana's lips. Tears streaked her cheeks. She had cried quietly during both services. Now she turned away from the grave, lowered her head, and allowed Carolyn to lead her back to Phyllis's car.

Phyllis noticed that Ben Loomis hadn't come to the cemetery. Either he had gotten a ride with someone else who wasn't going to attend the graveside service, or else Barbara was going to leave here with one of her friends. The four of them stood there with wet, hollow eyes, waiting near Phyllis's car. Each of them hugged Dana in turn when she came up to the vehicle. Dana seemed to accept the embraces and return them with gratitude, but Phyllis was no longer quite so sure about that.

Jenna rested both hands on Dana's shoulders and said, "We're going to put all of this behind us now, Dana, do you understand? We'll be at Mrs. Newsom's tomorrow for Thanksgiving, and we'll see you there."

Dana managed to nod. "I wish I could put it all behind me," she said. "I really do."

"You can," Jenna told her. "It may take a while, but you can and you will."

"I don't know. I just don't know anymore."

Phyllis watched closely. Did Dana suspect that her friends had been involved with Logan? She couldn't tell. Dana didn't act like it, but Phyllis had already been forced to consider the idea that Dana was a consummate actress, always keeping her real thoughts and emotions deeply buried.

More drizzle began to fall. "We'd better go," Phyllis said.

"What time do you want us to show up tomorrow?" Kendra asked.

"Oh, it doesn't really matter. Carolyn and I are delivering canned goods and turkey dinners in the morning, and the rest of you are, too, I believe. Just come on over whenever you're finished with that. We should be back by eleven or so, and even if we're not, my friends Eve Turner and Sam Fletcher will be there." Sam had offered to help them with the deliveries, but Phyllis didn't think that was going to be necessary.

Dana was going to go with them, though, Phyllis decided. She was going to keep a very close eye on Dana Powell from here on out.

Chapter 34

The cold front moved on out of the area Wednesday evening, taking the clouds and drizzle with it. The skies cleared during the night, so Thanksgiving morning was clear and crisp, with blue skies and temperatures in the upper thirties. As Phyllis walked out into her front yard to pick up the paper, fallen leaves rustled and crunched under her feet. All this day really needed to be perfect was the smell of burning leaves in the air, she thought as she took a deep breath, but of course no one burned leaves anymore, and certainly not in the city. It was against the law.

So was murder, but that didn't stop people from committing it, she thought.

She had still drawn no conclusions about Dana's guilt or innocence. She wanted to believe that Dana was innocent, but it was hard to get around the pile of evidence saying otherwise. First thing Monday morning, she was going to call Juliette Yorke and tell the lawyer about the NorCenTex Development deal. The sooner that was fully investigated, the better. It might wind up clearing Dana's name.

Today, though, was all about giving thanks and doing good. Phyllis had gotten up a little earlier than usual to fix breakfast and get the turkeys in the oven. For breakfast she made bacon and eggs with cranapple rolls. The turkeys could cook during the morning while Phyllis, Carolyn, and Dana were delivering canned goods and turkey dinners to the less fortunate.

Sam and Bobby were talking football at the kitchen table over breakfast when Sam bit into one of the hot cranapple rolls and sighed. "Bobby, your grandmother is the best cook in all of Texas." Then he went back to talking about the Cowboys, who would be playing the Washington Redskins in the traditional Thanksgiving Day contest. "It's nearly always a good game," Sam told the little boy. "Sometimes it goes right down to the final play."

Phyllis enlisted Eve to keep an eye on the turkeys as they cooked. Eve was a little leery of the idea.

"You know I've never been much of a cook, Phyllis," she protested.

"You won't actually be cooking anything," Phyllis said. "Just make sure they don't start to burn. They shouldn't."

"But what if they do?"

"Take them out," Carolyn suggested drily.

"Well ... all right." Eve's reluctance was obvious. "But I have somewhere to go later this morning, so you'd better be back by eleven like you said."

"You're going somewhere on Thanksgiving?"

"Yes, but I'll be back for dinner."

"All right," Phyllis said. She didn't pry. What Eve did was her own business.

Dana wasn't sure she wanted to go along on the deliveries, but Carolyn wouldn't take no for an answer. "It's a beautiful day," she insisted. "It'll do you good to get out and about for a little while. Anyway, you devoted a lot of time and effort to preparing for this, Dana, and you deserve to reap some of the rewards."

"What rewards?" Phyllis asked.

"The smiles of the people we're helping, of course," Carolyn said. "Especially the little ones. How can you not feel good about providing a Thanksgiving to remember for them?"

She was absolutely right about that, Phyllis thought.

Helping others was just about the best feeling in the world.

Phyllis had told Sam they wouldn't need his help with the deliveries, but she did accept the loan of his pickup when he offered it. She had driven the truck before, so she wasn't worried about handling it. It would certainly be easier to load and unload the boxes of canned goods and the boxed turkey dinners from the back of the pickup. Carolyn took her car, too, though, so all three of them woudn't have to crowd into the front seat of the pickup.

Satisfied that everything was under control and proceeding as it was supposed to at the house, Phyllis headed for the Methodist church with Carolyn and Dana following her. When they got there, they found the place busy as people pulled into the parking lot and backed up to the side door of Fellowship Hall to load the boxes they would soon deliver.

Dolly Williamson was there supervising, of course, standing beside the open door with a clipboard in her hand. Everybody was talking and laughing, and holiday spirit filled the air.

"Good morning," Dolly greeted them. "Happy Thanksgiving."

"Happy Thanksgiving to you, too, Dolly," Phyllis said. "We're ready to make our deliveries."

"You have your list of addresses?"

Carolyn took it from her purse. "Right here. I even looked up the streets I wasn't familiar with on the Internet." She sounded proud of herself, and Phyllis thought she had a right to. Carolyn had never been that comfortable navigating her way through the Web.

"All right." Dolly stepped just inside the door and pointed to one of the stacks of boxes lined up along the wall. "Those are yours right there."

None of the boxes was all that heavy. It didn't take long for the three women to carry them out of the building and place them in the back of Sam's pickup. When they were ready to go, Phyllis said to Carolyn, "You lead the way, since you have the list. I'll follow you."

Carolyn nodded in agreement and got into her car, along with Dana, while Phyllis climbed behind the wheel of the truck.

Little old lady, indeed! she thought with a smile as she started the pickup and listened to the throaty roar of its engine. She'd like to see a little old lady handle a beast like this.

The next two hours went quickly as Phyllis followed Carolyn from address to address. At each stop, they unloaded a box of canned goods and other nonperishables, along with a boxed turkey dinner. The families receiving them were grateful, although some were more effusive in their thanks than others. Some of the people seemed a little uncomfortable, and Phyllis didn't blame them. It was hard for some people to take charity. They were willing to do it, though, in order for their children to have a good Thanksgiving and also so they could eat well for a while. In some cases, the donated food might be just what a family needed to tide them over until their situation improved.

They finished the deliveries shortly after ten thirty. Carolyn said, "I need to swing back by the church and let Dolly know that we dropped off everything just like we were supposed to. Do you want to come with me, Dana, or would you rather go back to the house with Phyllis?"

"I think I'll just go on back to the house," Dana said. She looked at Phyllis. "If that's all right with you?"

"Of course it's all right with me," Phyllis said. "I'll be glad for the company."

"See you in a little while, then," Carolyn called as she got into her car.

Phyllis unlocked the pickup's passenger door for Dana. As they started back toward the house, Phyllis suddenly realized one of the things she had forgotten at the store a couple of days earlier.

"Oh, darn," she said. "I've been meaning to pick up some candy for you."

"Candy?" Dana repeated.

"Peppermints," Phyllis said. "I assume since you had

them all over your house, you liked them, too. Unless—"
Phyllis broke off for a second, then said, "Oh, goodness,
Dana, I'm sorry! I didn't even think. Under the circum-
stances, you probably don't want any."

"I don't want any, regardless of the circumstances,"
Dana said. "I don't like peppermints."

Phyllis glanced over at her. "It was just Logan, then,
who ate them?"

Dana nodded. "That's right. Oh, I had some from
time to time. He was always trying to get me to eat some
of them, especially when we were out. I guess he thought
it wouldn't look as odd, him sucking on them all the
time, if I was doing it, too. I didn't hate them or anything, so I'd usually take one or two just to keep from
causing a scene when we'd be at a PTO meeting or
something like that." She laughed but didn't really
sound amused. "If I never eat another peppermint in
my life, that'll be just fine with me."

"Well, then, I guess it's a good thing I got distracted
at the store the other day and didn't buy any of them. I
would have felt foolish offering them to you when you
don't even like them."

"Oh, I probably would have taken them. I'm in the
habit, after all."

Phyllis didn't say anything else about the peppermints and wished she hadn't brought up the subject in
the first place. She was more suspicious of Dana than
she had been, but at the same time, her instincts com-
pelled her to make a guest in her home just as comfortable as possible.

It was a few minutes before eleven when they
reached the house. Phyllis parked the pickup at the curb
in front and took note of the fact that there weren't any
strange cars parked in front of the house yet. Some of
the guests would probably start showing up soon,
though. Dolly wouldn't arrive until all the volunteers
had checked back in and let her know that their deliveries had been carried out.

They went in through the front door. Eve was waiting
in the living room with her purse. "I have to go," she

said. "I'll be back in a couple of hours. The turkeys didn't burn."

"Thanks," Phyllis said, but Eve was already on her way out the door. Phyllis shook her head. Just when things looked like they might get back to normal, more strangeness reared its head.

The wonderful smell of the turkeys cooking filled the house. "I need to get the dressing started," Phyllis said to Dana. "Come into the kitchen and give me a hand?"

Dana hesitated, then nodded and smiled. "Sure, why not?"

Sam and Bobby clattered down from upstairs and came into the kitchen right after Phyllis and Dana. Bobby said, "We watched the parade! Santa Claus was there, Gran'mama! And a bunch of great big balloons, and Sam says now there's gonna be a dog show! I like doggies!"

"I do, too, Bobby," Phyllis told him.

"Everything go all right with you ladies?" Sam asked.

Phyllis nodded. "Yes, we made all our deliveries without any problems. Thanks again for the loan of your truck."

"You're welcome. Need a hand here in the kitchen?"

"No, I think we can handle things just fine. Carolyn will be back in a few minutes, too." The phone rang, so Phyllis nodded to Sam and added, "You can answer that, if you want to."

Sam picked it up, said "Hello," listened for a moment, then turned to Phyllis. "It's Carolyn. She wants to know if somebody named Jenna is here."

"Jenna Grantham?" Phyllis asked with a frown. "No, not yet, but she should be soon." She held out her hand, and Sam gave the phone to her. "Carolyn, what's this about Jenna?"

"She never showed up to make the deliveries she was down for this morning," Carolyn said at the other end of the line. "Dolly says she tried to call her but didn't get an answer. One of the other volunteers took those deliveries when he came back to check in."

"That's odd. Maybe Jenna's sick."

"I know where she lives," Carolyn said. "I can go by there and check on her."

"That's probably a good idea. Let me know if you need any help."

Phyllis said good-bye and hung up the phone. Dana asked, "What was that about Jenna?"

"She didn't show up at the church this morning to take her deliveries," Phyllis said. "Dolly was worried about her, and I think Carolyn is, too. She said she'd go by Jenna's place and make sure she's not sick or anything."

"I hope she's all right," Dana said, and she sounded like she meant it.

Phyllis got to work on the stuffing she intended to make: a cranberry stuffing ring and a pan of traditional corn bread stuffing. So she didn't think any more about Jenna. As usual when she was working in the kitchen, her thoughts seemed to clear a little. There was nothing like doing some pleasant but familiar activity to focus the brain. There were so many little things that had bothered her over the past week, but she brought up the most recent one.

"You said that Logan always tried to get you to eat some of his peppermints?" she asked Dana.

"That's right," the younger woman answered with a puzzled frown. "I'm not sure I want to talk about Logan, Phyllis. Everything about him is still really painful."

Phyllis nodded. "I know, and I'm sorry. Did he only do that when the two of you were out in public?"

For a long moment, Dana didn't reply. Then she said, "Now that I think about it, I believe that's right. They were always around at home, of course, but he didn't try to persuade me to eat any of them there."

"I wonder why that was the case."

"I'm sure I don't have any idea," Dana said.

"And you never found your missing keys, did you?"

"No." Dana shrugged. "They're gone for good, I guess. I need to get the locks on my house changed. I should have done that already."

The pieces of a theory were shifting around in Phyllis's head. Mentally, she tried them one way, then another, and although they were beginning to form a picture, it wasn't a recognizable one yet.

"Are you in good health, Dana?"

"What?" Dana looked really confused now. "My last checkup, the doctor said I'd live to be a hundred. Why in the world would you think I was sick?"

"Logan was, but he didn't look it."

"No, that's true—"

The phone rang again, and Phyllis recognized Carolyn's cell number on the caller ID as she picked it up. "Hello?"

"Jenna's not at her apartment," Carolyn said, and there was a definite edge of worry in her voice. "Or at least she's not answering. Do you think I should call the police?"

The doorbell rang before Phyllis could answer. She didn't know whether Sam and Bobby had gone back upstairs to watch TV in Sam's room, but she didn't hear the set in the living room. "Hold on a minute," she told Carolyn. Carrying the phone with her, she walked up the hall from the kitchen and went to the front door.

When she opened the front door, relief went through her. Jenna stood there on the porch, a smile on her face and a rectangular plastic container in her hands. "Sorry if I'm late," she said. She lifted the container. "I baked some muffins of my own."

On the phone, Carolyn asked, "Is that—?"

"Yes," Phyllis said. "You can stop worrying. Jenna's here."

Chapter 35

"Who was worried about me?" Jenna asked as she came into the house, carrying the container of muffins.

Phyllis had said good-bye to Carolyn and broken the connection. "That was Carolyn," she said. "She'd gone to your apartment to make sure you were all right because you didn't show up at the church to make those canned-goods deliveries."

Jenna's eyes widened. "Dolly didn't get my message?"

"I guess not. She seemed surprised that you didn't come by."

"Oh, no," Jenna said. She shook her head. "I left a message on her phone telling her I couldn't make it after all. Or at least I thought I did."

"No trouble, I hope?"

"No, no. I just got an e-mail from my mother saying that she wanted to call me and talk to me this morning. My great-grandmother is at my mom's house today, and she wanted to visit with me on the phone. I felt bad about letting Dolly down, but my great-grandmother's getting really old, you know, and I haven't talked to her in a while. I felt like I couldn't say no, so I had to stay home and take the call."

Phyllis didn't see any reason why Jenna's mother couldn't have called after Jenna was back from making her deliveries, but she supposed Jenna might not have thought of that.

"Let me take those muffins out to the kitchen," she said.

"I can go over to the church right now—," Jenna began as she handed Phyllis the container.

"That's not necessary. Someone else took those boxes and delivered them."

"I'll apologize personally to Dolly for letting her down. I sure didn't mean to."

Phyllis heard car doors and looked past Jenna to see Taryn Marshall getting out of a vehicle at the curb. Another car pulled up behind hers, and one stopped in the driveway. Phyllis recognized the teachers who got out of them carrying covered dishes. They were just acquaintances, but for today they were her guests, so she smiled and waved at them and called, "Come on in, folks."

That was just the beginning of a period of joviality as people continued to arrive bearing food. It really did feel almost like a good old-fashioned Thanksgiving with a houseful of friends and relatives, Phyllis thought as she greeted guests, found places on the kitchen counter for the food they brought, tended to her own cooking, and supervised the preparations for dinner. Carolyn came in and said, "I spoke to Jenna out in the living room. We must have just missed each other."

Sam and Bobby, perhaps wisely, stayed out of the way.

The only problem was that Eve wasn't there. She had called to say that she was running late and might not make it for dinner but would be there as soon as she could. Phyllis had tried to find out what was going on with her, but Eve had already hung up.

With the whirlwind of activity, Phyllis didn't have time to worry about Eve or to think any more about the nebulous idea that had come to her earlier. In fact, she barely had time to pause and take a breath until dinner was on the table. When all the food was ready and everyone was gathered around, she asked Sam to say grace. He obliged by thanking God for the bounty in his deep, rumbling voice that appropriately reminded Phyllis of what an Old Testament prophet must have sounded like.

Then, when Sam said, "Amen," everyone echoed, "Amen," and then sat down to stuff themselves.

It was a wonderful Thanksgiving dinner.

Afterward, with the guests sitting around the living room and talking while the announcers on the TV set the stage for the Cowboys game that was about to kick off, Phyllis found herself in the kitchen surveying what was left of the food. They'd made a big dent in the two turkeys, but there was still plenty of meat on the bones for leftover turkey and dressing sandwiches, one of her favorites. The various desserts had been heavily sampled as well.

A tiny frown formed on Phyllis's face as she looked at the counters. Something was missing, she thought, but she wasn't sure what it was.

Carolyn came up behind her and said, "It was a beautiful dinner, Phyllis. You outdid yourself this year."

Phyllis smiled. "You did plenty yourself, you know."

"Not this year," Carolyn said. "Too much else was going on. All this horrible business with Dana ... At least she seemed to enjoy herself today. There's some life in her yet, thank goodness. For a while there, it looked like whoever killed Logan might as well have killed Dana, too."

Phyllis stiffened. With an almost audible click, the pieces finally fit together in her brain. She turned to look at Carolyn, who must have seen something in Phyllis's eyes that caused her to take a hurried step backward.

"Oh, my God," Carolyn exclaimed quietly. "Phyllis, what's wrong? You look— Oh, my." Carolyn's eyes widened. "I've heard Sam describe that look. You just figured it all out, didn't you? You know who killed Logan."

Phyllis drew in a deep breath. "I think so, but I'm not sure. Is everyone in the living room?"

"That's right. Jenna just brought those muffins of hers in there and was going to pass them around before the football game starts, even though everyone's insisting that they're too full to eat anything else."

Phyllis leaped into the hall and headed for the living room at a dead run. She barely heard Carolyn's startled cry behind her.

Now she was sure.

And that was confirmed as she reached the living

room and saw Jenna handing a muffin to Dana, saying, "Here, I made this one especially for you."

"Dana, no!" Phyllis said as she came to a halt, startling just about everyone in the crowded living room. "Don't eat that!"

Dana and the others in the room looked at her in confusion. Not Jenna, though. Her eyes locked with Phyllis's, and they burned with the cold fires of hatred.

"Dana, put that muffin on the coffee table in front of you," Phyllis said. "Don't eat it. The rest of you, don't eat your muffins, either. Don't take even a little bite."

With a shaking hand, Dana placed her muffin on the coffee table. "Phyllis, what . . . what's going on here?"

Dolly Williamson said, "Yes, what's the meaning of this?"

"We're just about ready to kick it off here, folks," the football announcer said on television.

"Jenna killed Logan Powell," Phyllis said, "and I think she was just about to try to kill Dana again, and maybe everyone else here."

A stunned silence hung over the room for a couple of seconds that seemed much longer. Then Jenna said in a curiously flat voice, "You meddling old bitch," and suddenly lunged at Dana with her arms outstretched, obviously intending to lock her hands around Dana's slender throat and choke the life out of her.

She didn't get the chance, because Sam brought her down with a tackle as good as any that would take place at Cowboys Stadium that afternoon. They crashed to the floor, and as Jenna started to scream and thrash around, Sam grabbed her wrists and pinned them to the floor.

"I've already called 911," Carolyn said from behind Phyllis. "The police are on their way."

"You're going to have to explain all this to me," Detective Isabel Largo said as she sat across the living room from Phyllis and Carolyn an hour later. Chief Whitmire was there, too. The guests had all left, and Sam had taken Bobby upstairs again. He was full of questions about what had happened, and Phyllis didn't envy Sam the job of trying to explain it to the little boy.

Dana was upstairs as well, lying down. She had taken one of the sedatives that the doctor had given her when she was being released from the hospital a few days earlier.

Jenna had been taken into custody as soon as the police arrived and was locked up by now.

Detective Largo arched her thin, dark eyebrows. "Well?"

"I was gathering my thoughts," Phyllis said. "This isn't easy."

Chief Whitmire said, "Murder's usually a simple crime. You never seem to run into any of those, do you, Mrs. Newsom?"

"This one was simple in its motivation," Phyllis said. "Love. Jenna Grantham was in love with Logan Powell. She'd been having an affair with him. She wanted him to leave his wife and marry her, especially when she found out that Logan stood to make a lot of money off the new mall that's going to be built here in town."

"New mall?" Largo repeated. "I haven't heard anything about that."

"You will," Phyllis told her. "Also, someone might want to check the bank accounts of the members of the Planning and Zoning Commission. There might be some large, unexplained deposits in some of them ... but that doesn't have anything to do with the murder."

"No, but we'll have to talk about it later," Whitmire said. "What about Powell and the Grantham woman?"

"Jenna decided that since Logan wouldn't leave Dana, she would get rid of Dana herself. She decided to murder Dana Powell."

Detective Largo said, "But it was Logan Powell who died."

"That was an accident, and his own fault, in a way. You see, Logan told all the women he was fooling around with that his wife was really very sick and that he had to spend a lot of time with her because of it."

"Wait a minute. Women? You mean he was having an affair with someone else besides Jenna Grantham?"

Phyllis nodded. "I think so. There were probably several of them. I don't know who they all were." That wasn't strictly true, since she suspected that Kendra Neville and

236 · LIVIA J. WASHBURN

Taryn Marshall had been involved with Logan, too, along with Barbara Loomis, but she wasn't going to ruin their lives by revealing that unless it was absolutely necessary. "You see, he used Dana's phony illness as an excuse to give himself time to juggle all his affairs. He told the women that she would slip into a coma from her low blood sugar unless he made sure she kept it up by sucking on those peppermints he carried around. He told the women he carried the candy for her, when really he was the one who needed it. He was just too vain to admit that."

Detective Largo leaned forward. "So Jenna Grantham substituted the sugar-free peppermints thinking that by doing so, she would cause Mrs. Powell to fall into a coma and die?"

"That's what I think happened, yes," Phyllis replied with a nod. "She stole Dana's keys from the school office Friday afternoon. I think she probably intended to use them to get into the Powell house on Saturday, while Logan and Dana would both be at the festival, so she could switch out all the peppermints there. Before that, though, she used them to get into Dana's car while Dana was at the park arguing with Logan because she'd started to suspect that he was cheating on her. Jenna probably figured that Dana carried peppermints in the car, too, and she was going to switch them out. Jenna didn't know that Dana doesn't even really like peppermints."

"This is all speculation," Largo said. "You can't prove it."

"Jenna might still have Dana's keys," Phyllis suggested. "Check what she had in her pockets when she was arrested, and if they're not there, I'm sure you can get a search warrant for her apartment."

Chief Whitmire lifted a hand and said, "Let's worry about proving it later. Just tell us the rest of what happened, Mrs. Newsom. How do you know the Grantham woman got into Mrs. Powell's car Friday night?"

"Because of the muffin," Phyllis said. "Remember, Jenna thought that Dana was the one whose health was bad, not Logan. She had already switched out the peppermints Logan carried in his pockets, probably the last time they had a rendezvous somewhere. She didn't know that his health was so precarious that his blood sugar would plunge quickly without them. By Friday night, he was already having trouble. Jenna met him at the park after everyone else had gone home. When she saw that he was having trouble, he must have confessed to her that he was really the one who was at risk of falling into a coma. She didn't want him to die. She'd been trying to kill Dana. So she ran back to her car and grabbed the pumpkin muffin she had swiped from Dana's car when she got into it earlier."

"Pumpkin muffin?" Detective Largo said, her voice rising. *"Pumpkin muffin?"*

Phyllis remained calm and nodded. "Yes, I had given it to Dana earlier that evening when she stopped by here to find out if I still had the keys she'd let Carolyn and me use that afternoon. I didn't, of course. Jenna had them because she'd taken them from the school office while Katherine Felton was distracted. Jenna and Barbara Loomis were there in the office when I brought the keys in and handed them to Katherine, who must have set them down on the counter and forgotten about them. So I knew Jenna was aware of who the keys belonged to."

"What about this Barbara Loomis?" Whitmire asked. "Couldn't she have filched the keys?"

"She could have," Phyllis admitted, "but she couldn't have given the muffin to Logan on Friday night because she was home with her husband at the time."

Detective Largo took a deep breath. "So you gave the muffin to Mrs. Powell . . ."

"Who put it in her car and took it with her to the park," Phyllis said. "But it wasn't there later, Dana told me when I asked her about it. If she was telling the truth, then the muffin disappeared while the car was at the park, and while maybe it was possible someone besides Jenna could have taken the keys—and the muffin—she was certainly the most likely suspect. It was a petty thing to do, stealing a muffin . . . but she had already tried to steal Dana's husband from her, and when that didn't work, she decided to steal Dana's life."

"There was no muffin in Ms. Powell's SUV when we searched it; that's for sure," Detective Largo admitted.

Whitmire nodded. "So when Powell starts fading and realizes that his blood sugar must have dropped, he tells the Grantham woman what's going on and she remembers that she's got the muffin."

"Which has quite a bit of sugar in it," Phyllis said. "She must have run back to her car and gotten it, then tried to feed it to Logan in hopes of raising his blood sugar. But she was too late. He had a heart attack and died."

"So that really was part of your pumpkin muffin in his mouth." Whitmire shook his head in amazement. "If that doesn't beat all."

"Okay, maybe we can prove some of that; maybe we can't," Largo said. "What about the blasted scarecrow costume?"

"Jenna found herself alone in that deserted park in the middle of the night with the body of the man she loved, the man she had just inadvertently murdered, and she panicked. She didn't know what to do. So she decided to hide the body in plain sight. She dressed him in the scarecrow's clothes, hauled the body and the hay bale down to the dogtrot, and set them up there. She wouldn't have had much trouble doing that, as athletic as she is. That gave her some time to think about it and figure out a way to dispose of the body later on. She must have planned to come back and get it Saturday night, after the festival was over and no one was at the park. But of course Carolyn and I discovered it Saturday morning, and that ruined the plan."

"It worked out for Jenna, though," Carolyn put in, "because *somebody* decided that Dana was the one who'd killed Logan."

"All the evidence pointed to her," Largo snapped. "We didn't know any of that crazy business about car keys and . . . and muffins!"

Whitmire said, "I've got to admit, it all makes sense, though, the way you explain it, Mrs. Newsom. But is it enough to convince a jury?"

Phyllis pointed to the muffin that still sat on the coffee

table, the one Jenna had baked and given to Dana. "It will be if there's poison in that muffin, like I think there is. In Jenna's twisted mind, she blamed Dana for Logan's death, and she was still determined to kill her. She may have poisoned all the muffins she brought today. She might have been willing to commit mass murder just to get her revenge on Dana. But more than likely, if she put anything in the others, it was just enough to make the rest of us sick without killing us. She might have been planning to eat one herself, just to make it look good. That way, when the rest of us got sick and Dana died, it would look like a case of tampering with one of the ingredients she used. Things like that aren't nearly as common as they once were, but they're not unheard of."

Chief Whitmire gestured toward the muffin. "Better bag that up, Detective. Get the others, too. We'll take them all in as evidence. Better mark 'em clearly, though. That bunch back at the office sees a bag of muffins, they're liable to help themselves."

"Yes, sir," Largo said. "I'll get search warrants for Ms. Grantham's apartment and car first thing tomorrow, too."

"You do that. And depending on what you find, I suspect I'll be calling District Attorney Sullivan on Monday morning and recommending that all charges against Ms. Powell be dropped."

"Now, that makes it a good Thanksgiving," Carolyn said.

The chief and Detective Largo stood up to leave a few minutes later. Largo paused in the doorway and said to Phyllis, "I don't know how you figure these things out, Mrs. Newsom, but I just hope it doesn't backfire on you one of these days."

"I don't set out to catch murderers, Detective. I just like to know the truth."

"Well, the truth is, I'm going to go salvage what I can of the holiday with my little boy." Largo managed to smile. "Happy Thanksgiving."

"Happy Thanksgiving to you, too, Detective."

Sam and Bobby came downstairs a few minutes later. "Cops gone?" Sam asked.

"They're gone," Phyllis said.

"And Dana's name has been cleared," Carolyn added.

"If everything works out."

"It will and you know it," Carolyn said. "When they tell Jenna everything that you figured out, Phyllis, she'll confess. She's smart enough to know she won't stand a chance."

"But not smart enough not to commit murder," Phyllis said quietly. It was a shame. She had liked Jenna. But the young woman's friendly facade had been just that: a false front that hid the hate she really held in her heart.

Bobby was obviously excited and had been holding something in. "The Cowboys are winnin'!" he finally burst out.

"Well, why don't you and Sam sit and watch the rest of the game down here?" Phyllis suggested. "I'm going to try to call Eve again. I can't imagine where she could be. She's already missed most of Thanksgiving."

"Not to mention all the excitement," Carolyn said drily.

Phyllis had just picked up the phone when the front door opened and Eve's cheery voice called out, "Hello, everybody! I'm so sorry we're late. Roy's plane was delayed—"

Eve stopped just inside the front door and looked around at the mostly empty living room. Behind her stood a distinguished, silver-haired man in a topcoat.

"Where is everybody?" Eve asked. "I know we missed dinner, but I thought we could have leftovers and visit with everyone."

"A lot happened while you were gone," Carolyn said; then she added with her characteristic bluntness, "Who's this?"

"Oh, my goodness, that's right," Eve said. "I have introductions to make." She turned and took the stranger's arm. "Come here, dear, and meet my friends." She smiled as she faced Phyllis, Carolyn, Sam, and Bobby, and went on. "Everyone, meet Roy Porter. Roy and I are engaged. Do you believe it? We're going to be married!"

Recipes

Pumpkin Cheesecake Muffins

Filling:
1 (8-ounce) package cream cheese, softened
1 egg
3 tablespoons brown sugar
1 teaspoon vanilla extract

Topping:
4½ tablespoons all-purpose flour
3 tablespoons brown sugar
½ teaspoon ground cinnamon
¼ teaspoon ground ginger
3 tablespoons chopped pecans
3 tablespoons butter

Muffin:
2½ cups all-purpose flour
2 cups white sugar
2 teaspoons baking powder
1 tablespoon pumpkin pie spice
½ teaspoon salt
2 eggs
1⅓ cups canned pumpkin
⅓ cup vegetable oil
2 teaspoons vanilla extract

Instructions:
Preheat oven to 375°F. Grease and flour 18 muffin cups, or use paper liners. Fill any unfilled muffin cups with water.

Filling: In a medium bowl, beat softened cream cheese until smooth. Add egg, brown sugar, and vanilla. Beat until mixed, then place bowl in freezer to set while mixing other ingredients.

Topping: In a medium bowl, mix flour, brown sugar, cinnamon, ginger, and pecans. Add butter and cut it in with a fork until crumbly. Set aside.

Muffin batter: In a large bowl, blend flour, sugar, baking powder, pumpkin pie spice, and salt. Make a well in the center of the flour mixture and add eggs, pumpkin, vegetable oil, and vanilla. Beat together until well mixed.

Place pumpkin mixture in muffin cups about ½ full. Take the cream cheese mixture out of the freezer and add 1 tablespoon of the cream cheese mixture right in the middle of the batter in the muffin cups. Having the cream cheese mixture chilled will help you keep the cream cheese from touching the edges. Sprinkle on the streusel topping.

Bake for 20 to 25 minutes.

Makes 18 muffins

Note: If you have dogs, add a heaping tablespoon of the leftover canned pumpkin to their meal. All of my dogs like pumpkin, and it's a healthy treat.

Carolyn's Caesar Sandwich

3 cups chopped romaine lettuce
½ cup creamy Caesar salad dressing
¼ cup grated Parmesan cheese
6 large croissants
1 pound cooked pork roast, thinly sliced

Instructions:
In a medium bowl, toss lettuce with dressing and cheese; set aside. Slice croissants. Layer sliced pork and then dressing-and-cheese-covered lettuce on croissant bottoms. Place croissant tops over lettuce.

Serves 6

Cranapple Breakfast Rolls

1 small peeled apple, diced
1 cup whole-berry cranberry sauce
¼ teaspoon ground cinnamon
1 container (12.4 ounces) refrigerated cinnamon roll
dough

Instructions:
Preheat oven to 400°F.

In a small saucepan, mix apple, cranberry sauce, and cinnamon. Cook on medium-high heat, stirring frequently, to reduce sauce and cook apples until soft.

Set aside icing packet from cinnamon rolls. Place rolls in ungreased muffin cups and bake for 8 minutes.

Using the back of a spoon, make an indention in the center of each partially cooked roll and fill with hot cranapple mixture.

Bake 4–5 minutes longer or until golden brown. Cool for 5 minutes, then drizzle with the icing that came with cinnamon rolls.

Makes 8 rolls

Toasty Pecan Pie

1⅓ cups pecan pieces
½ cup melted butter
3 eggs, lightly beaten
1 cup light brown sugar
1 cup light corn syrup
¼ teaspoon salt
1 teaspoon vanilla extract
Unbaked 9-inch pie shell

Instructions:
Preheat oven to 400°F.

Lay out pecans in a single layer on a nonstick cookie sheet or parchment paper. Cook for 5–7 minutes, turning the nuts over halfway through. Check them frequently after turning them over. The pecans are done when you see the color get darker and they smell like toasted pecans. Let pecans cool.

Turn oven up to 450°F.

Mix together the butter, eggs, brown sugar, corn syrup, salt, and vanilla. Whisk until smooth. Blend in pecans. Pour into pie shell.

Bake 10 minutes at 450°F; then lower heat to 350°F, cover crust edges with thin strips of aluminum foil to keep them from browning too much, or use a pie shield. Bake pie an additional 40 to 45 minutes at the lower temperature. Allow pie to cool before serving.

Serves 8

Tart Cranberry Streusel Pie

Filling:
1 pound fresh cranberries
1 cup white sugar
¼ cup all-purpose flour
Unbaked 9-inch pie shell

Topping:
½ cup chopped pecans
½ cup packed brown sugar
¼ cup all-purpose flour
1 teaspoon butter

Instructions:
Preheat oven to 350°F.

Filling: Chop cranberries. In a medium bowl, mix cranberries, sugar, and flour. Pour filling into pie shell.

Topping: In a small bowl, mix pecans, brown sugar, and flour. Cut butter in with fork or pastry blender. The mixture should be crumbly. Sprinkle over pie.

Bake for 45 minutes, or until streusel is light brown.

Serves 8

Rich Mocha Pie

6 (1-ounce) squares semisweet chocolate
1 cup unsalted butter
½ cup light corn syrup
½ cup pecans
1 teaspoon flour
4 eggs, beaten
1 teaspoon vanilla
1 teaspoon instant coffee
1 (9-inch) prepared graham cracker crust

Instructions:
Put the chocolate, butter, and corn syrup in a saucepan, and cook and stir over low heat for about 5 minutes, until the chocolate and butter have melted and the mixture is smooth. Remove from the heat, and let cool.

Preheat oven to 350°F.

Chop pecans and put in plastic bag with the flour. Toss until pecans are lightly coated. This keeps the pecans from sinking.

Pour the beaten eggs, vanilla, and coffee into the cooled chocolate mixture, stir in the pecans, and mix well. Pour the chocolate filling into the prepared graham cracker crust.

Bake 30 minutes or until the pie filling is cooked and set. Let cool before serving.

Serves 8

Dolly's Baked Mashed Potatoes

5 pounds potatoes
¼ cup butter or margarine
2 cups light sour cream
8 ounces ⅓ less fat cream cheese
Salt to taste

Instructions:

Wash and peel potatoes. Place peeled potatoes in a large bowl of cold water until you are ready to cook them. This keeps the potatoes from becoming brown. Use whole potatoes or cut potatoes that are similar in size so they will cook evenly.

Place the potatoes in a large pot and fill with cold water just covering potatoes. Put a lid on the pot. Bring the water to a boil. Boiling time is determined by size and freshness. Fresh potatoes boil more quickly than older potatoes. Smaller potatoes will take 10 to 15 minutes to boil. Large potatoes can take 30 minutes or more to boil. Watch to make sure the pot does not overflow. To see whether the potatoes are done, carefully poke a fork through a couple of potato pieces. If the fork slides through easily, the potatoes are done.

Drain the pot and add butter, sour cream, and cream cheese. Mash the potatoes until smooth of lumps, or whip with mixer. Season potatoes with salt to taste. Spoon mashed potatoes into a greased 2-quart casserole dish. Bake at 375°F for 45 minutes, or until bubbly. The deepness of the casserole dish may cause a difference in the baking time. These baked mashed potatoes can be made days in advance and refrigerated. It's also easy to halve this recipe to serve a smaller group.

Serves 10–12 people

Cranberry Stuffing Ring

Filling:
1 can (16 ounces) whole-berry cranberry sauce
2 tablespoons sour cream
1 teaspoon dry mustard

Stuffing:
½ cup butter or margarine
¼ cup extra-virgin olive oil
1 large chopped onion
1 cup chopped celery
4 cups corn-bread crumbs
6 slices oat-nut bread, cubed
1 tablespoon thyme
1 teaspoon salt
½ teaspoon ground black pepper
1 can (14½ ounces) chicken broth
4 eggs, beaten

Instructions:
Combine cranberry sauce, sour cream, and dry mustard in a medium saucepan. Over medium heat, bring to a boil. Cook, stirring occasionally, 10 minutes or until filling begins to thicken. Remove from heat and set aside.

Preheat oven to 350°F.

Melt butter in a large skillet over a medium heat and add olive oil. Add onion and celery, and sauté until onions are translucent. Remove from heat. In a large bowl combine corn-bread crumbs, bread cubes, thyme, salt, and pepper. Stir in celery and onions, chicken broth, and eggs. Mix until blended.

Spread half of the stuffing into a heavily greased 10-inch springform tube pan. Push an indentation along the center of the stuffing ring to make a place for the filling. Bake 30 minutes. Pour filling evenly in the indention over baked stuffing. Spread remaining stuffing evenly over filling. Bake 45–50 minutes longer or until top is brown. Loosen sides of pan, and turn over onto a serving plate.

Makes 12 servings

Southern Corn Bread Dressing

½ cup butter or margarine
¼ cup extra-virgin olive oil
1 cup finely chopped onion
½ cup finely chopped celery
6 cups crumbled corn bread
2 cups dry bread cubes or crumbled toasted biscuits
2 teaspoons dried sage leaves
½ teaspoon dried thyme leaves
¼ cup chopped fresh parsley
½ teaspoon pepper
1 large egg, beaten
2 cups chicken broth

Instructions:
Preheat oven to 425°F.

Melt butter in a large skillet over medium heat and add olive oil. Add onions and celery and sauté until onions are translucent. Remove from heat.

In large bowl combine onion and celery mixture, crumbled corn bread, bread cubes, sage, thyme, parsley, pepper, egg, and broth; toss gently to mix. The mixture should be very moist; if it isn't, add more broth or a little water. Spoon stuffing into greased 13 × 9-inch baking dish. Bake 30 to 35 minutes or until golden brown.

Makes 10 to 12 servings

Author's Note

The city park in which the Harvest Festival in this novel takes place is based on Holland Lake Park in Weatherford, Texas, a beautiful place where my husband, James, and I used to take our daughters to play when they were young. A number of renovations to the park have taken place since then, and for dramatic purposes I've taken a few minor liberties with the current geographical details, describing the park as a blend of what it used to be and what it is now. To the best of my knowledge, no such Harvest Festival has ever taken place there, and, of course, the events and characters of this novel are completely products of the author's imagination. If you ever find yourself in Weatherford, though, I recommend that you pay a visit to Holland Lake Park and enjoy a peaceful stroll through its beautiful surroundings.

As long as you're not with Phyllis Newsom, I think you'll be pretty safe.

Don't miss the next Fresh-Baked Mystery!
Christmastime has come again to
Weatherford, Texas, and Phyllis has cookies
to bake—and a killer to catch.
Read on for an excerpt from

The Gingerbread Bump-Off

by Livia J. Washburn

Available now from Obsidian.

$\mathcal{P}$hyllis Newsom lifted her head and frowned as she heard the unmistakable strains of "Grandma Got Run Over by a Reindeer" drifting through the house.

A baking sheet full of German chocolate cookies ready to go into the oven sat on the kitchen counter in front of her, but she left them sitting there as she walked out to the living room, wiping her hands on a towel as she went.

Sam Fletcher stood in front of the stereo system, which rested on a shelf next to the television. His hands were tucked in the hip pockets of his jeans, and his head moved slightly in time with the music. He was tall and slender, in keeping with his background as a basketball player and coach, and although his rumpled thatch of hair had a lot more white in it now than gray, he still didn't really look his age.

"Sam," Phyllis said, "you know I don't really like that song. It just doesn't seem very . . . Christmasy . . . to me."

He looked back over his shoulder at her. "Sorry," he said. "I thought with you out in the kitchen it might not bother you." A smile spread across his rugged face. "I got 'Jingle Bells' by the Singin' Dogs if that'd be better."

She was about to tell him that it wouldn't be, when she realized that he was joking. She wasn't going to give him the satisfaction of seeing that he had almost fooled her, so she just waved a hand casually and said, "Play whatever you want. I really don't care."

With that, she went back to the kitchen. By the time she got there, the music had stopped as Sam ejected the CD. A moment later, Nat King Cole started singing about chestnuts roasting on an open fire. Phyllis smiled. That was one of her favorites.

She looked down at the cookies on the baking sheet. The base was a dark chocolate cookie, each with a thumb-sized depression in the middle that Phyllis had filled with a mixture of German chocolate, grated coconut, and crushed pecans. The oven was ready, so she opened the door and slid the baking sheet onto the rack. If these cookies turned out well, she would make another batch. With any luck, this recipe would be her entry in the local newspaper's annual Christmas cookie recipe contest.

The past two years Carolyn Wilbarger, who also lived in the big house in one of Weatherford's tree-shaded old residential neighborhoods, had won that contest, with Phyllis finishing as a runner-up both times. That was fine with Phyllis—she just enjoyed coming up with recipes and sharing them with people—but it might be nice to really give Carolyn a run for her money this year. Not that there was any money at stake, Phyllis reminded herself, only prestige, and she didn't really care all that much about *that*, either. She had a good life here, with a lovely son, daughter-in-law, and grandson, and three good friends who were retired teachers like her to share this house with her.

But that comfortable, well-ordered life was about to be shaken up, and although she knew she ought to be happy about the circumstances, she still wasn't sure how she felt about it.

"Everyone, meet Roy Porter," Eve Turner had said when she brought the silver-haired stranger to the house on Thanksgiving. "Roy and I are engaged. Do you believe it? We're going to be married!"

That news had been a bolt out of the blue. None of Eve's housemates had had any idea she was seeing anyone. It shouldn't have been that surprising. Eve had been married several times before, and she always had her eye out for an eligible bachelor of the proper age. She had even pursued Sam for a while after he moved into the house to rent one of the vacant rooms. But she certainly had been more discreet about her courtship this time.

"We met on the Facebook," Eve had explained. "It turns out we have mutual friends. We started writing on each other's door—"

"Wall, dear," Roy had corrected gently.

"On each other's wall," Eve went on, "and, well, one thing led to another."

With Eve it usually did, given half a chance.

Thanksgiving hadn't necessarily been the best time to break the news of an engagement, but to be fair, when Eve and Roy came in, Eve didn't know that Phyllis had just solved one murder and prevented several more from occurring. That had turned out to be a very busy Thanksgiving indeed.

Now Christmas was coming up, but before then, a bridal shower on Christmas Eve, to be followed by the wedding itself on New Year's Eve. An abundance of Eves, including the bride, Phyllis thought as she stood there in front of the oven for a long moment, thinking about everything that was going on this holiday season.

"Well," she said aloud, "at least nothing else—"

"Don't say it," Sam interrupted sharply from behind her.

She turned her head to look at him. "Don't say what?"

"You were about to say that with all you've got goin' already this year, at least nothin' else can happen," Sam said in a warning tone. "Don't you know that's the surest way to jinx things?"

"Oh, goodness gracious. I'm not superstitious. Anyway, *you* just said it."

"Yeah, but that's all right. I can say things like that without all heck breakin' loose. You're the one who can't."

"That's not fair."

Sam shook his head. "Fair's got nothin' to do with it," he said with a solemn expression on his face. "It's just the way the cosmos is. Some folks seem to attract trouble to start with. You don't want to go makin' the odds even worse."

"Well, that's just silly."

But despite what she said, Phyllis had to wonder if there might not be something to Sam's idea. There had to be some explanation why she seemed to keep getting mixed up in murder cases these past few years.

That thought was going through her head when the doorbell rang.

Sam spread his hands. "See? There you go. Trouble at the door."

"Oh, hush," Phyllis said. She took her apron off and thrust it into his hands as she went past him. "Keep an eye on those cookies. Don't let them burn."

"Wait a minute. I don't know anything about bakin' cookies—"

"Take them out if they start to burn," Phyllis told him over her shoulder.

"But . . . they're chocolate. How will I know?" Sam asked as Phyllis went out of the kitchen and up the hall to the living room.

She patted her graying brown hair to make sure it was in place as she went to the front door. It was the middle of the afternoon, and she wasn't expecting anyone. Her son, Mike, who was a Parker County deputy sheriff, dropped by unexpectedly sometimes, and so did Mike's wife, Sarah. Carolyn was out somewhere, and so was Eve. Neither of them would have rung the doorbell, anyway. This big old house was home to them now.

When Phyllis looked out one of the narrow windows that flanked the door, she saw that the visitor wasn't family or one of her housemates. Definitely a friend, though. She opened the door, smiled, and said, "Hello, Georgia. Please, come in. What brings you here?"

December weather in this part of Texas could range anywhere from summerlike heat to snowstorms and wind chills well below zero. Today was on the warm side, but the air still had a pleasant crispness to it that came into the house with Georgia Hallerbee.

Georgia was what people once called "a handsome woman." She was about Phyllis's height and well shaped despite her age. Her hair was dark brown, and she insisted she didn't color it. Phyllis believed her. Georgia wore a dark blue skirt and a matching blazer over a white blouse. She was an accountant and tax consultant, and she was also very active in civic affairs.

"How are you, Phyllis?" she asked as Phyllis closed the door behind her.

"I'm fine. How are you?" They had known each other for at least ten years, and while they had never been close friends, Phyllis was always glad to see Georgia.

"Busy as always," Georgia replied with a smile and a sweet drawl in her voice. She wasn't a native Texan, having grown up somewhere in the deep South, possibly even the state that bore the same name as she did. Phyllis didn't know about that.

She ushered the visitor into the living room and said, "Have a seat." As Georgia sat down on the sofa, Phyllis stepped over to the stereo to turn off the CD.

"Oh, let it play," Georgia said. "Don't turn it off on my account. I love Christmas music."

"So do I." Phyllis settled for turning down the music to a level that wouldn't interfere with their conversation. She sank into one of the armchairs and went on. "What can I do for you?"

"Maybe I just came by to visit," Georgia said.

Phyllis shook her head. "You said it yourself. You're one of the busiest women I know. You're always up to your elbows in some project or other."

Georgia smiled and tilted her head. "You know me too well," she said. "I've come to ask a favor of you. You may know that I'm in charge of the Jingle Bell Tour this year."

The Christmas Jingle Bell Tour of Homes was an annual tradition in Weatherford, and in many other Texas towns, for that matter. Each holiday season, a dozen or so homes would be selected and beautifully decorated. Some might even say extravagantly decorated, both inside and out. Then, on one night a few weeks before Christmas, people could pay a small fee to go on a tour of those houses, with the proceeds going to one of the local civic organizations. There would be caroling, hot cider, and snacks at the homes on the tour, and it was a gala evening for everyone concerned ... except perhaps the homeowners, who had to go to the trouble of decorating and then opening their homes to the public.

"I did know that," Phyllis said. "I'm looking forward to it, like always. There are such beautiful decorations every year."

"Yes, there are," Georgia agreed. "And I'm hoping you can give me a hand this year."

"You mean in organizing the tour? I assumed all that was done already—"

"It was. Or at least, it was supposed to be. But this year we have a ... situation."

Phyllis frowned slightly. "Whenever someone says 'situation' like that, they're usually not talking about anything good."

"I'm afraid you're right," Georgia said with a sigh. "One of the homeowners had to drop out. Doris Treadwell was diagnosed with cancer yesterday."

"Oh, no." Phyllis recognized the name but didn't actually know Doris Treadwell. Still, it was a terrible thing to hear about anyone, especially at this time of year when everything was supposed to be festive.

Georgia nodded. "She'll be starting chemo right away and then radiation, of course. And naturally she's not going to feel like participating in the tour."

"Of course not," Phyllis said. An uneasy suspicion stirred in the back of her mind. "But you're not asking *me* to—"

"To take her place, yes," Georgia said, nodding. "We'd like for this lovely old house of yours to be part of the Christmas Jingle Bell Tour of Homes this year."

Phyllis sat back, surprised and unsure what to say. Georgia was asking her to take on a big responsibility on short notice. Plus there was the notion of allowing strangers to troop through her house, and the bridal shower to get ready for . . .

"Excuse me, ladies," Sam said from the door between the living room and the foyer. "I hate to interrupt, Phyllis, but those cookies are startin' to smell a little like they might be gettin' done. . . ."

Phyllis got to her feet. "I'm sorry, Georgia. I really need to check on that."

"Of course, go right ahead. I wouldn't want to be to blame for ruining a batch of Phyllis Newsom's cookies."

On her way out of the living room, Phyllis fluttered a hand in Sam's direction and said, "I don't know if you two have met. . . . Georgia, this is my friend Sam Fletcher. . . . Sam, Georgia Hallerbee."

Sam nodded, smiled, and said, "Pleased to meet you." Then he followed Phyllis down the hall to the kitchen.

Phyllis picked up a potholder, opened the stove, and leaned down to check the cookies. She reached in and took hold of the muffin pan, pulled it out, and set it on top of the stove.

"They're not burned," she said.

Sam heaved a sigh of relief.

"But they are done," Phyllis went on. "You did the right thing to come and get me." She lowered her voice. "Now, tell *me* the right thing to do about what Georgia wants."

"What's that?" Sam asked, equally quietly.

"She wants me to help her with the Jingle Bell Tour."

"You mean that thing where folks go around and look at all the fancy-decorated houses? That doesn't sound so bad."

Phyllis pointed at the floor under their feet. "She wants *this* house to be one of the stops."

Sam's eyes widened a little. "Oh. Well, it's kinda late to be askin' something like that, isn't it?"

"They had an emergency. Someone had to drop out of the tour."

Sam nodded and said, "Yeah, I guess that could happen, all right. What're you gonna tell her?"

"I don't know. It would be a lot of work . . . and we already have this business with Eve's shower and wedding coming up. . . ."

"It's gonna be a busy month, all right," Sam agreed.

"On the other hand, it's for a good cause. And I *do* like to decorate for Christmas. . . ."

"Yeah, but you'd almost have to go overboard for something like that, wouldn't you?"

"You can have a lot of decorations and still be tasteful."

"I don't know. I've seen some places so lit up with Christmas lights, I wouldn't be surprised if you could see 'em from space. But you know whatever you decide, I'll be glad to give you a hand."

"I know." Phyllis nodded her head as she came to a decision. "I may regret it, but I'm going to do it."

"I'm sure it'll be fine," Sam told her. "You want me to, uh, sample one of these cookies for you and tell you how it tastes?"

"Keep your hands off of them. They have to cool first. With that topping, you'll burn your mouth if you eat one now."

"I'll try, but they smell mighty good."

He wasn't the only one who thought so. As Phyllis came back into the living room, Georgia Hallerbee said, "My goodness, those cookies smell delicious, Phyllis. Nothing smells much better than cookies right out of the oven."

"I know. They're cooling now. If you can wait a few minutes, you can try one."

"I'd like that, but I really do have to be going soon." Georgia paused. "So, have you thought about what I asked you?"

"I have, and . . . I'm going to do it."

A smile lit up Georgia's face. "That's wonderful! Thank you so much, Phyllis. I can't tell you how much it means to me, knowing that you'll step in and do a good job, like you always do at everything."

"I don't know about that. I'm not going to have as much time to prepare as the others. But I'll do the best I can."

"I'm sure the place will be beautiful," Georgia said as she stood up and started for the front door. "Thanks again. I'll be in touch with all the information you need, like which stop you'll be on the tour and when you can expect people to start showing up. And if there's anything I can do to help you get ready, just let me know."

"An extra six or eight hours in the day would be nice."

Georgia laughed. "Don't I know it! I've been wishing for that for a long time now, but it hasn't come true yet."

Phyllis opened the door and followed Georgia out onto the small front porch. Georgia's stylish crossover SUV was parked in the driveway.

She paused and looked down at the pair of large ceramic gingerbread men that sat on the porch, one on each side of the doorway. "These are new, aren't they? They're adorable."

Phyllis nodded. "Yes, Sam and I were out driving around one afternoon, and we stopped at that place between Azle and Springtown that has all the ceramic things. These gingerbread men were cute, and I thought they'd look good up here."

"You were right." Georgia gave Phyllis a look. "You and Sam . . . are the two of you . . . ?"

"Goodness, no, we're just friends," Phyllis said. That wasn't *strictly* true, but she had been raised to believe that it was best to be discreet about some things.

"You know what you should do?" Georgia said, looking down at the gingerbread men again. "You should dress them up for the tour. You could make, I don't know, elves or something out of them."

"Or Mr. and Mrs. Claus," Phyllis said, getting caught up in the spirit of the thing. "I've thought from the start that one of them was male and the other female."

"Well, there you go. You see, I knew you'd be good at this." Georgia lifted a hand in farewell as she started toward her SUV. "I'll be in touch. Enjoy those cookies!"

"We will," Sam said from behind Phyllis, then added, "You think they've cooled off enough to eat yet?"